Women
Leading

Women Leading

MAKING TOUGH CHOICES ON THE FAST TRACK

NANCY W. COLLINS

SUSAN K. GILBERT

SUSAN H. NYCUM

The Stephen Greene Press
Lexington, Massachusetts

THE STEPHEN GREENE PRESS, INC.

Published by the Penguin Group
Viking Penguin Inc., 40 West 23rd Street, New York, New York 10010, U.S.A.
Penguin Books Ltd, 27 Wrights Lane, London W8 5TZ, England
Penguin Books Australia Ltd, Ringwood, Victoria, Australia
Penguin Books Canada Ltd, 2801 John Street, Markham, Ontario, Canada L3R 1B4
Penguin Books (N.Z.) Ltd, 182–190 Wairau Road, Auckland 10, New Zealand

Penguin Books Ltd, Registered Offices: Harmondsworth, Middlesex, England

First published in 1988 by The Stephen Greene Press, Inc.
Published simultaneously in Canada
Distributed by Viking Penguin Inc.

Copyright © The Stephen Greene Press, Inc., 1988
All rights reserved

Library of Congress Cataloging-in-Publication Data

Collins, Nancy W.
  Women leading.

  Bibliography: p. 181
  1. Women executives—United States. 2. Women
executives—United States—Biography. I. Gilbert,
Susan K. II. Nycum, Susan H. III. Title.
HD6054.4.U6C64 1988   658'.0088042   87-25130
ISBN 0-8289-0567-3

Designed by Deborah Schneider
Printed in the United States of America
by Haddon Craftsmen
set in Aeolus, Gill Sans Light Italic, and Goudy Old Style by
AccuComp Typographers
Produced by Unicorn Production Services, Inc.

We dedicate this book with much love—and also with great appreciation for the supportive role our husbands play in our life—to Richard F. Chapman, M.D. (Nancy Collins), Keith D. Gilbert (Sue Gilbert), and George H. Bosworth III (Susan Nycum).

Contents

Foreword

We have written this book about senior level women in our society for the professional woman who aspires to reach similar status.

In short, it is written for women who are intelligent, motivated, who plan to work hard, possibly sacrificing other phases of their lives, and who want to know, "Will it be worth it?"

NANCY W. COLLINS
SUSAN K. GILBERT
SUSAN H. NYCUM

Preface

Women Leading is about working women who are high achievers—women who have chosen to utilize their full potential in the male-dominated world of work and who are known as successful. "Successful women" is defined as those women in the work force who have all or most of the following: attainment of preestablished goals; power and influence with or over other people; high status among peers; notable ranking in their community; autonomy over their own work and actions; large financial rewards; and a high degree of self-satisfaction.

This is a book that draws on the authors' life experiences, observations, and insights and those of their professional colleagues, as well as the sample of 160 women listed in *Who's Who of American Women*, to illustrate their message. The book discusses the achievements and failures, the joys, problems, and disappointments that they encountered on the way to success and are still experienced in their daily lives.

The authors believe the role of choice is central to achievement. Thus, they discuss the choices they and others in this book have made and why they made them, the importance of timing, and the implications that the choices have made in their lives. They also comment on why they and their peers so often select a choice that is stressful.

The book consists of sections on work, the people with whom these women work, their families and personal friends closest to them, and their lives outside the workplace. The conclusion of the authors is that indeed the success that they and the other women in this book experience, and the rewards that follow, are well worth the sacrifices and personal life-style required to attain these goals.

Introduction: The Authors

These brief introductions are designed to give the reader an insight into the professional lives of the three authors. Collins, Gilbert, and Nycum have chosen different professional paths and each brings to this book a unique and distinct perspective that reflects her own experiences. Their lives are typical of many in the study and illustrate that career paths go in many directions and that those who are successful must overcome many professional obstacles as well as personal pain and misfortune.

Nancy W. Collins

Nancy W. Collins is currently the assistant to the president of the Palo Alto Medical Foundation, a position she has held for the past five years. Before that, she was an assistant director at the Hoover Institution, and prior to that she was at the Stanford Graduate School of Business for twelve years, both as the assistant director of the Sloan Executive Program for ten years and as the corporate relations officer.

Collins's current board positions include the Pacific Graduate School of Psychology (where she chairs the Development Committee), the Personnel Board for the City of Menlo Park, and the Chapman Research Fund (where she is the secretary-treasurer).

She is a recent member of the board of the Coro Foundation Women's Programs, the Girl Scout Executive Council of Santa Clara County, and the Charter Review Committee of San Mateo County.

Collins received her A.B. in Journalism from the University of North Carolina in Chapel Hill, followed by a year of graduate study at Cornell University. She returned to UNC ten years later and received her M.S. in Personnel Administration. She is the author of *Professional Women and Their Mentors* (New York: Prentice-Hall, 1983) and *Mentoring: Its Role in Career Development* (to be published in 1988). She is listed in *Who's Who in California, Dictionary of International Biography*, and *Who's Who of American Women*.

Susan K. Gilbert

Susan K. Gilbert is currently chief operating officer of a medical diagnostics company, Apprise, Inc., located near San Francisco. As COO, her duties include financing her company through venture capital, determining strategy, and building a fully integrated organization preparatory to market launch.

Before accepting her current position, Gilbert was vice-president of corporate development for Syntex Corporation, a $1 billion pharmaceutical company in Palo Alto, California, where she was responsible for planning, acquisitions, divestitures, and a venture capital program. Prior to this, she was vice-president of finance and administration for Syva, Syntex's Diagnostics Division, from start-up to over $100 million in sales. She has also worked as a consultant to the health care industry involved in market and technology assessment and strategic planning for health care companies, both major corporations and smaller start-up companies.

Gilbert has served on the board of directors of several start-up healthcare companies and is a former president of the Peninsula Professional Women's Network in the Bay Area. She is a graduate of New York University, with a B.S. in Foreign Languages.

Susan H. Nycum

Susan H. Nycum is currently a senior partner in the international law firm of Baker & McKenzie and is partner-in-charge of its Palo Alto office. She is a senior member of the firmwide practice group of high-technology law.

Nycum is president of the Computer Law Association and past chairman of the American Bar Association Section of Science and Technology (the only person to have served in both capacities). She is frequently a U.S. delegate to meetings of international organizations of which the United States is a member, such as the Organization for Economic Cooperative Development and the World Intellectual Property Organization. She has consulted to seven governments (including the U.S. government) on matters involving technology and the law.

Nycum is a member of the Board of Visitors of Stanford Law School and a member of the Advisory Board on Technology and Law for the law schools of Arizona State University, University of California at Berkeley, Harvard University, Rutgers University, University of Santa Clara, University of Southern California, and Stanford University. She has been a member of the Board of Advisors to the Math and Computer Science Section of the National Science Foundation, a member of the National Conference of

Lawyers and Scientists, and a committee head of several international bar associations.

Nycum's clients range from start-up companies to multinational Fortune 10 organizations and include both vendors and customers of high technology products and services.

She is the coauthor of *Your Computer and the Law* (New York: Prentice-Hall, 1975), and she is listed in *Who's Who in America, Who's Who in American Law,* and *Who's Who of American Women.*

Women
Leading

1 Our Work

> "To make a living is no longer enough.
> Work also has to make a life."
> —PETER F. DRUCKER—

The American woman is someone entirely different from her mother and grandmother: today she is pioneering careers that women never thought of thirty years ago or, in many cases, even ten years ago. Because of this, some of the past rules for expectation and fulfillment no longer apply. And the new rules for managing all three phases of a working woman's life—career, marriage, motherhood—are not yet written in final form.

Women today mean business. For the past fifteen years, the growing involvement of women in business has lifted the American economy to new heights. Until recently, society's expectation of women has been that they fulfill themselves with the duties of homemaking, a restriction that both frustrated women's ambitions and deprived the economy of their intelligence and resourcefulness. Now that the working world has opened to them, women are taking full advantage of the new opportunities by making a strong commitment to their careers with a willingness to accept increasing levels of responsibility. It is unlikely that women ever will be content to "stay home" again.

The modern woman is discovering that she can decide for herself the level of her work involvement. With effort, she can expand the best of both the new and the old worlds of home and work: the joy of marriage and motherhood need not be lessened by having a successful career. She is finding that she can indeed utilize her full potential with success in many areas. She is coming to know what men have known all along: *that work is of great psychological importance and is a powerful vehicle for fulfillment.*

As representatives of that growing number of executive and professional women, we, the authors, have both observed and experienced that fulfillment. We are now at a vantage point to offer insights to other women who aspire to success in the world of work. The book draws insights from our own experiences and from our survey of 160 high achievers throughout the United

States listed in *Who's Who of American Women*. Our unique survey examines the work experience and life-styles of these 160 women, who are at senior level in their profession. In addition, we personally conducted interviews with some of America's most successful women. Central to our research was the single issue: was their success worth the price?

In carrying out this study, we meticulously selected a representative number of women from law, medicine, academia, business, government, health services, and nonprofit organizations. Our sample was further selected to include a wide geographical representation as well as a spread of birth dates. We were gratified by the high percentage of questionnaires returned, the honest feedback, and the enthusiasm that was expressed for our research.

Although the responses varied tremendously, the categories that describe our typical respondent are as follows: between forty-one and fifty years old, advanced degree, working in the same field as academically studied, salary well above average (over $50,000) — including some in the six figures — married (and in the first marriage), financial status average as a child, mother did not work, one sibling, first in the family birth order, married from sixteen to twenty years, and with two children but no stepchildren. The advanced degrees most frequently listed were law, business, math, and computer sciences.

As would be expected of those included in *Who's Who of American Women*, our respondents are in the upper echelon of females employed in the United States. Of the 160 responding, 13 percent are CEOs/presidents; 34 percent vice-presidents, partners, managers, supervisors; 25 percent attorneys and judges; 6 percent professors or principals; 3 percent physicians; 2 percent psychologists; 4 percent biologists/scientists; 3 percent personnel/public relations; and the remaining 10 percent from mixed categories (such as USN Admiral, dentists, editor, news anchor, performing artists, and jewelry designer).

The fields of expertise in which they work fall into the following categories: 29 percent business, 25 percent legal, 16 percent computers, 12 percent medical, 6 percent educational, 5 percent music/arts/theater, 4 percent government, and 3 percent engineering.

Throughout the book, we examine the role of work in the lives of these women, who in many instances have been trailblazers in their professions, as well as the role of work in our own lives. We also explore another important element of life — how to deal with our surroundings, which, in turn, can become a supportive environment where we can develop. As we discover, women lead in many ways.

THE PLACE OF WORK IN OUR LIVES

Work is central to our lives, and like successful men, we have always identified ourselves by what we do. Said a scientist in our study, "It's my whole life. Is there anything else?" Adds Collins, "Work has always been central to my very core." But as many professional women know, that work-oriented sense of identity can conflict with more ingrained ones.

In identifying ourselves as professionals and in becoming high achievers, we had to be capable of managing several roles. And like other successful women, we faced innumerable obstacles. A once common obstacle is expressed in Gilbert's reflections: "When I started to work, the ability to have a successful career, children, and a stable marriage had not yet been proved by most women I knew. I wanted it all rather than having to make trade-offs by choosing among these options. I was somewhat lonely in this choice, since I had few role models or associates to whom I could look for support. At this point I sought some counseling; I finally accepted my personal needs as well as the fact that it was all right to want success. Luckily for me, I had chosen for my counselor a woman who had her own degree of personal success as well as a family. We could relate to each other and our needs. Other women I know have not been so fortunate and have reported a lack of understanding by the counselor from whom they sought help."

Working at a serious career in the early seventies was still unusual for a woman. At that time, we felt different and slightly misunderstood by both our female friends and most men with whom we worked or socialized. That lack of understanding is almost comical in retrospect, but at the time it was often painful. In a telling instance, Nycum had to explain patiently to her fellow volunteer group members that she couldn't go on a scheduled day trip with the group because she worked. Members were shocked that her work had *that* kind of priority. The irony of the situation was that several of the members' husbands worked for her. The social stigma connected with a serious career during that era might be summed up by a comment that Collins overheard, as two women discussed her and an eligible bachelor, "Oh, don't get him a date with her—she *works*."

Obviously the workplace has changed over the past few years, and now there are many female high achievers in business. Women who were once critical of us at the beginning of our careers are themselves now choosing to combine work and family. Some are the same women who formerly focused their efforts on managing church bazaars, running Junior League events, and chairing the PTA. Or, if they are much older, they are encouraging their daughters to prepare for a career. We are gratified to see women start out, even late in their lives, on meaningful career paths.

The eighties have made it acceptable in our society for a woman to have both a career and a family. The percent of women in the work force has risen dramatically, so that 44 percent of the total work force are now women. Women especially made steady advancement between 1970 and 1980, with the numbers of working women growing by 41 percent, so that for the first time a majority of all women are in the labor force. In 1986, there were 52 million working women, compared to 67 million men (Barbara R. Bergmann, *The Economic Emergence of Women*; New York: Basic Books, 1986).

The number of children whose mothers work has now surpassed the number of children whose mothers are at home. In fact, so many mothers work today that only 7 percent of all households fit the traditional American stereotype of a working father and a stay-at-home mother with young children. The conventional stereotype of Mother (who baked cookies after school) is clearly an anomaly of the post–World War II era.

Although society now agrees that women can have both a career and a family, and statistics show that many women are doing just that, simple approval and sheer numbers do not ensure an easy route. Success in both areas still requires determination, some sacrifice, and many choices. In making work central to their lives, in committing themselves intensely to their careers, young women need to realize that the demands of work can take them in a direction that often conflicts with other parts of their lives.

Consider, for example, Nycum's past position as director of the Stanford University Computer Center, a facility that served the university and twenty or more outlying schools and colleges (including some 5,000 diverse local and remote users) with a yearly budget of $2.5 million in 1970. "During a period of campus unrest, I needed to be on call all night, night after night, because of firebombs and other attacks by disgruntled students to the computer center. The strain of thinking of leaving my eleven-year-old only child alone at night (no other adult was available) to go to the center to face campus unrest was untenable. Had there been anyone to whom I could have delegated either of these responsibilities, I would have done so. But I literally had to be in two places at once, and the choices were wrenching.

"When an attack did occur and evacuation was necessary, I was the last person to leave and the first person to be permitted back inside by the police and fire departments. Because of the danger of hidden bombs, suppliers—including IBM—would not permit their employees to enter until I had first walked through and surveyed the areas."

Thus, from the beginning, women are courting stress and emotional tension in being committed to their careers. Women now realize if they want to succeed in three roles—parent, wife, and high level professional—it will be much more difficult than succeeding in one or even two of these roles. And the challenge of fulfilling three roles is further intensified by the fact that it is more difficult for a woman to achieve success in the still male-dominated work world than it is for a man.

Betty Harragan agreed with this assessment in an interview with Gilbert on November 10, 1985. Harragan, a noted business consultant, job counselor, and lecturer on women's issues, writes a monthly column for *Working Woman* and has authored two career-strategy books, *Games Mother Never Taught You* (New York: Warner Books, 1977) and *Knowing the Score* (New York: St. Martin's Press, 1983). In the interview, Harragan identified some major issues that women still face. After citing the fact that women still do not collar the top jobs, she enumerated other problems: "Personal problems still overwhelm women—divorce and marital relationships being the primary ones. Unfortunately, there are not enough men around prepared to live in a marriage with a successful woman. The work force still includes a generation of women who were raised to take care of home and children, not careers. They don't feel employment discrimination. Recent female graduates also are unaware of discrimination because they have not faced overt discrimination at entry levels during the short time they have worked.

"What needs to change before women seek heavy responsibility in the workplace is for attitudes toward family responsibilities to change. These conflicting loyalties are a growing menace, yet there are few role models for the younger women to follow. Our superwoman nonsense has to stop!

"Change will only come from a change in obsolete attitudes. Why do so many women echo, 'I am nothing without a man'? Women still have a long way to go to feel truly independent."

Priorities

As we try to find the place for work in our lives, we are forced to examine what is important to us. We often ask ourselves what is the balance that is most fulfilling? This examination requires us to constantly review and sometimes change our priorities, which can be a difficult task.

Once we admit that our work has a very high priority, we can handle it more openly without feeling as much conflict. Once we are honest with ourselves, it becomes easier to be more open with the people closest to us, who have demands on our time. Men who make a serious commitment early in their lives to a career have a clear understanding with those they love that their career will have a central role from that point on. "Yet women tend to experience guilt or feel that they are looked at differently when they allow themselves to do the same," stated an engineer in our survey. "Women who do acknowledge the personal importance of work will ultimately experience more ease than those professionals who deny its place."

Theoretically, women can order priorities for themselves as they relate to work and family quite easily, but when reality intrudes, they need to make unexpected daily choices. Although those choices usually don't carry life-or-death consequences, they can be fraught with the emotional tension of divided duties, as illustrated by an incident in Nycum's life, early in her relationship with her husband, George Bosworth. She was being interviewed by *Forbes* magazine, while the hour of her dinner reservation with George was creeping uncomfortably near. George was uneasy, but Nycum felt compelled to finish the interview, which she did, developing a migraine that expressed her inner conflict and lasted well into the dinner they did *not* miss.

Nycum sums up this process: "Juggling priorities so that no one else loses has sometimes taken a toll on my equanimity. At times I wish I did not want to have it all at once and juggle so much at one time. But as a friend's T-shirt loudly proclaims, 'So much to do, so little time!' "

Divided duties frequently emerge, pitting work against children, and some of the most difficult daily compromises that career women make involve their offspring. When the school nurse calls and says that your child has a fever of 102 degrees and you are about to give a major business presentation, what do you do? Gilbert's solution is first to call her husband; they compare schedules to see who is best able to leave work. "Sometimes I go home. Sometimes I take a business client or associate with me to pick up my daughter and then go home, proceeding with business there. And sometimes, when the illness is minor, my daughter stays at home alone." One key, then, to these unexpected daily decisions is flexibility.

We can try to confine our work to certain hours of the day, but putting too many limits on working hours hampers career growth. As professional men have long known, we may have to travel at inconvenient times, we may be given a project that requires weekend or evening work, or we may be involved in evening business discussions, luncheons, or dinners.

Shared a lawyer, "Priorities may vary even in the course of a year. The 'squeaky wheel' theory works, and often the situation in crisis gets shifted to the top, if only temporarily. The successful woman's overall challenge may be different from the male peers' on her level, and she must be a master at seeing the whole picture and making the necessary changes in priorities to adapt to her current situation."

Many of the women in our study resent the way the domestic system seems to work against them: if there is a crisis at home, they are still the ones expected to deal with it. Others, however, have accepted this role and realize that while their children are small they may be the ones required to give less to their profession in the face of domestic crises or extraordinary home problems. Still others have negotiated or decreed that their career needs will come first for a prescribed period. Nevertheless, it still seems to be the female who at least organizes the main domestic responsibilities.

Collins, who raised her three sons—Chip, Chuck, and Bill—single-handedly for many years, assumed that responsibility that went along with her role as a single parent. Now remarried, she finds that she can share many of the problems at home with her husband—arranging for yard work, calling the plumber, or doing the shopping—and this makes life much easier.

Gilbert and her husband, Keith, share equally in the management of their home and in the care of their daughter, Amanda. The twist in Gilbert's experience is that everyone *else*—teachers and administrators at school and parents of her daughter's friends—automatically expect that Mother will take care of the problems. "They expect that," Gilbert says, "even when I am out of town."

Nycum, who was a single parent for most of her daughter's growing years, now finds that she and her husband continually work out the home situation and that they share at least equally in handling responsibilities. If she takes the cat to the vet's, he picks it up. Yet, she philosophizes: "Dealing with crisis simply comes with the territory of being a woman. No matter whether it is a cut knee of a child or a bomb in the office, I find I am the one elected to deal with the matter. The bottom line is that responsibility for the care of others is a duty that women have eternally assumed."

Frequently, in discussions of how we manage to balance our priorities, we tend to overlook some factors. Sheer luck and chance play a part for all of us. These may exhibit themselves through the choice of a husband who grows to understand us and our needs and is willing to share our burdens, children who are easy to care for, an especially supportive work climate, or an understanding and facilitating boss. To some degree we each choose and find our luck, but sometimes we need to acknowledge that fortunate things happen that are beyond our control and have a hand in our success.

Why We Work

Nycum says, "I have always worked for the challenge of it. Money is important, fame is fun, but the real satisfaction comes to me from accomplishment. Whether it was managing a group of smaller children as a teenager, running the world's most prestigious computer center, or directing the largest high-technology law practice in the world, accomplishment is the key. I am easily bored by repetitive tasks and easily intrigued by new ideas. 'I wonder if I could do that' is quickly followed by trying it.

"I also work because it satisfies my need for financial independence. If I want to buy jewelry or take a trip, I can do it without asking for permission or worrying about the impact on the family resources. In working, I feel like a contributor—to the family and to society. It is important to me to advance the state of knowledge and to help others in whatever I do. The sphere of influence is larger in the work arena than at home. I feel it is also important to use the talents God gave us. He dealt me more work-oriented talents than domestic talents. I am notoriously poor at flower arranging and Christmas-package wrapping—my only domestic enjoyment comes from doing the laundry and concocting desserts, usually chocolate."

Collins says, "I work hard because I enjoy the tremendous satisfaction I experience from a peak performance. I am, by nature, an energetic, driven, and aggressive person. I also work to make a contribution and for status and recognition in the community. Making money has never been a major goal, and while I admit I like to be surrounded by comfort, I have never thought of work as just a means to acquire wealth. But I must admit, few of my friends work as hard as I do or for such long hours. But like me, those who do seem to thrive on competition, deadlines, and stress. One of my friends sums it up by saying, 'It's not the work or responsibility that kills. It is the lack of control and challenge.' "

Gilbert notes, "I have always worked, and started when I was fourteen. Looking back on my life, it appears that there was one event which was so significant as to change its entire course. Though there are many events which shape our lives, none was so consequential for me as the death of my father when I was fourteen. Although I did not realize it at the time, it appears the way I worked through my grief was to get out of the house and keep busy. I got my working papers, required then by the state of New Jersey, and went to work in a local drugstore.

"There was no particular financial need within my family that required me to work, but I enjoyed the feeling of independence that came from earning my own spending money. I also enjoyed the fact that I had more than enough money for my needs, and I got into the habit of saving quite early in life.

"I work today for some of the same reasons: independence and the freedom of choice extra money can bring. I am not a big spender, other than on clothes, but I like the feeling of security that comes from having money in the bank and other investments. Perhaps one of the most important lessons I learned was to juggle a lot of different responsibilities early in life. This taught me to manage the many situations which came later.

"I can't imagine *not* working. Work is such an integral part of my life that I can't even contemplate my life without it. I have always felt that working is what I was meant to do and have enjoyed considerable success and fulfill‑ ment from it. There are few substitutes for the feeling of accomplishment that comes from making a contribution to the business world."

Many women in our study went to work initially because they finished school and it was "the thing to do," especially if they had no immediate plans for marriage. Most of these women "drifted" into one of the first available jobs and did not have a clear plan of where they wanted to be in five years, much less a road map of how to get there. This is different from today's women graduating from school and from those in their twenties and thirties who know they want a career.

Although many women today may have clearer intentions, the process of choosing a career still has some built‑in inadequacies. From Collins's view‑ point, "When we are young, selecting a career is one of the most important decisions we make, but most of us are forced to do so before we have much experience of work and the knowledge of our capacity to perform. Yet, as we grow up, most of us have a dream of ourselves in the working world. In our dream, we fantasize about our exciting work and accomplishments, but when we reach young adulthood, the immediate problems of survival don't always allow us to work in an area that contains this dream."

In fact, as we explore women's careers in this book, we discover that few women are actually living out their dreams as they envisioned them in their early twenties. But, on the other hand, our research shows that some young women who made a strong career commitment early in their working lives often regretted it later, when they realized how many other options they could have exercised.

Although dreams and vision play a part, the overwhelming reason most women work today is economic. Their paychecks are simply essential to take care of the family needs. Most young couples getting married today realize that one paycheck will not support two people, and this means work is no longer an option. Other factors also contribute to women joining the work force today in such large numbers—the advent of birth‑control pills and legal abortions, the demands of the feminist and civil rights movements, the emphasis of the 1970s on the quest for personal satisfaction, and landmark job‑discrimination lawsuits that have opened up new opportunities.

Several women in our study have been fortunate enough to have made a lot of money in their early career years. Once their economic needs were filled, a few retired early, took up golf, studied music, and traveled. But the majority chose to work even harder, *continuing* to select those options in their lives that they know in advance would be difficult, stressful, and anxiety-causing. Wrote an engineer in our study, "Unless we are lucky enough to have a large inheritance or to marry into wealth, hard work is about the only way women can attempt to acquire a lot of money. Many of my acquaintances are high enough up on the professional ladder to have acquired the tangible symbols of wealth: expensive homes, luxury cars, designer clothes, and jewelry. Accumulating great wealth normally requires taking large risks—and this takes a certain kind of a person who is willing to make the great personal sacrifices that are normally necessary."

Another told us, "For many of my friends, hard work and risk-taking mean building their own businesses. Many forfeit leisure time and other aspects of their personal lives to meet their goals. In the early years of building a business, they often are paid no salary, devote themselves fully to their work, and give up all social life. If their husbands are involved in the business and share their goal, the marriage may have a better chance of success. Otherwise, unless they are careful, the price for success may be the marriage."

While the women in our study agree they want a serious career, the other side of the coin also needs examining. In *The Cinderella Complex* (New York: Summit Books, 1981), Colette Dowling told of giving up her job, and along with it, the startling collapse of her work ambition soon after she started sharing her home with her male lover. Dowling wrote that both she and her boyfriend believed a woman ought to be responsible for herself, yet she seemed to prefer being dependent upon him. It was almost as if she had a psychological need to avoid independence—a wish to "be saved." However, this attitude was *not* prevalent among the women we studied.

Total Commitment

What do senior level women put into their jobs? "Total commitment!" state a large number of our sample. We find that most successful working women were first ambitious, hard-working college students. Many did not realize at the time what field they would end up pursuing, but all had a zest for life at an early age and a competitive drive that propelled them into always striving to do their best. Nycum reveals, "I have a mental image of myself at the top of a ski slope or diving tower or the start of a broad jump, thrilled at the opportunity to see how far I can go and how well I can do."

Formal education, early discipline, a willingness to work hard, and dissatisfaction with mediocrity are crucial as the female executive climbs up the formerly male-dominated ladder. For example, like others, Nycum uses every minute to the fullest and loves the pace: "I work a twelve- to fourteen-hour day as a matter of course, and those hours are full and often stressful. I am a white-knuckle flier, yet log hundreds of thousands of air miles to all parts of the world for client meetings."

For women who have achieved success over the past ten to twenty years, commitment is the major factor that has dominated their lives. Most got their start before the road for women was paved, and the level of commitment that was necessary then was higher than it may be today. Nycum finds, "To-day's woman has few of the barriers that impeded women when I began my career. It is so much easier to accomplish things now. The drive and skill necessary in the old days for any success take me much farther much faster today."

Said a psychologist in our study, "What younger women need to realize is the sacrifice that senior [level] women have made to get to their present level. Because it may look 'easy,' junior [level] women often do not see the years of evening work, travel requirements, weekend conferences, and working meals, where senior [level] women were required to give a lot of their energy and creative planning in addition to their routine eight-hour day. Many successful women, now in their forties, found it necessary to delay marriage, spend money for extra training, move from their home territory, and alienate their parents, *especially their mothers.*"

"Placing work in a central place in our lives does not mean that we cannot also have other central focuses in our lives—husbands, children, friends, or other interests," says Collins. "However, in order to be successful in many areas of our lives, there are difficult choices we have to make, and many adaptations are necessary."

When we asked the women in our study what they thought was most necessary to be successful in all the different facets of their lives, the answer (next to sheer intelligence) was, inevitably, *good health, energy, perseverance, and an intense desire to achieve.* But they added that success seems to require not only the gift of good health but the commitment to maintaining it. Others noted, "And a little luck and good timing along the way."

The president of San Jose State University (the only female to hold this title in the California State University system) attributed much of her success to the exceptionally high level of stamina that she carries to her job. She feels up to handling personal problems and to interacting with those at home even after her most harried day.

In contrast, another woman, who is treasurer of a high-technology company, confessed, "After getting up early each day, arriving at my job before most of my peers, looking well groomed and attractive, and working hard for ten-plus hours, there was simply nothing left of me when I arrived home. The last thing I was ready for was cooking dinner and being pleasant for my family. I just became no longer willing nor able to make the effort to play the 'Ms. Competency' role twenty-four hours a day. I am now divorced."

Said one respondent, "Along with commitment goes belief in your-self—that you can 'get the job done' and that the time spent in doing it is worthwhile."

Gilbert adds, "Even in a supportive work environment, where work is done within a culture that recognizes the need for time for family and self, we find we occasionally slip out of balance when our job becomes too domi-nant in our life. There are many weeks when we find that too much of our energy is going into our work rather than into the rest of our lives, and we find that we need to pull back and regain the balance. Even twenty minutes to ourselves to sit extra long with coffee and the newspaper can work won-ders." However, the women in our study commented that this balancing act is a struggle that will probably be ongoing for as long as we work.

Identity and Purpose

What we get from our jobs can be expressed in many ways, and identity and purpose are major factors. For Collins, "Work is exciting. It's a joy and a turn-on. I flourish on competition." Nycum in particular feels rewarded by professional accomplishment. She comments, "Where else could I find this stimulation and challenge?" Gilbert adds, "I get a feeling of completion from my work and of using all the capabilities that I have. We all have multiple facets to our personalities—I like to develop in all areas of my life."

High-achieving men have never questioned if *they* could "have it all," and they have certainly made trade-offs. No one seriously proposes that men relinquish marriage, choose not to have children, or least of all, give up their work. Women, too, should stop thinking in "either/or" terms. We believe a woman's well-being, like her male counterpart's, is enhanced when she takes on multiple roles.

The majority of senior status women in our survey seem to find work fulfilling in itself. When asked who they *are*, they answered, "I am *vice-president* of marketing"; "I am *president* of the company"; "I am a *controller*." These women very much identify themselves by what they do, and salary and title serve as an important scorecard by which they continuously measure them-selves. Said a government official, "Women who are high achievers need their work to feel whole. Our work gives us identity, a purpose in life, and gives our path meaning and direction. Through our work we become independent, have our self-concept reinforced, find an accepted outlet for our creativity, and gain recognition and influence within the community."

If a woman feels fulfilled in her job, much of this satisfaction may spill over into other areas of her life. When she feels like a winner in a major part of her life, the other areas of her life reflect this also. The woman who is successful in her field can also appear competent in areas totally unrelated to it. For instance, membership on one prestigious board often brings opportunities to serve on boards for organizations in completely different fields.

"The key element for feeling successful comes from our job," wrote Helen Gurley Brown in *Having It All* (New York: Simon & Schuster, 1983). She further wrote, "A job is the ticket to money and position." She counseled against quitting the job to get married or have babies and said, "After all, the job will still be there after the divorce!"

Nycum sums up the rewards: "I get from my work a sense of 'putting it all together.' Education and training are used, dress and appearance count, and strong moral and physical stamina are tested." For the high-achieving woman, then, the exhilaration of *stretching* herself to meet multiple challenges is unmatched.

In conclusion, women who are high achievers work to be fulfilled. They associate themselves with their work, which gives them a purpose in life; their work gives their path meaning and direction and establishes their place in society. Through their work, and only through their work, they become independent, have their self-concept reinforced, gain recognition and influence within their community, and experience the exhilaration of power. The need for large financial rewards, prestigious titles, high status among their peers, and satisfaction from performance becomes a very important—if not the *most* important—drive in their lives.

"SUPERWOMAN IMAGE"

It is still hard for us to admit that because we work we are not able to manage all the things that other women do who do *not* work! The "superwoman image"—I can do it all and do it all well—is still strong with us, as it seems to be with most of our professional women friends. No doubt we will continue trying to do it all for as long as we work; however, we are glad to find the world is slowly changing to accommodate the working couple.

In the book *The Superwoman Syndrome* by Marjorie Hansen Shaevitz (New York: Warner Books, 1984), a superwoman is defined as "an extraordinary ordinary woman, someone who is trying to fill a number of roles and fill them all to perfection." The superwoman idea emerged when large numbers of women began to enter the work force, and instead of shifting from being homemakers to being career women, they simply tried to do it all.

Shaevitz noted that it is fine to have a career and be a wife and mother, but the problem is when the woman sets very high standards, tries to do everything herself, and ends up exhausted, guilty, and angry. She further pointed out that frequently the husband has no idea of what is involved in maintaining the house, and his attitude is that his home is his castle and place to rest. To the woman, her home can represent a never-ending project and an impossible list of things to do.

We believe women may not get men to agree to perform 50 percent of the housework but could consider other options—such as doing away with some tasks, hiring help to perform all that can be delegated, and relaxing standards during certain peak work times.

Scheduling Our Time

For the professional woman who is trying to combine a variety of roles, time is the most significant, scarce commodity. For most of us, there simply is not enough of it. Once we are committed to our jobs and to our families, there is not much time left over for ourselves, much less for other pursuits. Although time-management courses are available to assist those who have trouble managing time, ultimately there probably will not be enough time in the day to do everything we would like to do.

Since most of our time and energy go into our work, it becomes necessary to schedule time clearly for activities that are not work related. We do this as much for those with whom we live as for ourselves. It can become too easy to spend all our waking hours on job-related activities—for our work, if we love it, can be seductive.

The key to Gilbert's system is simplicity. She uses *one* "To Do" list that includes home, family, and work priorities. In describing the use of one list, as opposed to several, she says, "This is a small but important tactic. Some people keep their home list separate from their work list, and then get so focused on their work list that the insurance doesn't get paid." Gilbert has an innate sense of time and timing. "When I receive a project, I know immediately whether I can do it or not do it and how much time it takes." This, plus her one-list system, makes handling her time relatively easier.

Nycum describes her scheduling process as follows: "Management of time is something I am still trying to master. I usually juggle at least four or five work projects at once and several social tasks and 'errands' as well. My main goal is to have some time just for me. I handle that by trying to schedule at least one evening of those weeks when I am in town to do nothing. That 'evening' may not start until I reach home at 8:30 P.M., but I do with it as I choose—dinner with my husband, then a good book; a swim or hot tub; or just a long, hot bath. Then, when the alarm rings at 4:30 or 5:00 A.M. the next morning, that new day looks exciting, and I feel fresh.

"Weekend evenings are social times, but George and I do business and household projects during the weekend day. Many of our busy friends have similar life-styles when they are at home. A few confess to working twenty-hour days during the week and sleeping twenty hours a day on the weekends."

Collins, too, has an effective strategy for handling her schedule. "There are many adaptations necessary when one gives work such a high priority. Time is my most limiting factor, and as I take on more responsibilities, I try to be very, very organized. While I juggle a lot, I try to concentrate my time and energy to complete one task at a time and to prioritize by doing first things first. I also try to be realistic about what I am able to contribute to the various organizations in which I get involved, and not to allow myself to be used for 'window dressing.' I have learned to say no if I do not feel I can make an honest contribution. Once I accept, I am very goal-oriented, and I quickly try to find out which players I will be able to mobilize to get the job accomplished."

An accountant shared, "Handling time wisely is the toughest thing I do. I try to schedule a specific function for each night of the work week. For instance, I reserve one night a week for 'catch-up time' on my job. This means the freedom to stay at the office until a certain amount of work is completed, and this can last up until 10:00 P.M. Another night is scheduled for an intellectual event or for serious reading time. And one night goes for community work or committee or board meetings. Organization is the key."

A high level government employee said, "On most Monday mornings, if I thought about all the things I was responsible for that week, I'd probably never get out of bed. I would just lie there and think discouragingly, 'I can't do it all.' So what I do is pep myself up by the reminder that I have *five* days in the week to do it all, and I try to divide my priorities so that I have a schedule that is workable. Sometimes activities can be combined, eliminated, or rescheduled in a manner that is convenient to all involved."

Since good health and a high level of energy are absolutely essential for the professional woman, we need to schedule time for our physical well-being into our busy lives also. This may have to be worked in at odd moments. Some of the women in our study carry sports clothes with them so they can take advantage of any free moments to exercise. Other women join exercise groups or schedule tennis or other recreational pursuits at lunchtime or right after work. Nycum agrees that exercise is a must for any serious executive, but finding time to fit it in is a problem for her. Her solution: "I take early morning walks or do aerobic exercise. My most recent Christmas present was a cross-country ski machine."

Collins maintains her health and energy level by jogging most mornings with her husband for one to two miles. Her comment, "I hate it, but I do it," means that it is sometimes difficult to get going, and not much fun while doing it, but afterwards she feels energized and is always glad she made the effort. And she feels it is good for her husband! She adds, "But what I recently discovered at La Costa, a San Diego health spa, is the trampoline or rebounder. This is something I really enjoy, and I try to exercise daily."

Gilbert, too, acknowledges the value of exercise, despite her proclamation: "I hate, loathe, and abhor exercise. When people at parties enthusiastically spring up to play volleyball, I want to slide under the table." Her remedy is to jump rope in twenty-minute stints. At times she slacks off from this routine, but inevitably disciplines herself to return to it, working up to the twenty-minute periods again. For most women, discipline plays a part in keeping committed to their own health and exercise regimens.

One woman, a physician, said, "I always take time to schedule something in my day to look forward to. This may be a delightful luncheon with a friend, a good book I am looking forward to reading, even a television show. But I always have something each day that is just for me. I find that this helps me keep my emotional balance."

She gave the following advice: "Taking care of yourself is very important. Remember that you are 'number one' and give yourself permission to be good to yourself. Take time to watch the colors of sunsets, enjoy the power of waves, feel the warm sun on your body, and listen to the song of birds without a sense of beginning or end."

Shared a marketing director, "To make the best use of your time, first set realistic goals. Then determine the priorities. Of those duties to be accomplished during the week, tackle the short-term emergencies first. Then schedule the weekly priorities into segments to be handled each day. Try to be realistic—don't give yourself so much to do that you leave the office each night feeling discouraged and more behind than ever."

Tips from the Top

Dianne Feinstein, mayor of San Francisco, in correspondence with Collins in late 1985, offered some insight into her own commitment to work and how she manages her schedule. She gave some advice to women rising through the ranks: "As mayor, efforts to manage my personal time do indeed present 'special problems.' Basically, I view my office as a seven-day, twenty-four-hours-a-day position; I don't leave it between 9 and 5. There are simply too many pressing issues that are quite unpredictable to confine the office schedule to normal business hours. What I try to do, though, is save Sunday for my family."

She also said, "With respect to advising women new to senior management, I guess my bottom line is to do your homework; know your subject thoroughly; and be willing to be available whenever you are needed.

"I advise women aiming for leadership positions to develop very thick skin. You have to be resilient and prepared for the fact that you will win some and lose some. Stamina is critical."

Mary Brem Templeton, one of the very able women on Wall Street, is vice-president and general counsel for SPC Securities Services Corp. In an interview with Susan Nycum in February 1986, she made a number of important observations about professional women that she learned from working in New York.

Templeton commented on the frequent tendency of women to equate amount (or hours) of work with effectiveness. She said, "I have learned that one doesn't have to work all the time to be on top of the job. Indeed, the person who is or becomes indispensable in a job may not be promoted and ends up staying there. My advice is to be sure to constantly groom a successor, so you will be free to move on. Men figure this out earlier than do women. The Old Boys' Network takes the younger men under its wing and teaches them what they need to know. Women don't have these advantages."

Templeton passed on some pragmatic advice learned from her father, a surgeon. He said, "You don't have to walk on water to be successful, just walk a half step ahead of the guy behind you."

She continued, "Among the burdens working women carry that working men don't are the perception in the community that if one visible woman fails, all women fail, and the perception that all women support each other (when, in fact, there are women managers who are prejudiced against women). These latter are frequently women who have never had female peers and tend to identify with traditional male viewpoints. We also have to cope with the fact that child care and maternity leave is not as accepted as military or reserve leave.

"Wall Street is still very male chauvinistic — women are still looked upon as a 'piece of fluff' in spite of the fact that they are chairing more and more of the important meetings. Women obtain credibility later in their careers than men, and I have read in the *Wall Street Journal* that when there is a merger, the women are released first and then accept lower jobs than they had before while their male peers hold out for higher offers."

Templeton concluded with some practical tips, "Be the best prepared person at each meeting and keep on your toes during it, communicate upward, and blow your own horn for a change. A person who is focused upward and communicates upward usually moves upward."

When we asked the 160 women in our survey to share their "tips from the top" on the organization of their time, they responded:

- *Every block of fifteen minutes counts; use it wisely.*
- *Learn to delegate—this is essential.*
- *Do the most difficult tasks early in the day when you are rested.*
- *Learn to prioritize, and shift priorities when necessary.*
- *Keep a daily list of things to accomplish, and check it off.*
- *Have an annual plan, a monthly plan, a weekly plan, a daily plan.*
- *Never attend meetings without a clear understanding of the agenda.*
- *Pay close attention to the bottom line.*
- *Try not to waste time regretting a past action or decision.*
- *Learn to say no firmly.*
- *Set aside one night to stay late and complete the overflow.*
- *Avoid reading mail and other memos that come across your desk more than once; make a decision on each as you open it.*
- *Accomplish as much as possible by telephone.*
- *When you accomplish your goals, reward yourself.*

One woman wisely summed up, "When you have more to do than you think you *can* do, do it now; do it fast; delegate, delegate, delegate." Said another, "Always keep an appointment book at hand. In the office put it by your telephone; otherwise, keep it in your purse. Make daily lists, check them several times a day, and don't allow yourself to get sidetracked."

And another concluded with, "Keep your office and especially your desk *clean*. File everything except what you are currently working on, and don't spend too much time on any one item."

The *New York Times* published an article in 1985 entitled, "A Survey of Women Officers of America's Largest Corporations," a poll of 107 executives conducted by Kane, Parsons and Associates. Among other issues, the women commented on their lack of time to do all that they wanted. Some 63 percent responding stated that in order to be successful, they had to give up their marriages, family plans, time with their families, social relationships with friends, as well as such pleasures as travel, cultural activities, and leisure time.

The women questioned were employed by corporations included in the Fortune 500 and listed by *Standard & Poor's Register of Corporations, Directors, and Executives.*

Most women in very high-pressure jobs find that even when setting aside time for themselves, a minor change in schedule can throw all their plans awry. It helps to talk to many acquaintances and friends to compare how they manage their lives. We haven't yet found any woman who can honestly claim that she manages it all perfectly. Finding an appropriate balance among ourselves, our families, and our work seems to be a lifelong pursuit.

STRESS

Almost all of the respondents to our survey report some stress in their lives, but less than 15 percent reported feeling in a state of almost perpetual stress.

The working world produces a unique stress of its own. Many professional women we know leave their offices with stuffed briefcases, fight the traffic to get home, unwind with a drink and a late meal, and then work for a few more hours before collapsing into bed. As one woman wrote, "Ever feel stressed? Of course, it comes with *all* high level jobs!" Another wisely added, "I have worked with many top people, and I've yet to see one succeed who couldn't handle stress and handle it well. Early on it is essential to learn to 'let things just roll off your back.' And it is important to adopt the philosophy that you can't win them all—remember, 51 percent can be a majority."

Some women reported that a certain level of stress can even be useful. The late Hans Selye coined the word "eustress." He described this as "stress, which if handled correctly, gives one a competitive edge, and enhances one's creativity." We have found that eustress can have a positive effect on our career and can psych us up for presentations or for situations with others in which we need to do our best.

The women in our study, often under great pressure to advance in their professional career, reported handling their stress in different ways; for many, control was a key issue. Notes Collins, "We manage well as long as we know our boundaries and are in charge. If someone encroaches on our territory, and tries to take over, it causes great anxiety. Normally our work goes fine as long as we feel we are in charge of our 'area of control.' "

When asked what their physical symptoms were when stressed, the respondents' replies were varied. Lesser stress symptoms included flushing, sweating, dry mouth, shallow breathing, chest pain, heart palpitation, fatigue, internal distress, and diarrhea. If stress was severe, some women experienced amenorrhea (loss of menstruation), premenstrual tension and headaches, postpartum depression, melancholia, and even anorexia. Many reported that these symptoms made them feel agitated, irritable, panicky, shaky, and depressed. Several also said that they had a hard time getting to sleep, and when they did, they experienced nightmares and, in extreme situations, some even had a fear of death.

While our sample reported certain stress accompanies their jobs, Metropolitan Life has discovered in a recent study of 2,352 women listed in *Who's Who* that their annual death rate is 29 percent lower than that of their contemporaries. Indeed, the groups of women who have had the highest rates of heart disease are secretaries and saleswomen—women in the jobs with little security, status, or say over their work situation.

What Causes Stress

The causes of stress are diverse, but there are several persistent themes we found among high-achieving women. For many, stress revolves around the demands of the job. Frustration arises from unfulfilled desires, a lack of satisfaction with career progress, perceived discrimination due to sex, and the day-to-day decisions at work. Politics at work are reported by many to be a cause of tension, and the difficulties of managing people cause problems for others.

Shared one respondent, "The biggest stress I ever had was when I found out through the grapevine that a colleague was aiming for my job. And because it was not in the open, I was at a loss to know how to fight."

Time, or the lack thereof, is a big stressor for many as we try to juggle responsibilities at home and at work while leaving some time to pursue personal interests. Many of us feel that we do not spend enough time with children, husbands, or lovers. Demands caused by long hours or deadlines, too much responsibility, and travel are blamed as being the principal causes of stress.

Occasionally, events in other people's lives are stressors for us. One woman reported her mother's illness as causing stress, and several mentioned the death of a peer as the ultimate stressor. Others commented on the difficulties they are having with their teenaged children, especially drug-related problems.

A recurring theme was having the responsibility of caring for their parents. Wrote one, "Women traditionally have been charged with the caring functions of the family, and thus it is we who most often feel the strain. While I expected someday to care for my aging father, the timing couldn't have been worse; he arrived to live with us the same month my youngest of four went off for college."

Single women, especially single mothers, find loneliness and the lack of another person with whom to share problems can cause stress. For some, the demands of building and sustaining a romantic relationship are causing problems.

Money was reported to be a cause of stress by less than 10 percent of respondents, but these felt they were financially undercompensated at work. Several women were close to retirement and concerned about monetary security in their futures.

We were surprised to find weight control mentioned as a stressor by several women. Some of these respondents are currently overweight and struggling to diet. Said one, "I am more stressed by breaking promises to myself to diet, than I am by the actual increase of pounds." Only a few are fighting to gain weight. Thus appearance seems to cause problems for some women.

One respondent reported public speaking early in her career was a major stress, especially the unpredictability of her voice. She said, "If I got through the first ten sentences, I relaxed and knew I would be OK. But I never knew how my voice was going to come out, and I find I coughed and cleared my throat a lot before my turn."

Several women seemingly have insight into their own personalities and believe that their own reactions to their lives or their too-high expectations for themselves are causing distress. One reported that she "overprograms" herself and is "too diversified in activities." Another cited her need constantly to control as her primary stressor, and a third mentioned *success* itself as being stressful and a lot more demanding than she had envisioned.

While the causes of stress were varied among our survey respondents, we see the persistent responses of juggling responsibilities in many diverse areas, discrimination, over-high expectations, and the lack of time as consistent themes. But some concluded that a certain level of stress was positive and, if handled correctly, could produce favorable results.

How We Cope

The ways we cope with stress are varied. Nycum has an approach that almost always works for her. "When I feel stress at night, I sit in a hot tub filled with expensive scented bath oil, sip a glass of dry white wine, and read a murder mystery. A great way to rescue a morning off to a bad start is by a shorter soak (sans wine). The idea is to break the chain of tension by doing something deliberately nice for myself and figuratively thumbing my nose at the pressures."

She also humorously adds, "In addition, I unwind by making ever richer chocolate desserts. As an unreformed chocoholic, who is always on a diet,

I have to take the desserts to my office. I have corrupted an entire work force!"

Gilbert adds that she handles stress in the following manner: "I try to determine if my life is manageable today. If the answer is no, I figure out what I need to do to be in control. Usually I see that things will shortly improve or that I may have to make a major adjustment. I spent many years fearful of losing something because I couldn't do it all perfectly. I now have a different perspective. If I'm miserable and no relief is in sight, I will do whatever is necessary—including a job change or a temporary time out. Nothing under my control—and the choice to work *is* under my control—is worth either my health or that of my family."

Collins has her own approach to handling stress. "If things get *really* bad, I conjure up a picture in my mind of an uncaring nursing home for the elderly, which I think is very depressing. I then ask myself, 'Well, would you rather be yourself with all your problems, or would you rather be sitting in a wheelchair with very few decisions to make?' This helps get my life in perspective and gives me a great appreciation for my health, vitality, and the fact that I am fortunate to be where I am. And this perspective almost always makes my problem-solving a game."

Slightly over one-half of our sample said that they exercise routinely to cope with stress and felt that it helps in providing some relief. Interestingly, many of those who do not exercise routinely also felt it helps to cope with stress, but either do not schedule the time or do not choose to exercise. The methods of exercising employed are varied. Some women reported jogging or running routinely, and walking was mentioned by many. Most women who exercise choose several combinations, such as ballet and walking, aerobics and weight training, biking and swimming, calisthenics, and sailing. No one listed only one method.

Less than 15 percent of the women we surveyed smoke, which compares favorably with the national average for women. According to a 1985 Gallup Poll, 35 percent of the U.S. population smokes, and of these, 32 percent are women. Only two respondents in our study smoke more than one pack per day. Half of the smokers would like to quit, and the other half are presumably content with their smoking behavior and reported no plans to stop.

Although 80 percent drink socially, less than 25 percent of our respondents said that they use alcohol to cope with stress. We asked these women how many alcoholic drinks they take in a week, and answers ranged from one drink to twenty. Only two women felt they drink too much, and five had someone in their lives who they felt abuses alcohol. Only one woman admitted to being a recovering alcoholic now active in AA; another described herself as a potential alcoholic and chooses not to drink. As Alcoholics Anonymous estimates that 10 percent of the people who drink are alcoholics, our data suggest that our sample is much lower than the national average.

Less than 15 percent of our sample reported occasional use of drugs (other than alcohol) to cope with stress. Valium was used by several, and marijuana was used by one. Several reported using medications to help them sleep. One reported using vitamins for stress, and a few others used over-the-counter stimulants for late-night meetings.

When we asked what other coping mechanisms our sample used for dealing with stress, the answers were highly individualistic and diverse. Some try meditation or prayer for psychological relief. Talking with friends is helpful for some, and forcing one's mind to other matters or keeping events in long-term perspective works for others. Relaxation techniques, including self-hypnosis, are useful, as are stress-reduction programs.

One respondent was quite creative in how she handled stress and confided, "Once a year, I go to Great America and ride the most exciting ride—I find that screaming my lungs out, normally socially unacceptable behavior, is incredibly purging and rejuvenating!"

Said an investment counselor, "Awareness of your body is important. Occasionally taking stock of stressful events is helpful. I schedule long-weekend breaks—by taking three Fridays off in a row—and I find this the most relaxing; sometimes a longer vacation is exhausting! Also, I have other activities and interests *totally* removed from work and people at work—mine is the world of opera. Thus, having a private life separate from work life gives a breather."

Diversionary activities help many. Some said that reading, especially "trashy" novels, helps them unwind. Physically removing ourselves from a stressful situation may help, and days off from work or vacation meet this need. One woman wrote, "When I feel stressed, I consciously pull in and try to find time for *myself*, which is the most difficult time to find. The vacation that works best for me is to take twenty-four hours, register into a nearby luxury hotel, spend the day shopping in elegant stores, and have room service for a late dinner in bed while watching TV—things I enjoy but never seem to get to do at home. As I am married with several children, this takes a special kind of husband, but he is willing to extend himself for this crucial twenty-four hours several times a year for my sanity."

Self-indulgence, or being good to ourselves, is a common response to stress. Shopping, especially for such "treats" as expensive clothing, and eating chocolates provide needed relief. Others mentioned that "touch" helped—getting their hair done, having a facial, manicure, or a long massage.

And still another wrote, "For stress I advise doing something physical for a few hours: exercise, garden, paint something; if no time for the above, at least go to the women's room and breathe deeply for twenty times or so—this is great short-term therapy."

It is a very rare high level woman, we have found, who has not at some point in her life gone to see a professional counselor for outside help. This can be either a psychiatrist, psychologist, or other professional helper. For some people, this is a difficult step to take, either because they are conditioned to think only unstable people see psychiatrists or because they don't like to admit they cannot solve their problems on their own. One mark of an executive is to know when to consult experts.

Said a company president, "I do not believe it is an admission of failure to see people who can help me with my emotions, and this experience can be a tremendous opportunity for personal growth. My advice is that if you find that you need such help, there are many ways to find a competent professional: references from friends (you will be surprised at how many people will tell you of their own good experiences in therapy if you ask), a referral by a doctor whom you trust, or a local health-services agency. And it is quite acceptable to interview them, both for fees and for their personality and outlook, before you agree to retain their services."

An entrepreneur warned, "It can sometimes be difficult to find a competent professional person with the experience and background to successfully understand and help a successful woman with unique problems. I made several tries before I found someone who could relate to a patient other than a typical male executive or a traditional woman, but then it was well worth the effort."

Vacations are perhaps one of the best ways to deal with stress. However, many of our respondents said that they seldom take all the time that their firm allows. But when we find ourselves getting somewhat out of balance, exhausted, abusing alcohol or drugs, or being irritable, one of the first questions we should ask ourselves is whether we need a vacation. Even a few days can work wonders, unless there are underlying emotional or physical problems that need professional care.

We believe career-oriented women need to relearn what all school children intuitively know—that vacations are to be looked forward to and cherished! Vacations may be the most important scheduling we do for ourselves. In addition, many senior level women travel, and one or two days' vacation can be added to the end of what would otherwise be a stressful trip. Relaxing in a different part of the world with no telephones, mail, or normal interruptions can do a great deal toward restoring vitality.

Nycum finds, "A real vacation is too difficult to schedule, so I take an extra day or two on a business trip when George can join me. This year we have been in Denmark, Israel, Singapore, and France—not bad at all for fun, and just enough time to rest without losing touch with the office. Also, from time to time, George and I take a weekend off in nearby Carmel and just forget all our daily commitments."

Collins's personal vacation plan is to "find the sun" for a week at the end of each January, either in Hawaii or Mexico, and to take several shorter trips during the year. She considers herself lucky to be able to plan as flexibly as she does with her husband, a psychiatrist who governs his own schedule.

Gilbert finds that vacations in her family are difficult to schedule and says, "I find it hard to get away. I know I put the pressure on myself, and I'm trying to change this." She does, however, take some vacation time, usually a week at Christmas and one or two weeks in the summer, but not ever more than two weeks at a time. Her final word on time off: "When I really get to the end of my rope, I go see a movie."

Our approaches to vacation differ, but we all agree on the need for refreshing breaks and for planning them into our schedules. Many executive women plan and schedule their vacations at the beginning of the year for the entire year. While we may have to be flexible and change plans, we have learned that it is best to make a vacation something that, barring accident or serious illness, is going to happen on schedule.

There are many causes for stress in each of our lives, and it is important to find the means to cope—both short term means, such as reading, exercise, or other relaxing techniques, and long term ones, such as vacations or time off from work. Successfully handling stress can literally ensure our survival.

THE "NEW GIRLS' NETWORK"

Male executives have long proven how valuable the "Old Boys' Network" is for them. Networking is building a community of professional peers across professional and occupational lines. Networking helps women become more effective in the work world and gain clout, money, more know-how, and more self-confidence. It helps us beat the system, which tends to isolate women as we move up in a male-dominated environment. In short, it is getting together to get ahead.

The importance of networks goes far beyond friendships; networks are an important part of the total work environment. Those people in our network have the power to effect many major business decisions, and sometimes an important choice is made on the golf course or over cocktails. Top level women are discovering what men have known all along, and that is, ambitious people profit greatly by associations with equally successful people on an informal basis.

It is important for younger career-oriented women to understand the value of networking. According to Mary-Scott Welch in *Networking* (New York: Harcourt Brace Jovanovich, 1980), "Women hold only 6 percent of the top managerial and administrative positions, the category where we're supposed to be making such huge strides. The other ninety-four percent of the people in these jobs are male." She concluded, "We need each other! Only through networking can women be a real bond and support to each other which is needed for advancement."

Network groups are formed to develop and use contacts, to get inside information, to share ideas, and to lend moral support when the going gets rough. But as one climbs higher, the select network circle becomes smaller. One respondent commented, "Most of my friends are in similar professional positions. We understand our personal standards are higher than those of most others around us. We also know we place higher demands on ourselves than on others at work and at home."

The motivations for selecting new friends are many. Nycum reveals hers: "As I get older, I find that things don't get easier, but they do get clearer. What is clear to me now is that if I am ever going to meet people outside my professional field, it is time to make that effort. So I am seeking out people who bring some new dimension to my life; people who have achieved something that I don't know anything about, or who are in fields with which I am not familiar such as mountain climbing or working in Scotland Yard. The criterion is people who have achieved a very high level of expertise because they are the people who are compatible with my existing friends."

Collins says, "We personally know many friends who have taken the initiative to form groups of women like themselves with comparable job responsibilities and experience. In fact, Sue, Susan, and I were instrumental in helping to guide such a group, the Peninsula Professional Women's Network, through its formative years. We have now formed another group, Forum West. We are convinced that busy women need a small circle of active friends with whom they can share their careers. We all need other women who talk our language as equals."

Wrote a respondent on the importance of networking: "For women who make it beyond a certain level, there is a great need to spend informal time with a peer group which cuts across age and occupation. Senior [level] women are limited in their numbers. We need nurturing acquaintances who keep us from feeling so isolated. It is important to discuss how others juggle their homes and jobs and if they feel guilty over not spending more time with their husbands. We need friends like us, who don't apologize if they haven't cooked a meal in two months or changed a bed in three!"

In testimony to that last remark, Gilbert recently experienced the benefits of a network: "I've much enjoyed the New Girls' Network concept. When I recently decided to change jobs, many of my female network associates really went to bat for me and tried to use their contacts to help me. Several things about this experience impressed me. First, women have now achieved positions of sufficient influence to help other women; and second, many women were delighted to help a 'sister.' I intend to repay their kindness by helping other women throughout my entire career."

One woman in our study who manages a large shopping center told us about the importance of her select circle of professional contacts when she recently went through a job crisis. Because she was not one of the 'boys' at work, she really did not have anyone connected with her job to turn to in confidence who understood what she was going through. She told us, "Fortunately, I had several close friends who held similar jobs with different centers. To deal with my crisis, I invited them for an emergency dinner meeting to discuss my options. I received excellent feedback and advice on the power I already had and how I should best use it. My story has a happy ending, and the advice from my network was used in a very crucial time, enabling me to 'land on my feet' after a time of turmoil in my career."

As one woman wrote, "When I am with my network, it is one of the few times I can brag about my victories, and my peers feel pleased and proud, rather than envious, resentful, or threatened." Wrote another, "Competitive women acknowledge each other's abilities, drives, and ambitions. They provide reinforcement and encouragement for each other. They spur each other on. Competitive women give their best work when pitted against each other."

Senior level women are realizing more than ever that we need and can be useful to each other. Men have long enjoyed the benefits of their Old Boys' Network, and now women are beginning to establish the same kind of organizations. Relating to our female peers in a professional and social sense is as valuable and beneficial for women rising in their fields as it is for their male counterparts.

Although we believed we could guess the answer, we nonetheless decided to poll the respondents in our survey to see if they belonged to networks or other organizations for women only. Seventy-five percent replied they did, and some added that they found such groups very useful and helpful.

Of the 24 percent who said no, several stated they would like to if more time were available. Only 1 percent did not answer. We recommend taking the time: the rewards are well worth the effort.

In summary, many women in our study make work central to their lives with an intense commitment to their career. However, giving work such importance does not mean women cannot also have other focuses—husbands, children, and meaningful friendships. The balancing of roles is difficult and often stressful and will probably be ongoing for as long as women have high level careers. Organization of time, the establishment of networks, as well as good health and energy are crucial and act as limiting factors on what can be accomplished.

2 The People with Whom We Work

"It is not enough to have great qualities,
You should also have the management of
them."
—*FRANÇOIS LA ROCHEFOUCAULD* (MAXIMS)—

As women climb in organizations, gaining position, power, and responsibility, we must become increasingly adept at leading and managing people. But no matter how excellent our personal qualities of leadership and management are, we have found that it is hard to get to the top solely on our own. If we cannot fit into the organizational structure, we will not advance beyond a certain level. Most executive women have learned how to work effectively and supportively with subordinates, peers, and bosses. And they were open to being coached, groomed, and mentored into higher positions, until they were bosses themselves.

The sobering fact is that no matter how *willing* women are to work for those high positions, the dynamics of organizations play a critical role, as Gilbert notes: "I find that being a woman and an executive is still sometimes an issue in organizations. I have worked with many supportive bosses, peers, and subordinates; I have also worked with (luckily few) people who made life, and the accomplishment of our objective, difficult. Some, of course, are simply difficult people, and gender plays no role in the interpersonal relationship. In other cases, problems arose because I am a woman.

"One problem occurred when I worked briefly for a man who had never had a female executive in a direct reporting relationship before. He didn't know whether to treat me as one of the boys or to try to establish a personal relationship, and he tried both tactics. His confusion added to a difficult working relationship.

"Also, several times I have had to demand a difficult assignment that would naturally have been part of my job but that was going to be assigned to a man in order to 'protect me.' Assumptions were made about my ability to travel or work long hours because of my family responsibilities. However, over time, people learned that I could and would hold my own."

Rear Admiral Grace M. Hopper, recently retired from the Naval Data Automation Command of the United States Navy and holder of forty-six honorary degrees, is one of the best-known women in the country. She is responsible for having trained countless people, and as one of our sample, reflected on leadership in a November 8, 1985, interview with Susan Nycum. Rear Admiral Hopper stressed teamwork and the bond that is needed both up and down in an organization. She also differentiated managers from leaders; managers may manage projects, but they do not lead people. Leaders inspire, motivate, and lead those below. Rear Admiral Hopper stated, "We went overboard on management, and now we've got to remember leadership."

She said, "Good leadership is important no matter what job you're in. I go back to the things I learned at midshipman's school. Leadership is a two-way street, with loyalty down as well as up." She stressed those below should "respect your superiors and keep them informed." And she advised those in leadership positions to "take care of your 'crew'—and this especially applies to those in charge of younger people." Rear Admiral Hopper is currently a consultant at the Digital Equipment Corporation in Washington, D.C.

Throughout this section, we comment extensively on the differences between men and women's positions in the workplace. This acknowledges the dominance of numbers of men in business and the accommodation of the environment to men. As the numbers of women in the work force increase, so, too, will the environment change. However, we expect a number of years to pass before participation is more equal at all levels.

THE BOSS

The most important person in a career, besides oneself, is usually the boss. Our experience validates that women need to understand the power he or she can wield in making or breaking their advancement in the short term. The boss can also have long-term influence. The boss evaluates us for promotions and salary increases and carries or suppresses the message of our abilities to superiors, thereby establishing our reputation throughout the company.

In discussing why the boss is so important, Betty Harragan stated in *Knowing the Score* (New York: St. Martin's Press, 1983), "Given that tremendous breadth of control over your present peace of mind and your eventual career destiny, it is little wonder that the boss relationship is so highly charged with emotional reactions towards the *person* who is in that position relative to you."

She added, "Absolute deference to the authority invested in your immediate boss is the undeviating number one rule of the (working) game. There is no way you can leapfrog, bypass, overrule, ignore, challenge, disobey, or criticize your boss and not get penalized in the game."

Once you have decided to become a career woman, selecting the right boss and a good organizational climate to facilitate your move upward is crucial. In later years many of us have the good fortune to be in a position actually to choose a good boss, but in the early working years, having a good boss is often a matter of luck.

Collins's thoughts are backed by her own earliest experience of a boss—her father. "He influenced me at an early age by taking me under his wing and teaching me about his business and his philosophy of making a livelihood. At one time he owned three furniture stores, and when I was in high school, I worked for him on Saturdays and Wednesday afternoons as well as full-time during the summers. I learned as much as I could—from ordering, cataloging, and bookkeeping to displaying and selling. While there was a certain prestige in being the boss's daughter, I soon discovered that my father did not treat me any differently than he did the other employees.

"Some of what I learned related to basic 'profit and loss'—Saturday night closing time was a lot happier when the books showed a large gain. Bourbon would be passed around on special occasions, and everyone—both drivers and salesmen—would slap each other on the back and offer congratulations. During this time I was allowed to be part of their adult male world and share their comradery.

"Working for my father furthered my desire to be equal to men in the working world. I found out I could be just as helpful to the customers and sell the same quantity as could the male salesmen. Thus the potential for commission could be the same—this was an enormously valuable lesson."

Collins's first experience with a boss, regardless of the family tie, was a positive one in that she was allowed the freedom to work to her own potential and was given the opportunity to learn.

Nycum comments, "I once worked for a boss who used his relationship with me much as a teaching doctor would in a teaching hospital. He would tell me after he'd done something why he'd done what he'd done, and then we would review how successful he had been. He thought that it was helpful for him, as well as enormously beneficial to me, to go through this learning experience."

The value of a good boss cannot be overemphasized. This sentiment is echoed by other senior level women, who state that they scrutinize the prospective boss almost as closely as they do the actual job. They try to select a situation in which their boss is very competent at what he or she does. They look for a boss who is well respected by their peers, as well as one who has vision and is not threatened by subordinates' good performances. They also look for a boss who rewards achievement and is willing to delegate, a hard task for some.

Nycum says, "In the days when I had a boss, I chose to work for the person who brought the most 'value added' to my career at the time. By 'value added,' I mean anything in addition to the opportunity to do the job and get paid money for spending my time at it. In my case, I always was looking for someone who would teach me something that I didn't already know or would update what I knew—that would include psychological education as well as substantive education. For instance, how does Mr. Jones handle this new situation at a level higher than the one with which I'm comfortable? This knowledge would allow me to grow into the higher level."

Gilbert adds, "I once had an opportunity to work for an established firm where I felt the job would not be permanent, but I took it anyway. I did this first to do direct selling of the firm's services and second to perform consulting assignments because my analytical skills had grown rusty. This gave me a chance to work with someone I greatly respected and to brush up on analytical techniques, as well as to have the opportunity to gain selling skills. This proved to be a crash refresher course in business and was a very valuable experience."

Our advice to professional women, then, is to choose the boss carefully, if you are at liberty to do so, and select a person from whom you can learn *something*. Everyone who has worked under an exceptional boss treasures the experience. Nycum recalls her first boss at Stanford. "He taught me the necessity of always solving a number of problems with each solution—be it technical, managerial, or just the use of time. He taught me to be a strategist rather than a tactician and how to cut through the layers of what he termed 'foo-foo dust' to get to the central issue."

Although we'd all like to choose our boss, we're not always able to do so. The negative boss is someone we can unfortunately encounter in our career. How is a bad, or negative, boss defined? In general terms, a bad boss is one who stifles a subordinate's growth and initiative, does not recommend a deserved promotion, and worse, hides the subordinate's ability and performance from other superiors. Such a boss can sometimes be afraid that he or she will be overshadowed by the subordinate or that his or her own career will somehow be damaged by the loss of the subordinate's work. A bad boss can also be defined as one who is powerless and therefore unable to command the necessary resources to accomplish the job.

Early in our careers, many of us experience a boss who we feel is a selfish tyrant, an ogre, or not terribly bright. It sometimes helps to get the relationship into perspective by remembering that the company thinks the boss has good qualities or he or she would not have been elevated to that position.

Said one respondent, "The pain of betrayal which I felt, caused by a former boss, a person I had totally trusted, was greater than any I experienced before or since."

What a negative experience can teach us is perseverance. It can also make us wiser. If we can learn to work for a tyrant (and keep in mind it is temporary), the exercise will strengthen us in future years. Learning to take criticism and even some abuse without getting upset is important. Although most of us will always learn best from bosses we admire, it is possible to get some valuable lessons while waiting for the right time to move away from those we dislike.

In evaluating our relationship with a boss, chemistry can also be a big factor. Sometimes we work for a person we just do not like, and this immediate, "gut" response can become a permanent negative feeling. Understanding the person's prime motivation will often help us deal with the situation on a more rational basis. Because it is so important to work for someone we like, admire, and trust and with whom we are comfortable, we shouldn't hang on to positions where we do not like or respect our boss. Chances are, because he or she outranks us, he or she will be there longer than we will.

Collins finds that she has been fortunate in having had mostly outstanding bosses. She notes there was an exception, however. "I once worked for a man for whom I had little respect. During this short period in my career, both he and I spent a lot of energy openly undermining each other's reputation and in trying to get rid of the other. I had a loyal group of supporters, as did he. This was my first experience with office politics and the male ego. Although this person was my boss, he was several years younger than I and was behind in experience and judgment. This was a most unpleasant and disfunctional time.

"In later analyzing the situation, I realized this man had never supervised a professional woman before, nor had he ever achieved any great recognition in his own career. He felt threatened by my experience and visibility, and as my boss, he was not able to be nourishing or facilitating to my own growth."

Gilbert, also, through experience has come to be particular about her boss. "I was once in a situation in which I did not have my boss's support. Due to circumstances over which neither of us had control, I was asked to report to a man whose management style and thought processes were very different from mine.

"With some misgivings, we agreed to the arrangement and tried hard to make it work. I'm afraid that my underlying lack of comfort with his style showed, and his feelings that I wasn't quite what he had in mind for the job were apparent to me and a few others. My self-confidence was undermined to a point that was untenable.

"In retrospect, I should have never agreed to work for someone about whom I had such misgivings. He left the organization before I did, and thus the problem was solved, but I would not willingly repeat an experience that was so personally discomforting. Bosses, and their support, are crucial to us all."

Nycum comments, "I outgrew bosses as fast as my child did her clothes. Two incidents come to mind as examples of when I knew it was time to go. One was when my boss criticized my attire as being too fashionable when, in fact, it was both more appropriate and in better taste than his own. The comment disclosed his insecurity in the relationship and his need for control. The second time was when a boss who, instead of looking pleased with my handling of a delicate matter in his absence, looked threatened. Each of these events was a start of the 'prickling of the thumbs' that tells me when it's time to move on.

"My few experiences with bad bosses have been short-lived. I simply cannot function with people who are dense and unfair. It is reassuring to learn that as one nears the top the density lessens dramatically and that unfair as such is rarely tolerated by the system because it is wasteful of human productivity."

On occasion bosses or others with whom we work won't leave the sexual possibilities of the relationship aside. Says Gilbert, "If we are at all attractive, we will certainly find ourselves in sticky situations. All senior level women I know have had to fend off advances on business trips or social occasions. Leaving our personal moral standards aside, it can be career suicide to yield to these temptations."

Gilbert remembers, "Years ago I actually had a boss tell me his wife 'didn't understand him.' A proposition soon followed. I'm afraid I wasn't too tactful in my refusal, but the incident was not repeated—at least not with him."

One corporate executive in our study wrote, "As our business pressure grew and profit fell, my boss's personality changed. He began to make life miserable for those under him. He became ruthless, short-tempered, and yelled a lot. We lost all respect for him, which was unfortunate. Had he created a different atmosphere, I think we could have succeeded, but unfortunately under his negative leadership, our ability to function diminished, and the division took an even steeper nosedive downward and was soon disbanded."

Fortunately, it is our experience that bad bosses seem to be the exception rather than the norm in the business world; yet most of us seem to encounter at least one bad boss during our career.

One of our prime responsibilities in working for anyone is to make him or her look good. The better we make our boss look, the more responsibility he or she will get, which, in turn, will lead to increased responsibility for us. Collins sums this up: "Early in my career, when I was learning the 'rules of work,' I used to expect credit for my efforts. During the years that followed, I learned the importance of not demanding recognition, but instead of putting a lot of effort into making my own boss look good. I believe promotions will follow just as fast this way, and with this attitude, you can guarantee there will be a lot of people higher up wanting you on their team."

Ralph Waldo Emerson once said, "Make yourself necessary to somebody." We find this to be especially good advice for women in the working world, and this is a valuable tactic in supporting your boss and in securing your position. One way of becoming necessary to your boss is to be an expert in at least one phase of his or her job, so that your ability in this area far exceeds his or hers. Thus, when your boss needs to make a major decision or report, you will most likely be consulted. A future benefit of such expertise is that when your boss moves up and duties are shuffled around you will be the logical one to assume responsibility for that area.

Gilbert found early on that she was good at finance and accounting and understood the principles better than one of her bosses. After she saved this man from making a potentially embarrassing error on the financial statements, he consulted her on all matters and eventually promoted her and delegated all the finance functions to her.

Another woman in our study wrote, "One important way to be valuable to our boss is to learn to deal effectively with people he doesn't like. Not only does this shield him from those with whom he has a conflict, but our ability to get along makes us a *very* valuable part of his team. Sometimes his success in a project depends on moving a certain phase of it through someone he hardly speaks to; then we become the logical one to assume this responsibility and his gratitude."

Collins remembers a boss who was often called upon with very little notice to give reports in a certain area. "I constantly updated this data so that he could count on me for this type of information, even though it was not formally part of my job. He knew he needed these facts in making reports to *his* boss, and I performed a valuable service for him."

Here are some suggestions that our survey respondents made regarding bosses: Know what their short- and long-term goals are and then be part of the *solution* not part of the *problem*. Keep them informed. Reinforce both the organization's and their positive self-image. Learn all you can from them and let them know you appreciate and need their help. Don't give them any negative surprises if you can avoid it. Let them know (and often) by deeds as well as words that you support them and their ideas and that you speak well of them throughout the organization. Keep their confidences and cover for them when necessary. And have the right attitude, attitude, attitude.

Shared one respondent, "I've worked for many brilliant people, and those that helped the boss most are those that do not point out *why* we couldn't do what the boss wanted. How bosses value employees who always say, 'I'm sure we can do it—I don't know how, but let's roll up our sleeves and go to work.' "

Shared another, "We can help our boss accomplish his/her job by really listening carefully when he/she talks. Many people think of how they are going to reply, and they lose some of the important message. Also, when given a project, stay with it until it is completed."

MALE ATTITUDES TOWARD FEMALE AMBITIONS

Male attitudes toward female ambitions in the work world are greatly changing, although not so quickly as most women would like. Our society is still in transition, as Gilbert's experience points out: "I have unfortunately been subject to some discrimination as a woman. I have had prospective employers say, 'I'd hire you in a minute if you were a man.' Recently an executive-search consultant told me that he frequently presents qualified executive women as candidates for a job, but they are usually not the person hired. This same person wanted to present me as a candidate for vice-president of finance for a company, but was told by the president he didn't feel the environment was ready for a woman. This was in 1985!"

In Betty Harragan's estimation, "Women are still not headed for the top jobs. Most women are still going into staff positions." She told us, "At senior level there is a wall across the workplace that we have not been able to penetrate. Men do not *want* women on their turf. When they can't fault a woman on her performance, they get her on her style. And I think younger men, including recent graduates, are just as bad as the older ones. They constantly threaten and knife the younger women. And we are easy targets because we are too trusting and naive."

Dianne Feinstein, San Francisco mayor, voiced some optimism over male attitudes. When asked if she thinks that American men have changed in the light of more women working, Mayor Feinstein said, "Yes, I think men have become more sensitive. I think men's attitudes are vastly better. Along with renewed sensitivity, there is a new willingness to listen to women."

That willingness may come more easily to younger men. It seems that many men over fifty do not take women as seriously or feel as comfortable with female executives as younger men do. Because men in their thirties had a large percentage of female classmates in the professional schools, they learned early on that not only will they be competing with women, but that women are as smart and certainly just as ambitious. Perhaps, though, this very fact contributes to the competitive ruthlessness that Betty Harragan sees, becoming a double-edged sword: because younger men *do* take women seriously, they are keenly competitive as they themselves struggle for position in the corporate workplace.

Gilbert offers another perspective on male attitudes: "One man, who was my boss for ten years, was especially supportive and encouraging. He is a man twenty-two years older than I and has two daughters. I believe that men who would like to see options available for their daughters are particularly helpful to women in business. Under this man's leadership as president of our company, close to half the management were women. Over time, these women were highly successful and accepted as equal players on the team. The company itself was extremely successful, growing profitably at 55 percent per year for many years."

Earmarks of transition and acceptance, however, don't alter the fact that a woman's presence affects corporate environments. Executive men are the first to say that business meetings and lunches have a different atmosphere if a woman is present. Not only are men more at ease if no women are there, but the topics are discussed more freely.

Nycum says, "Making people feel at ease is a skill still more essential to a woman in business than to a man. I work at it every day and try to learn from such experience—why a meeting went well or poorly. Increasingly, I find that a sense of belonging or comradery has little to do with gender, but much to do with age, status, ethnic ties, and similar agenda—all of which apply equally to men and women."

Some men still feel that off-color jokes and strong language are their prerogatives. We've heard of situations where women officers were the brunt of jokes, even when they were present. A woman's skill at extricating herself from awkward situations while keeping her cool (at least outwardly) is a skill as valuable as any accounting principle.

Collins, frequently the only woman at meetings, has learned to accept the fact that the talk before the meeting starts can center around sports and sometimes off-color stories. "I simply accept this as a fact of life," she says. "I have also learned that if I sit quietly and do not comment, the men share a laugh and the subject soon changes. I once was present when another woman tried to be 'one of the boys' and entered into the conversation by telling an even stronger off-color joke, and this seemed *very* inappropriate. Even the men seemed embarrassed! Instead of cementing her relationship into the group, which was her goal, the story seemed to have a reverse effect. The sad part was that I wasn't sure she even realized this."

Such men can also be quick to put down strong public figures who happen to be women, such as Margaret Thatcher and Jeane Kirkpatrick. Bruce Serbin, a New York–based writer, wrote an article for *Working Women* (May 1983), in which he said, "I once heard Kirkpatrick referred to by a high-level male as 'the girl at the U.N.' And this was when she was in the midst of her troubles with the former Secretary of State, Alexander Haig!"

How do men explain their resentment toward women and the inconsistency it represents? Serbin, in the article mentioned above, wrote it off as a matter of upbringing, saying that men are the ones raised on war and are better prepared as youths to lead. "Men are simply more competitive than women," he wrote. "Sometimes I don't know how to treat a woman executive—as a woman or as a man. It often comes down to a question of old world versus new world, basic things I'm used to doing for a woman like holding the door and waiting for her to be seated. Women threaten men when they depart from their traditional roles."

However, Nycum senses a move toward a much greater acceptance of women, including herself, as world-class figures. "I attribute much of this change in attitude to effective role models, such as Margaret Thatcher and Sandra Day O'Connor. It also appears easier for men to accord senior status as women reach forty and lessen as sex symbols."

Fortunately, most of us have found an increasing number of men to be secure in their talents and abilities and discovered they welcome the opportunity to work beside equally self-assured women.

In researching male attitudes toward female ambitions, we surveyed both men and women. First we surveyed fifty women in midlevel managerial positions (as contrasted with the 160 senior level women in our study), with salaries ranging from $30,000 to $50,000. When asked how they thought their bosses see them in relation to their male peers, the women listed as their common complaints (in order of frequency):

- *Are not treated seriously.*
- *Make less than our male peers in salary.*
- *Are assigned to more routine jobs.*
- *Are given staff rather than line promotions.*
- *Feel our skills are not fully utilized.*
- *Are overprotected.*
- *Are often excluded from social functions (especially sports events).*
- *Don't get credit for a project we pioneered.*
- *Are often interrupted in meetings.*
- *Frequently have our ideas passed over to have a senior level male recommend the same idea with acceptance.*

And one told us, "It is the pits to deal with my boss's misconception of 'you only got promoted to this job in my division because you are a woman.' "

The survey taught us three things. First, *very* senior level women have already learned, by personal experience as well as by viewing others, how to deal with most of the above situations. They have worked out those problems so that they seldom occur in their career. Second, midlevel women are the ones experiencing the above and other similar types of problems; and third, junior level women are not yet listing many of these situations as problems.

It is unclear why the junior level women do not relate to the above situations with which midlevel women are having problems. We can surmise only that they are working mostly with junior level men who may have learned to work more easily with women. Also, it may be because they are not high enough to be in contact with the seasoned veterans in the organization, who are chauvinistic and firmly entrenched in the Old Boys' Network. Or as one of our senior level women stated, "The junior level women are not yet visible enough to be targets."

To complete our survey of male attitudes regarding female ambitions, Collins surveyed twenty male corporate directors. She talked about the problems that they have personally observed younger women having as bosses. After a lengthy discussion, the men agreed that younger women who are recently promoted often have quite a few hurdles to jump. Below are their answers (in order of most serious to least):

- *Has a hard time delegating.*
- *Not good team player.*
- *Doesn't communicate as well informally.*
- *Not as skilled in team building or human relations.*
- *Complains too much.*
- *Doesn't handle problems by using established lines of authority.*
- *Behaves unpredictably.*

One CEO summarized: "The problem I have seen so many younger women have with their first major promotion is their belief that their work will continue to take them upward. An outstanding performance is no longer enough—they now need to master office politics."

While the directors were senior in age (as well as experience), we have found their answers are somewhat typical. Fortunately for women everywhere, younger women coming out of the professional schools are so well trained that they are helping to change the image of women in general.

The responses above apply mostly to midmanagement. Senior level women have already learned the rules, and junior level women—better trained and in larger numbers—will not face as many of these problems.

Gilbert shares her experience: "Several years ago there were more differences between men and women as bosses than there seem to be today. When I first moved into senior management about fifteen years ago, it seemed that women had more trouble adapting to the realities of the business world than they do today. I've seen tremendous growth in young women in terms of their needing to understand the rules of the game before they start playing. Our business schools are doing their job of coaching them, and the younger women are doing a better job of networking and asking the questions that get them the information they need to succeed. But I think the perceptions of some senior level or older men have not changed with the times."

Nycum adds, "I feel strongly that the mistake younger women bosses make, to the extent that they make them differently from younger men bosses, is to come on too intellectually, too stiffly, and not to roll with a situation or act as a human being. We're too concerned about the image of being emotional."

In our perception, this description of not showing emotions fits many older men we know. Nycum adds, "In my experience, women bend over backward not to show any feelings or take any sense of hysteria into the working relationship. That is wrong. There is a time to show anger and a time to show remorse. Men use emotions all the time, but women just stifle them. When they do so, they can lose one of the dimensions of being a good boss."

Marilyn Machlowitz, author of *Workaholics* (Cranbury, N.Y.: New American Library, 1980), said in a 1983 interview with *U.S. News & World Report* (quoted here as reported in the *San Francisco Chronicle*, August 25, 1983) that it is more difficult for women than men to compete for top jobs. "One theory," she noted, "is that women who have been put in middle management are those who do not have the traits for senior management. A study at Wellesley College showed that the characteristic of women in middle management and the characteristic desired for people in senior management do not overlap. The women in middle management were selected for their ability to carry out orders and not rock the boat. Exactly the opposite skills are needed for senior management."

Given that the workplace has been in transition for years, how will things get better? Betty Harragan gave us a direct, firm response, "We will have to count on women who have reached age forty-plus for the following reasons: they know about discrimination and have survived. They have passed their childbearing years. They have their personal problems at bay. They understand men and won't take the bullshit."

As Harragan emphasized, every successful career woman has experienced discrimination and has survived it. And as important as dealing with it is your own attitude, as Nycum expresses: "My war stories could fill a bitter book of frustrated ambition and despair if I chose to recount them. Frankly, I think most of the episodes were and—because they keep on happening—are funny. Humor is often the result of bizarre happenings, and male frustration of female ambitions simply because of sex differences is bizarre. Unfortunately, discrimination is real and must be dealt with. It strikes me that, like divorce, it is a possibility in every relationship and happens often. Yet to dwell on the horrible things that one's 'ex' did is to risk poisoning new relationships. I prefer to treat everyone equally and to require a rational reason for any discrepancies in that approach from others.

"For an ambitious woman, the key is to win the war, not necessarily each battle. It has no doubt taken me ten years longer than an equally gifted man to achieve what I have, but now I can see the detours and setbacks have been useful and even rewarding."

Women's success can also be difficult for our male colleagues, and we have known men to be especially resentful if they had a hand in training a woman, only to have her promoted over them. They can feel both stuck in their own inability to move upward and bitter that they were passed over. Men especially feel irritated if the women has "leapfrogged" several times and has not stayed in jobs long enough to "pay her dues."

There can be negative discussion on how she got the new job. The two most often used retorts seem to be "She got the promotion because she's a woman, and they are filling a quota" or "She got the job because she is sleeping with so-and-so." A banker told us about the time she got her first significant promotion. One of her male colleagues, miffed because he didn't get it, made some sly remark questioning whom she slept with to be promoted. "I was so mad," she said, "I told him the president, the vice-president, and all the senior members of his division."

The double standard also exists in language that we hear used. If a woman is aggressive, she becomes a "pushy broad." Men with similar behavior are labeled "high achievers" or hard-chargers" and are considered forceful, a positive connotation.

In contrast to the well-publicized discrimination of the business world, the military gets credit from Rear Admiral Grace M. Hopper for giving women opportunities. Rear Admiral Hopper is an excellent example of someone who encourages those below her. She summed up her experience: "I've had everything anybody could have wanted. The navy's been very, very good to me. Every opportunity. I think many people do not realize that probably one of the fields in which women are most accepted is the military. We always get the same pay, the same stripes [as men]. I've been in the academic world, the business world, and in the navy world. Certainly the navy has done more than the other places in providing opportunities for women."

Rear Admiral Hopper further cited computing as having opportunities for women: "It's a very good field for women because it didn't exist till World War II. When the companies first started at the end of the war, the men were all coming back from the service, and going to college, so they hired the women. And we've always been there. The programmer or systems analyst doesn't have any gender connotations at all. Never had it."

MENTORS

Mentors, like bosses, can have an enormous impact on our career. They can also give us direction, make us visible to higher-ups, introduce us to organizational politics, boost our self-image, and give us counsel in attaining the promotions we want. Because of the female social conditioning, women may need more support and encouragement at the beginning of their careers than men.

Commented one woman, "I attached myself in an unobtrusive but firm manner to my mentor. As his prestige and sphere of influence rose, so did mine."

The role of a mentor differs from that of a boss. First, we believe we should never select our boss as a mentor, mainly because we need a mentor with whom we can discuss our strategy and relationship with our own boss—especially if there are conflicts.

Second, we feel we should not have a mentor in our chain of command (i.e., our boss's boss). A mentor's career should not be affected by our following his or her candid advice in our work or in accepting another job (within or outside of the organization), or the advice being offered may not be solely in our best interest but may reflect what is best for the mentor.

How are mentors best defined? According to Collins's book *Professional Women and Their Mentors* (New York: Prentice-Hall, 1983), there are five criteria. First, mentors are higher up on the professional ladder, or ahead of us in our career. This is necessary if they are to be effective in helping us in our climb upward.

Next, mentors must be authorities in their fields; almost always they are older, but they must clearly be ahead in experience and knowledge so that we can learn from them. Third, mentors must be influential. They must have a recognized "voice" in their profession, be close to the lines of authority, and have the power to command the resources to accomplish their job.

Furthermore, mentors must have a genuine interest in our personal growth and development and be able to recognize our future potential both for the benefit of ourselves and our organization.

And last, mentors must be willing to commit time and emotion to the relationship. It can be an intense one, and it can be one of great devotion. There is mutual trust and caring and a willingness to devote time to help foster and develop the career of the protégée.

The working mentor relationship is not designed to be permanent and usually lasts several years. However, the contact can last a lifetime. Collins believes senior level people throughout the organization will be willing to act as our mentors if we are committed to our jobs, are open to being coached, and let it be known that we are willing to work hard to succeed and that we are ambitious and want to be promoted.

That a mentor is valuable and even necessary is unquestioned, as Nycum shares: "I have changed mentors as often as bosses, perhaps because their influence and perspective were dependent upon a specific job. I believe that the Lancelot who can ride through the world doing good, banishing evil, and coming out ahead exists only in Camelot. One simply must have the mentor or advisor to get through the underbrush of politics and rivalries and lack of information that block the road to advancement in most organizations.

"A few years ago, my last mentor came up to me after I had given a major speech and simply said, 'You have now put it all together. When are you going to be your own boss?' Since I am, by upbringing and training, inclined more to the role of the first mate than the role of the captain, the comment was a jolt, one that no one else would have cared to deliver, and one that I was unprepared to hear.

"Later, when we talked in depth and I described my comfort at being the first mate, my mentor told me, 'Then be sure you select the right captain; don't just shop for a good first mate's berth.' Switching to his own metaphor, he made his point. 'Organizationally, you will look as funny as a large goose trying to stick her big head under a little mother hen's tiny wing.' Suddenly the thought of taking charge made sense and felt right—and has ever since."

As one respondent said, "After I left the company, the mentor relationship ended. But to this day he is the first person I call when I get a significant promotion, and he still gives me an insight into certain problems."

Collins's three mentors have had a profound impact on her career also, significantly influencing her progress. According to her, "My first mentor relationship occurred when I was in my early twenties, living in New York, and working for a Fortune 500 company. My mentor, a senior vice-president, made a contribution to my career that has lasted my entire life. He helped shape my personal philosophy and formulate my desire to have a serious career, not merely a job. This was *very* unusual for a woman in the mid-1950s." So often, the first mentor is the most important person in a young working adult's career; certainly this was true for Collins.

"I later learned that for an ambitious woman like me, a mentor is even more crucial for her career than to her male counterparts'. It took another twelve years and a move to Stanford before I found another mentor. This relationship was significant in terms of my personal growth and development. His solid backing of me in the business arena was one that I will never forget, and we spent a lot of time discussing office politics and the male ego. As I knew I could always count on his loyalty and support, I worked twice as hard not to let him down.

"Some ten years later, I was fortunate enough to have the guidance of my third and what I consider to be my final mentor. I met him during a period of change in my career, and he was able to share with me that men better accept the fact that their careers will have more ups and downs than do women's. Perhaps this begins with the whole milieu of male competition and team sports. He helped me get my career in focus, which resulted in my making a very wise career move. A job change often results when a mentor works with a protégée who is approaching senior management."

It is interesting to note that Collins's three mentors were men, which is the typical experience of most women. As women still hold only 6 percent of the top jobs, more men are in positions enabling them to act as mentors.

However, today as more women are gaining positions of responsibility, they are becoming increasingly willing to assist those below. There are some advantages of having a female mentor; because they may have experienced similar situations, female mentors understand and can be responsive. As one woman in our study said, "When my female mentor told me, 'I know just how you feel,' I knew it was true." Female mentors can also have greater insight in pointing out which people, or groups of people, are the most facilitating in promoting women into areas of senior management.

Since we feel mentors are so important, we urge women not to wait to be discovered. We actively seek someone at a senior level to help guide our career and steer us through the organizational maze. We do this by working hard and letting it be known that we want to move up. Also we have learned to listen—especially to those whose breadth of experience exceeds ours—to show appreciation, and to follow up with those who express an interest in our work.

Gilbert has often been a mentor and says, "The main thing I try to do for those I mentor is to give them the benefit of my experience. However, I realize that some women have not been quick enough to pick up on what I was trying to do.

"There is a distinct culture in each organization, as well as in organizations as a whole, and often younger executives coming in do not understand this. This introduction to organizational life is one area where I can be most helpful.

"When I mentor someone, I mentor to both their strengths and weaknesses. What I try to do is tell them when they are performing well and then, when they approach something incorrectly, I try to help them by suggesting a more appropriate way. What characteristics do I look for in selecting women to coach? I look for people who are good—very good. And then I try to get them on a faster track than they might otherwise be on."

We were interested to learn what role mentors played for the women in our survey and whether they attributed their success to a mentor. Only 55 percent of our sample replied that they had a mentor. While we thought this was a low number, we feel women are not as knowledgeable as men in the concept of identifying, working with, and knowing the importance of mentors. We do not think many people, men or women, get to senior ranks without extra help and recognition along the way, and thus, we also wondered if our sample labeled those helpful to them as mentors.

When asked what their mentors' contributions were to their careers, our sample gave the following responses:

- *Thought of me as a person first; a woman second.*
- *Helped my orientation and assisted me in "learning the ropes."*
- *Gave motivation and guidance.*
- *Enhanced my reputation.*
- *Shared their philosophies.*
- *Instilled determination and desire to excel.*
- *Developed my long-term strategy.*
- *Gave access to powerful people.*
- *Helped me to take risks.*
- *Groomed me to be a boss.*

We also urge women to understand better the whole mentor concept, including such aspects as how many mentors we should have (men have from three to five, women from one to three and could undoubtedly benefit from more); and when to end the relationship (men's relationships average two to three years, women's last much longer and sometimes even after they are no longer effective).

Warned one respondent, "Keep the mentor relationship strictly business. The intellectual intimacy can sometimes lead to a physical intimacy, but as this is such an important career relationship, you should keep it professional. This way you will not be open to criticism from your peers for any special tutoring or favors you receive, and they will agree that you deserve this due to your competency."

PEERS

After getting firmly established in an organization, we need to turn our attention to our peers in responsibility. Men have long demonstrated their belief in the importance of belonging to an Old Boys' Network of men on the same level. Good relationships with peers can facilitate the transference of information, a feeling of belonging, and smooth day-to-day operations.

As we climb in an organization, we find that we sometimes pass our "age-mates" and former peers. In such circumstances, it is not always possible to maintain good relationships. Some of these people will be happy for us; however, others will be jealous and envious, if not overtly hostile. To them, we will suddenly become "the enemy." Gilbert comments, "I was once promoted from controller to vice-president of my organization. Along with the promotion came new responsibilities, new organization, and many more subordinates. The smaller group with which I had previously worked became jealous that our relationship could no longer be as close as in earlier times, since I did not have the time to spend closely managing as many people. I had to accept their disappointment (and some ill will) in order to grow in my job."

Trying to stay buddies with colleagues can backfire, and it is wise to define early guidelines. As John Sculley said of his relationship with the president of Apple Computer, when he was hired as the new chairman, "I wasn't hired to be [Jobs's] friend. I was hired to run the company" (from *Business Week*, "The No-nonsense Era of John Sculley," January 27, 1985).

Promotions almost always bring new challenges in working with our peers. Women are often seen as more idealistic than men, preferring compatible environments and personal relationships that evolve from trust as opposed to lines of authority. Women want to believe their colleagues who were once friends will remain friends; however, friendship can evaporate when the chain of command changes. We believe women should not let friendship get in the way of using authority to delegate, which is a crucial tool of success.

The senior level professional woman who has overcome most of the obstacles of being female and is accepted by the ranking males can be most helpful in counseling junior level women in peer relationships. Betty Harragan, in *Games Mother Never Taught You* (New York: Warner Books, 1978), explained very well the problems that women have in joining organizations and in being team players. She stressed team cooperation and noted that frequently women have not been brought up to play sports when they were younger. Thus, they are used to the role of individual contributor rather than that of a team member. Most organizations run on team cooperation, and these are skills at which a women needs to be adept when working with her peers.

Noted a respondent, "Women rising above their peers in responsibility often find they are also breaking other barriers. Men on the way up are referred to as 'crown prince,' 'favorite son,' or 'fair-haired boy'—there are no such analogues for women."

And, as Gilbert says, women may have to take the initiative in those relationships: "The work experience for executive women is different from men's, and sometimes our feelings are unintentionally wounded. At higher levels, some men are of a chronological age where they do not know how to behave with a female peer—they have never had the experience before. I have found I need to take the initiative in inviting male peers to lunch—even when I'm the 'new kid on the block.' My female peers and I are sometimes not included in some social occasions—such as drinks after work or family get-togethers on weekends—unless we do the inviting.

"In cases where peers felt threatened or would have ignored me if they could, support from the rest of the organization usually sufficed to generate respect. If the boss makes clear his or her respect for people, the organization usually responds. To me, this support from the top is crucial to our success."

Nycum, also, maintains that gender need not be a negative factor. "I have enjoyed thousands of excellent relationships and encounters and have had problems with peer relationships only three times in my career. I think it is easy to work with peers. It is simply a matter of finding commonality—of goal, purpose, style, insight, or other aspects of the relation. I rely on the 'prisoner's dilemma' as my working model—treat the peer as you would be treated until he or she acts unfairly, then hit back fast and hard."

Because women are rising to new levels within organizations, they especially need the support of those who understand their roles. The support of other women who are in comparable positions has an untold value.

Gilbert, in stressing what that means to her, sums up the sentiments of most senior level women: "Relationships with female peers (where we are lucky enough to have them) can be sanity saving. I find that senior level women are, by and large, quite supportive of each other. The Queen Bee we saw five years ago has been surpassed by women who realize that we need to help each other succeed. Also, when the inevitable waves of loneliness overtake us, our women friends and colleagues understand and empathize with what we are facing."

THE QUEEN BEE SYNDROME

No book on women at work would be complete without some comment on the "Queen Bee Syndrome," a term familiar to most working women. The label "Queen Bee" refers to a woman, usually somewhat older than the other female workers, who has worked very hard to get where she is and who is unwilling to be helpful to other women who are coming along behind her in the organization. The Queen Bee usually feels that she has made it by herself, taken a lot of hard knocks along the way, and had little or no outside support. This attitude accounts for her unwillingness to support others.

When a woman attains a high level position in her organization, she can be more scrutinized than her male counterparts (where normally there are several on the same level). Not only does she have to perform exceptionally well to have her presence noticed, but she must continue to work hard to have her accomplishments accepted in the future. The Queen Bee identifies herself to others at this point by bending over backwards so as not to be interpreted as giving special favors to or assisting other women. Sometimes she will even quietly sabotage the career of any female below her who is perceived as a fast riser and may be a threat to her position.

Said one respondent, "The Queen Bees often feel more identity with their male colleagues who have accepted them than with the women who are below. It is as if their specialness and self-esteem are eroded if another woman achieves the same success. I learned this the hard way as unfortunately my organization had a Queen Bee who felt there was room for one woman *only* in the corporate dining room, and she was *it*." Added another respondent, "The Queen Bee, because of her access to power and her visible role within the organization, is in the best position to advance the careers of women. But the irony of the situation is that she is the least inclined to do so." In examples like this, women have been labeled "women's worst enemy." And, unfortunately, situations like this occur time and time again.

Nycum's experience with "women's worst enemy" gives some added insights into how dangerously subtle these women can be: "I have met two Queen Bees in my career, and in each case I have been surprised. The person's reputation with her male colleagues had been great. They urged me to meet her because 'you two have so much in common.' Spare me! The Queen Bee is the worst of the career blockers because she is so credible to others. While a man can see that another man could be a horrid sexist, the idea that dear Janie or Joan or Ms. Smith whom he has admired for years thwarts her own kind is hard for him to swallow."

Sometimes a Queen Bee is given the unfortunate role of speaking for all women. This happens when she advances to places not occupied by a woman before—for example, membership in an all-male club, lunch in a former male dining room, invitations to hold board memberships or to social functions attended previously by men only. She is then sometimes asked to give a "woman's view," which, of course, no woman is able to do, nor should feel she can.

There still remains a threefold range of opinion among senior level women regarding the Queen Bee attitude. Some women still are not willing, nor do they feel an obligation, to go out of their way to help younger women. Other women are willing to be helpful to younger people's careers, but treat men and women equally. And still others approach helping and mentoring younger women almost as a crusade.

Gilbert offers her perspective: "I have often found myself in the position to help female subordinates or others in my organization largely because of a sense of 'If I won't, who will?' However, it is sometimes difficult to help the women by hiring or promoting them because such actions can be deemed biased by others. Younger women looking for help along the way may not always discern the conflict that the executive woman faces."

Collins comments, "People do have a tendency to label the highest-ranking person in a group as a Queen Bee, no matter who she is. I am aware of this, and when it happens to me, I bend over backwards to shed the image. I get rid of the Queen Bee label by giving power to those below."

Many women in our study echoed their belief in the end of the Queen Bee era and applauded the new spirit for the eighties, characterized by women pulling together and supporting each other in their mutual progression to the top. With a more supportive environment, along with networking and increasing numbers of women in midmanagement, more visible and competent women will hold managerial positions. When this happens, the Queen Bee Syndrome will no doubt be a function of the past.

In the meantime, though, lest younger women look at senior level women too narrowly, Betty Harragan warned: "The Queen Bee is very much alive out there, but today she is different; today she is apt to be the grasping underling, not the successful senior. Young women complain they are not getting help, but the top lady is hanging on by her fingernails and cannot afford to 'let the bloodsuckers feed on her.' Younger women don't appreciate the precarious situations of senior [level] women."

BECOMING THE BOSS

When it is time to move up, many women in our study use both networking and outside headhunters to assist them in their search. And presuming we have a good relationship with our boss, we can also enlist his or her help in finding a suitable job that makes better use of our abilities. Promotions seldom just happen. It takes experience, planning, and plain hard work. It is important to be very honest with ourselves, though, so that we do not move prematurely because we are ambitious and overestimated our capabilities.

What is obviously more fun than having a boss, Gilbert believes, is being a boss. "The catch, of course, is that everybody in a large company always has a boss no matter how high in an organization one may rise. The chairman of the board may have the most difficult job of all since he or she is responsible to the many shareholders or trustees."

How does it feel to be the boss? For Nycum, "It's fun. No longer does one say, 'Why don't *they*?' One simply does it. One is measured by those below, around, and above or outside, and it feels good. On the other hand, the buck stops here, and mistakes are one's own, not to be placed on others. Many times I have found the subtle distinction between responsibility and authority. When I have had to fight, it has been to get the second to go with the first. Then I have to be sure to use that authority before the vacuum that is created is filled by another. Men are more oriented to that part of a new job. Women are still learning to direct and exert control over others."

Being the boss, then, requires skill and insight not always exercised in a lesser position. Exercising the authority that goes with responsibility is a relatively new experience for women in general, made more difficult by the fact that only 6 percent of the top level jobs are held by women.

For Collins, the challenge of senior level responsibilities and authority is fundamental to her career satisfaction: "In my current role as assistant to a president and CEO, some of my tasks are repetitive, yet there are enough new duties to make the job a continual challenge. It is my job to make sure all functions run at peak efficiency with a minimum of disruption and to help convey the organization's image to the public-at-large."

One woman in our study commented that when she became boss, she seemed to experience times when she got her job done under the power of what is called "peak performance." These are times when we do our job in total confidence, nothing seems to go wrong, and we function at our very best. Jerry Fletcher, Ph.D., president of High Performance Dynamics, a management consulting and training company in San Anselmo, California, is one of a growing number whose recent research shows peak performance needn't be rare and isolated experiences. Said Fletcher, "We've studied thousands of high-performing patterns, and they're so wonderfully diverse it's really extraordinary. If I had to come up with one common trait, however, the one thing that distinguishes high performers, it's that they take responsibility for their own lives. If things aren't going well, they do something about it. They don't feel victimized or powerless" (from "Secrets of Peak Performance," *Glamour*, December 1986). For a woman to experience peak performance, then, is to be all that we can be—our best.

In the last ten years, the number of executive women in U.S. business more than doubled, from 1.4 million to 3.5 million, and it is still climbing. A *Time* magazine article (December 2, 1985) quoted Harvard Labor Economist David E. Bloom: "The growth of women in the work force is probably the single most important change that has ever taken place in the American labor market. Their arrival at high executive levels will be the major development for working women over the next 20 years." In the same article, Rand Corporation Economist James P. Smith said, "Thousands of ambitious young women are in the pipeline in middle management now. It is inevitable that after 20 years of work experience, a good number of those women will be at the top."

While in 1985 women made 64 percent of what men made, they are on a path that, conservatively, will raise their wages to at least 74 percent by the year 2000, according to a *Business Week* article.

Nycum discusses her transition in moving up: "The days when I had a 'boss' in the corporate sense are long over. As a senior partner in a law firm and as the managing partner of an office of the firm, my upward focus largely has been replaced by lateral focus. Decisions are made by consensus, rather than fiat. Learning to deal in that environment has been just as challenging as learning to deal in the vertical structure.

Are women moving up or plateauing? In the March 4, 1985, issue of *Industry Week*, Jane Evans, president and CEO of Monet Jewelers, a division of General Mills, Inc., the highest-ranking woman in the giant foods company, was quoted as saying she thinks that women's earlier rise may be at a standstill. She believes one reason is that men still don't have women as friends and that this can cause difficulties for rising females.

Her explanation: top male managers still do not share what she calls a "comfort level" with women executives. "The major problem we face is that we are different. We represent change. My biggest concern is that CEO's are men, and very few have worked with women in any professional capacity. Men still view women mainly as wives and sweethearts." She termed it "latent discrimination."

Evans said she suspects that, in many industries, women won't reach the corporate pinnacle "until men can feel the same comfort—or friendship—level with women that they do with men, or until we get a generation of management men who have grown up with women in a professional capacity, who have worked with women, and who have daughters in their 20's and early 30's and have become much more sensitized to the issues and see the discrimination that goes on."

One woman in our study, who works for a Fortune 500 company in New York, wrote that she was promoted rapidly during the first six years of her career. But four years later, she felt blocked. "It's hard to get the job done. I'm increasingly aware of a ceiling," she told us. "I'm at that ceiling now, and I know it, but I just don't know what to do about it."

When we become the boss, understanding how power works in our organization is vital to our success. Organizational power, by its definition, allows us to control or influence another. It gives us authority, within specified limits, to have the right to be the decision-maker. As one respondent said, "It spells out 'who' decides 'what.' "

We cannot manage without power. To have power, we must discover ourselves what power is, and also, with how much power we are comfortable. Much has been written on power, and it is usually pointed out that women often do not seek power—at least not at the start of their careers—in the same way aggressive males do. However, it has been our experience that once a woman experiences power she handles it well, and it becomes a part of her.

Gilbert notes, "For some reason I do not fully understand, I have always felt powerful—at least as much as the next person. Consequently, I do not stand in awe of many people and am willing to assume leadership positions. I believe I do this with others' interests at heart and try not to infringe on anyone else's sense of his or her own power.

When a woman first moves up into a powerful position, there can often be a testing ritual to which women are subjected by their male peers to see if they will qualify. This ritual varies from complete nonrecognition to the other extreme of an almost unmanageable work load. Psychologist Marilyn Machlowitz, author of *Workaholics* (Cranbury, N.Y.: New American Library, 1980), wrote about this ritual. "The testing is reminiscent of a class full of kids faced with a substitute teacher—they carry on and see how far they can go. It's the ritualistic response of any group to an unwelcome authority figure."

Power and its use are so important for the successful woman that we made this subject a three-part question in our survey. While we felt they were, we first inquired if our respondents were comfortable in dealing with their power. Some 85 percent responded yes, as they have learned that power is vital for success. Only 12 percent wrote no, and the remainder said, "most of the time." Second, we asked our respondents to give their definition of power. Here are some of their answers:

- *Ability to make and implement important decisions.*
- *Prestige, influence, strength, and the prerogative of ruling.*
- *Control over environment and ability to affect others' lives.*
- *Influence and authority.*
- *Ability to advance goals and to protect one's turf.*
- *Ability to obtain needed resources.*
- *Authority to hire and fire.*
- *Significant bottom-line influence.*

The third question on power was regarding advice for younger women who aim for jobs enabling them to use power. We applauded their answers:

- *Have confidence in your own use of it.*
- *Use as a legitimate business tool—power is OK.*
- *Essential for survival.*
- *Don't let the male ego bother you when you use it.*
- *Use it—talent, genius, and education alone will not assure your success.*
- *Use it constructively for the betterment of the organization.*
- *Save it for important issues.*
- *Not to be manipulated.*
- *Use power to support other women.*

An economist urged other women who were getting power for the first time to "use it very carefully. I've seen younger women use it to destroy, not to build. When this happens, you can bet others will be gunning for your fall."

Women display power in all the traditional ways that men do, such as in dress, manner, and office decor. Posture is also important—if we carry ourselves in a manner that indicates a position of authority, most people will pick this up very quickly. Body language, facial expression, and control of our hands exhibit a certain assurance that we feel in charge of the situation. Also, pitch and tone of voice are important, especially when tempers are flaring. This display of self-control is important in getting our message across that we are unflappable.

Since looking the part is important in obtaining a professional response from the work world, we included this subject in our questionnaire. Much has been written about dressing for success—to the extent that one woman returned our questionnaire and wrote in the margin, "We now have a work force of women who tend to look a lot like each other with navy pin-striped suits, white blouses, and sensible navy pumps." Another wrote, "We look like an army of mice in our matching shades of gray suits!"

This conformity does not give the impression of authority, and within "professional attire," a wide range of style is acceptable. If we are serious about our job, we advise looking so, and this means dressing tastefully and professionally. Like men, most women at the top have developed their own customized distinctive style of dress.

We also believe that the surroundings of professional women should reflect a professional image. Like its inhabitant, an office should have presence. We have seen examples of young women managers "feminizing" their offices with small area rugs, lamps, and items that don't look businesslike in a professional environment. A tailored, tasteful office that is in keeping with the culture of the organization is preferred.

In conclusion, more women than ever are moving up. At a time when corporations are facing ever greater competition, especially from foreign firms, American companies are learning that they must reach for talent and ignore sex. Now that women make up half the U.S. labor force and are earning more than half of all bachelor's and master's degrees, promoting women into top positions and tapping that pool of skills is nothing more than good business sense. In a *Time* magazine article (December 2, 1985), Charles Brown, chairman of AT&T, noted, "Removing the barriers that prevent women from realizing their potential is of critical importance for the stability, growth and competitive position of American business."

INSPIRING SUBORDINATES

"Probably the most important thing I have done in my whole career is to train all the young people I have," judged Rear Admiral Grace Hopper. This frank and simple statement underscores the responsibility and reward in inspiring those who are subordinate to us.

Subordinates are those below us in rank, power, and importance. We have the authority to direct and control their assignments, and to play a large role in evaluating their performance. Thus our effect on their careers can be enormous.

Wrote a senior level manager, "When you become the boss, the greatest responsibility for our subordinates is in the following five areas: selecting for advancement, disciplining when needed, making competent replacements, providing opportunities to widen their experiences, and encouraging subordinates to develop to their full potential."

Another added, "If we are going to be regarded as good bosses, we must be good managers as well as good leaders. This means always having the best interests of our subordinates in mind and looking for ways for them to get ahead. Such treatment, in turn, brings us credit and respect from those still higher."

Collins explains her attitude toward subordinates: "Managing bright younger people, no matter how loyal, can be a challenge. I felt I have had a good relationship with those subordinates whom I have managed. I basically make sure they understand the lines of power as well as their line of authority and responsibility. Within their job description, I try to give them as much control and flexibility as possible.

"Several younger women whom I have supervised remain in touch, and we still discuss their career options. I continue to act as an influence in their working life, and I find this very satisfying."

Do subordinates expect women bosses to be different from men? A study by Natasha Josefowitz (published in the *San Francisco Chronicle*, August 25, 1983) stated that they do. Josefowitz wrote, "Subordinates expect women managers to be helpful, nurturing, her door always open, and that she can be interrupted at any time." These expectations can collide with the manager's own wishes and can sabotage her rise within the company.

Nycum says, "I believe that the nurturing image may be part of the emotional baggage of the over-forty female manager, but the under-forty female manager is expected to be as much or as little a nurturer as a man in a comparable slot."

Many in our sample pointed out problems they had faced that were unique to their gender. They felt some men do not want to work for a woman boss and found that women can face special challenges in getting the job done because of this. However, the problem often lies not with us but with those whom we supervise. Research suggests that women are often perceived as powerless. Thus, ambitious subordinates who believe this may *not* want to work for a woman boss. They want a well-connected, powerful boss who can command company resources and advance their careers. One woman made her point regarding subordinates, "First, establish your credibility. Second, be the 'good guy.' "

Gilbert remembers, "When I was a corporate executive, a young man was assigned to my group. He was a very nice person with whom I had worked in another context, but he had never worked directly for me. He had some concerns about women being overly emotional, or that he would be perceived badly because he was working for a woman. It hurt his macho image. I'm pleased to say that after six months of working with me, he told me that in many ways I was the best boss he had ever had, simply because, seeing his competence, I left him alone. Even though we've gone separate ways over the years, we still stay in touch and I know that he would work for me again."

While Nycum has not had the problem of being the boss to a reluctant male, she comments, "Years ago it was such a novel situation that men were more curious about women bosses than discouraged. They would not apply for the position in the first place if they were not comfortable with the idea of a female boss.

"However, for a female boss to discipline a male subordinate is a more delicate task than for a male boss. There is the perception buried in every man that he's dealing with his first-grade teacher, and that has to be overcome. It is a delicate situation. When a man is authoritative, it is a strong feature; when a woman is authoritative, the message can be lost in the presentation."

Another respondent told us about the challenge of dealing with people outside her company who are not yet used to women in responsible positions. She wrote, "I am in a senior position with a male subordinate who is several years younger than I, and frequently we deal together with outsiders. It is not unusual for an outsider to presume that he is the boss rather than I, although it doesn't take long before this is cleared up (usually by him)."

Shared a tax firm owner, "I cannot overemphasize the importance of high morale. If you create a level of expectancy that those under you will succeed, I have found out that a large number will."

Our survey respondents advised learning as much as we can early on about inspiring and managing others, since the ultimate responsibility of being the boss is to get the job done through other people. A lot of people who are new to management forget about getting the job done and concentrate on the duties of supervision. The responsibilities of supervising other people are challenging and complex, but we will be ultimately judged (as will be our subordinates) on getting the job completed.

THE ENTREPRENEUR

The entrepreneur woman as boss is often different from the organization woman as boss. Some women reach the place where they are frustrated by what they consider their slow progress in large organizations, and as a result, they leave to start and manage their own business. These women are often characterized as creative and competitive self-starters and have a high level of both energy and self-esteem. They are also willing to take the risk of starting a business for the sake of earning more profits than they normally would in a salaried position.

Some entrepreneurs have difficulty in coping with the structure, system, and rules of large organizations. Nycum comments, "In some twenty years of interviewing prospective associate lawyers, I have learned to spot the ones who need more 'space' than a highly structured large law firm provides new lawyers. These people have proved to be the happiest as entrepreneurial sole practitioners or as heads of their own firms. They seem to be most productive when making the rules, since they chafe at following the rules of others. In a larger firm, they are often called troublemakers and leave under a cloud. With independence, many of them blossom, prosper, and mellow."

One woman in our study reported working hard for sixteen years in a large corporation. "I hit the 'glass ceiling' and felt betrayed by the system for which I had worked so long. But because I am basically a risk-taker and have always had big ambitions, I decided to start my own company. Fortunately my track record enabled me to raise the necessary capital. I felt it *much* more satisfying to run my own show. Even though I worked longer hours, the psychic rewards were immediate. The financial rewards took longer, but eventually they came."

Others also reported being discouraged with the system they once fought so hard to be a part of and quit lucrative jobs to begin their own companies. Wrote one, "My friends thought I was crazy when I threw in the towel to a six-figure job, but five years later I have over eighty franchises on the East Coast and am head of a multimillion dollar company. It does take guts, nerves of steel, a high tolerance for stress, and good decision-making instincts. And also large doses of optimism help."

Several entrepreneurs shared such comments as, "Before starting your own company, you should have a solid background in your specialty and be a visionary—spot trends and carry out your dream."

Collins says, "It is important for the entrepreneur to select a well-rounded staff to support you. Often the creative boss spends all his or her time on the broad picture, developing the product and identifying the market, and it is vital to have people with opposite skills tending the day-to-day operations."

Wrote one respondent, "The entrepreneur frequently has to play many roles in her company and usually has more invested in terms of financial resources than the person who works for someone else. She often has to do whatever is necessary, especially while the company is small. This may include playing receptionist or answering the telephones. Many times I have greeted visitors and asked if I can help, only to be told that they don't want to see me, they want to see my boss. Overcoming these stereotypes is a challenge!"

The beginning entrepreneur, as boss, has to rely on subordinates, perhaps even more than those who do not have their own funds invested. One successful entrepreneur told the story of hiring three recently graduated MBAs from a top university who felt they could do a much better job than she could. She wrote, "They were arrogant, and I was not sure if it was because of the university they attended or because they were men. Perhaps they felt they were simply technically more competent. However, I was never afraid to hire people that were better in certain areas than I was, and at one time, I even paid them more than I was taking out of the business. This attitude is important because an entrepreneur needs to look at her company over the long term."

Between 50 and 70 percent of new businesses fail in the first five years, and since starting a new business normally takes long hours and a full financial and emotional commitment, it is clear that being an entrepreneur is not for everyone. Yet according to a 1984 study by the Small Business Administration, women started companies of their own at a rate that was three times higher than men in the period 1977 to 1980. And these figures have grown even more since then, so that *now* some 7 percent of all firms are owned by women.

Another entrepreneur in our study gave a final warning: "Be aware of power plays from outside investors as your company grows and becomes successful. The ultimate goal is to make sure you don't wake up one day to discover you are out."

In summary, the people with whom we work influence our early desire to have a serious career, our progression toward seniority, and our ability to get the job done once we become the boss ourselves. In all phases of our career, we find that we never work in isolation—even if we become an entrepreneur—bosses, mentors, peers, and subordinates continue to play a major role in our success at all levels.

3 Love Relationships

"What do we live for
If not to make the world
Less difficult for each other?"
—ANONYMOUS—

Women who lead have as many life-styles and love relationships as they do career options, and no dominant pattern seems to emerge. Some women in our study have been married to the same person for more than twenty-five years; others have had two or more marriages; and others responded that they have chosen not to marry, but to have one or more long and close relationships. Still others gave all to their career with no time left for a family life.

However, we discovered that, if given a chance, most women prefer a stable life with one partner, structured around a traditional family. Our study validated that women elect to give quality time to develop and keep permanent relationships with those they love, feeling this is an important part of their lives. These women believe they have much to offer a relationship as well as to gain from it.

What makes the mid-eighties different from the previous decades is that women now have acceptable choices in establishing these relationships, and equally important, they *know* this and are selecting a variety of life-styles that reflects these options.

MARRIAGE

The most complex of all relationships for a woman is often with those whom she loves best, and the decision to marry can sometimes be a difficult one. Yet most of our respondents feel it would be a great waste to journey through life alone without love. A loving relationship gives us companionship and purpose, makes us feel secure and needed, and lets us know we are not alone in this world. If we are fortunate enough to find a partner to share our lives, most women feel the joy and satisfaction is worth all the efforts, pain, and sacrifice that it takes to foster and sustain the relationship.

In compiling the data on marriage from our sample, we found that the largest group, 66 percent, were currently married. Two percent were widowed, and 18 percent divorced (for a total of 86 percent who married). Only 14 percent had chosen never to marry. Of the 86 percent who at one time married, 73 percent married only once, 13 percent married twice, and 3 percent married a third time (the remaining 11 percent did not indicate their number of marriages). Our sample also stayed married a long number of years. Some 59 percent of the women have been married over fifteen years, 27 percent have been married from five to fifteen years, and 14 percent have been married less than five years.

Most women in our society who are over thirty were taught to assume they would have such a relationship—any choice other than marriage was inconceivable. As Collins's upbringing points out, the idea of questioning whether or not marriage would fit into her life never even surfaced. "It never occurred to me that I might not marry and have children," she says. "I remember playing with dolls and looking forward to that magic day when I would have many children myself. Thus, my early life was oriented towards being a good wife and mother; not much thought was given to having a lifelong career. This attitude was the same for all my friends.

"Even though I worked as a teenager for my father in the furniture business, a serious career did not cross my mind. Few, if any, women my age took courses in business or engineering, and although some were enrolled in medicine and law, the numbers were still very small. Certainly I never thought I would spend two-thirds of my life in the working world."

In contrast, women who are today in their twenties have grown up with the idea of choice. Older women, too, are just beginning to feel that they have a choice—it is quite all right to get out of a deteriorating marriage, and it is permissible *not* to remarry.

Wrote a respondent, "Several aspects of marriage—including sexual gratification and financial security—can now be met outside marriage. Women no longer have to marry to meet their sexual needs, and with salaries slowly going up, many have less reason to marry for economic needs. Live-in arrangements, traveling with the opposite sex, and closer relationships are all a part of the eighties."

Still, traditional marriage seems to be the desired choice for the majority of women. Says Gilbert, "I never questioned that I wanted to be married; I knew that I wanted a partner in life, and I wanted to have children."

Nycum adds her perspective: "I have been married, and I have been single—married is better. I simply prefer sharing my life—but only if it is with an understanding and supportive person. I find that all the old sayings and expressions are true. Two heads are better than one on a problem; two people can be two places at once. And it helps to have someone help to see one's self as others see us."

In addition to being practical, sharing life with somone adds a bit of fun as we learn to live with another's habits and life-style. Nycum looks at her "learning process": "My husband, George, is organized. When we first met, I lived in happy chaos. Little by little, he restricted my mess, until now it is confined to the top of my desk at home. I am still happily chaotic—I work best that way; but George, who requires everything in its place, has the rest of our private world neatly under control. I am a hoarder; he throws out. One family joke has my daughter and me calling to each other as one of us arrives home, 'Are you still here or have you been thrown out?' "

Coupling marriage with career brings its own challenges. Work, by its nature, spills over into personal relationships. Feelings related to the job—stress, tension, and worry—are inevitably brought home, even by the most senior level woman. Our sample agrees that negative experiences at work affect their private life, just as do positive experiences.

Negative emotional effects are sensed by others as depression, while negative physical effects are sensed as fatigue. Thus, the dominance of a senior level woman's career in her life is felt by all who surround and love her. Shares one respondent, "When work becomes almost intolerable, it is important to have a sacred place where you feel safe and can go to 'recharge your batteries.' "

Catalyst, a national nonprofit organization that works to foster women's participation in business and the professions, says we must look at the *joint* importance of home and career. "Women's entry into the work force is irreversible; already their numbers almost equal those of men. Women will not go home again. The focus must be on helping to effect change, change that will strengthen the new patterns of family life and make them succeed in the home and in the workplace" (from Catalyst's annual review, September 1, 1980–August 30, 1981).

The 27 million married working women in the United States constitute the female half of the first generation of two-career couples. In the 1970s, women were echoing the popular concept that they could have it all, and that quality time, not quantity time, was what counted. In the 1980s, for some of these women, life has become a struggle that can be physically exhausting and emotionally draining to her partner.

Several recent studies bear out the fact that women *are* succeeding as both homemakers and professionals. Mary Anne Devanna, research coordinator of the Center for Research in Career Development at Columbia University's Graduate School of Business, discussed her findings with Collins on May 12, 1987. Devanna conducted a study of men and women who graduated in the classes of 1969 through 1972 entitled "Male/Female Careers: The First Decade," published by Columbia in 1984. She found that 65 percent of the more successful women—those earning more than $50,000—were married. Equally significant, two-thirds of those women had children. "I would guess that the proportions have not changed significantly since this time," she told Collins in an interview.

And in another similar study, author Liz Roman Gallese took a look at the women in the Harvard Business School Class of 1975, the women who had the first chance to make it to the top. Gallese discovered in her book *Women Like Us* (New York: Morrow, 1985), that there was no correlation between a woman's degree of success and her choice of lifestyles. Many women who were married and had children were among the most successful. Gallese—in an interview with Nancy Collins on October 11, 1985—said, "Men do not have to make a choice, and it is time for women to have these options also. Women *can* combine careers and families."

We asked our sample a two-part question regarding their marriage. First, if they were *glad* to be married. Of those married, well over half responded yes; 4 percent stated no; 13 percent replied, "most of the time." For some reason, the remainder chose not to answer the question.

And secondly, we asked them how, if in any way, they would change their marriage. These are some of their answers.

- *Play more.*
- *Take more time for each other.*
- *Wish he liked and would take more vacations.*
- *Have better communication.*
- *Would get more help with decision-making aspects of home.*
- *Have him share child-raising responsibilities more equally.*
- *Have a less chauvinistic husband.*
- *Have him be more ambitious.*
- *Would have established my own identity early on in marriage.*
- *No way—it is a great relationship.*

Added one: "I would not change anything after nine years; my husband is my soul mate—without him I would be nothing. While I appear independent and self-confident to my colleagues, I am not at all and constantly need my husband's encouragement."

STAYING SINGLE

Rather than make the adjustments that balancing home with career demands, some women opt to remain single and uncommitted. One reason for the female high achiever not to marry is the time required to have a meaningful relationship versus the time required to be successful in one's career. If work is her first love, then she may be unwilling to take the hours away from her first priority—especially if it means that her chances for getting ahead are lessened.

Most relationships require several nights a week for courtship. Romance is further affected by such career variables as travel and transfers. For these reasons, many women are simply not willing to devote the necessary time and energy to relationships at key points in their careers. Collins describes one point when work was more important to her than dating. "During this time, I was beginning to be labeled as a workaholic. I thought nothing of telling a date I had to be home by 10:00 P.M. as I had several more hours of work to complete. I remember another occasion when my date told me if *he* could complete his work by 5:30 P.M., I, a *woman*, should certainly be able to do the same. When I emphasized how much I enjoyed working, he did not call me again."

Said a publishing executive, "I am presently uncommitted, which gives me the freedom to zero in on what is important to advance myself, which is my goal. It is easier to give more of myself to my work when I don't have to worry about fulfilling the needs of another person or handling a conflict situation at home." This is not to say, however, that a woman cannot have a successful career and a happy, committed marriage.

Women choose to remain single for a variety of reasons. We discovered that the successful women in our survey, in a four-to-one ratio, did *not* stay single because of their high career aspirations. Many responded that they "always had men friends," and others wrote they still hoped to marry "if the right person comes along." Others made such comments as, "Possibly, but as I get older, not as high a priority."

One woman wrote, "Most educated women of my era were expected to operate through the confines of the homemaker rather than being 'out' fulfilling their mental and/or professional capacities, and I wanted a real partnership in travel and work."

Gilbert reflects on her experience in being single and uncommitted for a while: "I was single for a year and half between my two marriages. I found that meeting men and dating took a great deal of time and energy that detracted from my job performance."

Another woman confessed, "What I missed in being single was having a 'wife.' This includes someone to listen and to help with the chores and the children, just like my male counterparts had."

Collins shares, "The many years that I was a single parent were by choice. Once I almost married, but unfortunately, he died of an unexpected heart attack. While I sometimes had a 'steady beau,' the thought of again being bound in a relationship less than ideal just wasn't worth it. As it turned out, I later met a man just right for me, and I entered my second marriage with the feeling not of 'giving anything up,' but of 'finding freedom.' "

And, for those who choose to stay unmarried, a kind of relationship other than male/female is also being displayed more openly today. Although this trend is still not accepted by many in the older and more conservative generation, those who are younger are turning their backs on adverse opinions and are behaving in a manner that seems appropriate for them. Females having close relationships with other females—as well as males having close relationships with other males—is becoming more accepted. And within these relationships, partners of the same sex are making lifelong commitments, as well as permanent living arrangements, with each other.

MARRIAGE AND ITS TIMING

The timing of marriage is important in terms of how successful either one's marriage or career will be. In the decade between twenty and thirty, when most partners are finishing their education and striving in their first jobs, there can be a lot of pressure put on the marriage because initiating a career consumes so much personal energy.

Gilbert's second marriage occurred just before she began to accelerate in her career. She says, "I felt a great sense of stability after my remarriage and benefited from having my husband, Keith, share my goals and aspirations with me. I believe he, too, found the same benefits."

And Nycum's marriage happened when her career was entering a critical phase of professional expansion and resulting challenge. She comments,

"Rather than the career putting pressure on the relationship, the relationship eased the pressure of my career. This guidance and support at home were invaluable to my upward mobility."

When women marry before they are successful in their careers or before they even seriously pursue a career path, the marriage will undoubtedly make a mark on the career. Whether that mark is negative or positive depends on the choice of spouse and the clarity with which the relationship was established. The awareness and acceptance of each individual's needs, expectations, and goals need to be reconciled and met.

Collins's experience as a single woman and later as a married woman illustrates the importance of this clarity: "Soon after college when I was still not ready to settle down, I decided to see if I could find a job in Europe. Once there, I had that overpowering sense of freedom that one rarely experiences and felt I could always be in charge of my destiny. In one's middle years, one learns this is not true—but in our early twenties we don't yet know this.

"Once settled in London, it became easy to find work. I turned to the career I knew best—journalism—and was soon certified by the military as a correspondent. During my three years in Europe as a journalist, I had apartments in Paris and Frankfurt as well as in London. As a young American woman, I learned a lot while living abroad for several years. First, I learned that I could take care of myself wherever I lived; and second, I learned how small most problems are, when separated by time and space. Third, I learned how similar people the world over are and of the importance of committed relationships between friends and extended families.

"While I was in France, I met my future husband. He was a captain in the air force and a fighter pilot. While we were engaged, he became an aide to the four-star general who was commander of the air force in Europe, and we married while he was stationed in Germany.

"After I married, I went through a period of feeling somewhat frustrated by the traditional model of marriage. In fairness to my husband, he was a product of the times that expected men to make all the decisions. And as often happens, he was following the pattern for marriage that his father had established with his mother, who was a true homebody.

"For a woman like me, who had for so many years been a free spirit, this attitude was a shock. The repetitiousness of housework, and the fact that I was expected to fit the mold of the other officers' wives was sometimes hard to accept. What was interesting was that I soon discovered many of my married female friends felt the same way. And while I had several jobs during the marriage, it was 'a given' that I would quit each time he was transferred.

"Still, I am not sure I would have returned full-time to the working world so soon had fate and circumstances not played an unfortunate role. After we had been married five years and had three sons, my husband was tragically shot down in 1965 over Vietnam on one of his missions as a fighter pilot, and we were told he was undoubtedly dead. Our air force base even held a memorial service for him. It was not until almost eight years later that we learned he had been taken a prisoner-of-war (POW) and was alive."

The dramatic circumstances of Collins's life when she first learned that her husband had been shot down, once more propelled her towards a career, with the sobering responsibility of providing for three sons.

In speaking of her first marriage, Gilbert notes, "In a relationship, clarity of joint goals and expectations is as important as each partner's individual ones. Lack of awareness and agreement over shared goals can bring disaster and impede careers. My husband and I had severe conflicts about our expectations. Eventually I wanted an affluent life-style, not unlike the one with which I was raised, and I was willing to work to get it. He wanted a less pressured, unstructured life involving a minimum of personal effort. Unfortunately, we did not possess sufficient communication skills or maturity to come to terms with our differences. Instead, we intensified our commitment to separate goals.

"I felt resentful about the unequal efforts in our marriage. At one point, I was working fifty hours a week and going to school full-time at night while he took a minimal (less than half load) number of college courses and didn't work. I thought that if we could both get through college, he would change, and we would be on the path of upwardly mobile people.

"Instead, he left me as soon as he received his college degree. He took with him our car, savings, and everything he could carry. Unfortunately, he did not say goodbye or leave a note, but left me standing on a street corner waiting for him to pick me up after work. I knew he was permanently gone when the bank called several weeks later to tell me my checks were bouncing because he had drawn all the funds from our accounts.

"Needless to say, I did not intend to repeat this mistake of choice in partners, and I'm happy to say I did not. After a move across the country, a new job, and a divorce, I met my current husband. We are compatible in just about all ways: we have the same expectations and goals, and we come from very similar backgrounds. We anticipated from the start that we would be a two-career couple, have children, and support each other's goals."

Up-front agreement on careers and goals, as Gilbert established with her second husband, is invaluable to a woman who is developing a career.

In working to become successful, we sometimes need all our energy to go into our job and being creative—and this can literally "wipe us out" at the end of the day. It takes enormous effort to work on a new project, whatever it may be, and this can cause much stress. It is difficult during certain stressful periods of achieving our goals to give very much of ourselves to anyone. Personal relationships take extra effort to maintain in high-stress situations.

One woman in our study, who had climbed to vice-president of marketing for a small computer company, told us that she was engaged and, once married, planned to continue working *very* hard. She wrote, "I can't imagine marriage without a career—but I can imagine a career without marriage."

Another woman who married before she became successful told us of dating many men before ultimately finding her "prince." With a sense of humor, she described a date that she had with a man who she thought was real marriage material. He was an executive with Hewlett-Packard, which meant to her that he was even "geographically desirable." He made a high salary, was approaching forty, was a graduate from an Ivy League school, had an MBA, and on top of all this, was very attractive. "We were having a great evening, both of us talking about our work, when he suddenly asked me what kind of a husband would be ideal for me. Blushingly, I described someone like him, and then asked him what kind of wife he was looking for. With great seriousness, he described an 'old-fashioned' woman, who would put him, his career, and his needs first. He went on to say it would be someone who at most, worked half time for a charity cause. I didn't know what to say. I voiced my shock that he wouldn't find a bright woman, who hoped to have a successful career, an interesting companion. He voiced surprise that I saw him in this light. I didn't know what to say after this, and I never saw him again after that evening."

Many women marry while they are achieving success. A manufacturing executive in our study and her husband are a good example of a rare couple who achieved success together. As their business grew, they grew; even though they spent an incredible amount of time nurturing their company, their relationship remained close because they understood the demands and pressures that each was facing.

Still another woman told us she had married while she was working an eighty-hour week, seeking election in public office. She told us, "Politics is an especially hard arena to combine with a successful relationship—there are few visible women and double the stresses."

One respondent wrote, "It was difficult to achieve success after we had been married for ten years. As I began to achieve success, he never got over being jealous, although I would have to admit he loves the money that followed!"

Another high level executive woman realized soon after her marriage that her husband's success was supposed to be *her* success. He was president of his own company, and this was supposed to be enough for both of them! This came as quite a shock to her, as she had not gone into the marriage with this concept. She was still achieving success in her own career and had a hard time handling his attitude when she realized that her career did not count or was not as important in his eyes.

Another woman commented, "I married while trying to achieve success and was finishing my book. I was under extreme pressure from the publisher to turn in the manuscript. During this time I became engaged, and that relationship was very valuable to me. Yet during the next several months I knew I would not have time for both.

"I knew I needed my fiancé and the continuity of our love a great deal, yet during this time I needed to be a 'taker' from this relationship and spend almost all my hours outside my regular job on the book. My partner (now my husband) was wise enough to 'give me rein' and know that I would return to him when I could as an equal 'giver' and doer. He also knew there would undoubtedly be a difficult time in his career when he would have little to give to our relationship. And he was secure enough to know that when this time came, I would sustain the relationship, be the nurturing one, fulfill his emotional needs, and provide whatever support I could for him."

Love and relationships inevitably change and grow, especially during the early career years while women—and men—are expanding their talents to achieve success. The early ecstatic stage of a relationship cannot continue at the same pitch of intensity, and as Saint-Exupéry noted: "Love does not consist of gazing at each other, but in looking outward together in the same direction."

As one woman wrote, "I have discovered we cannot love our spouse all the time in exactly the same way; yet this is, unfortunately, what many of us demand."

Relationships, like jobs, are not static, and as the relationship matures both working partners are drawn back into their more specialized and functional roles in the working world.

When women marry after they have achieved success, the roles are already cast, and both parties enter the relationship with reasonably full knowledge of what to expect. They assume their lives will continue in the present as in the past. With marriage occurring after both partners are comfortably established in their work, their expectations will be more realistic, the time and energy needed for their jobs will be known, and their time priorities can be worked out in advance. Two people who have already achieved success will be on a path quite different from that of their earlier years. When one is well up the professional ladder, then many options are possible—travel, new life-styles of one's choice—all is within reach. And for most, money is no longer a problem.

Collins summarizes: "The timing of marriage is important for a career woman, and I discovered that many respondents in our study had experiences similar to mine. When I first married, I was perceived as someone who had worked, but not as one who planned a serious career. Many years later, after my divorce and a second marriage, I had a successful track record, and it was clear from the beginning that I would continue to work. There was no talk of my giving up my career, retiring early, or even resigning from some of my boards and committees. It was all a given. Thus, where you are in your career—and the success under your belt—sets the stage for the kind of relationship you will have and for the way in which your career will impact your marriage."

Nycum says, "After some time as a single parent, I had my 'pores' open for a new relationship. George and I met casually at a wine-tasting party prior to a professional society dinner meeting, and we exchanged cards. By our first date he had looked me up in *Who's Who* and I had checked him out with my personal friends in his company. We each knew what we were getting into and from the beginning talked openly about our work commitments, finances, career goals, and expectations of each other as a spouse."

KINDS OF
MARRIAGES/RELATIONSHIPS

In a marriage, as in all kinds of relationships, whether personal or professional, the question of dominance soon arises. Either the individuals become equal partners (as much as this is ever possible) or one or the other clearly dominates. Since women today no longer automatically accept the traditional role of being solely their husband's "support system," this has caused new problems in marriages and thus the whole issue of balance needs to be reexamined.

In the book *Mating* by M. Ronald Minge, George Biuliane, and Thomas F. Bowman (Dixville, N.Y.:Red Lion Press, 1982), the authors stated that the most important factor in a marriage is a "parity" between the partners. Neither should feel shortchanged in the balancing of assets, defined in the book as "personality, appearance, economic status, social considerations, sexuality, or marriage values." The authors wrote, "Parity is lost if one or the other believes he or she is giving more than is being gotten. Then resentments build up, and the closeness of the relationship is lessened."

Equal Partners

Because two-career couples have only recently become a permanent social institution, information about their different relationships has become increasingly important. We have found that most successful women need equally successful partners. Although it is difficult to define the word "equal," it most closely applies to title, status in the community, education, and ability to earn money. It also refers to standards of life-style desired, background and upbringing, goals and ambitions, and even appearance.

Gilbert describes her marriage to her second husband, Keith, as one of equals. "We have remained truly equal partners and have literally no conflicts over who does what. In general, I see to the housework (we have a housekeeper) and cooking, and he takes care of the yard work, cars, and pool. Since we're both fair people, we fill in when required.

"We both tend to be conservative about financial matters and have never had disagreements about money. We both work hard and have been fortunate to have sufficient resources to meet our needs. We buy what we want without consulting the other (except for major purchases), and since neither is a spendthrift, this works for us.

"The life-style of a two-executive family does give rise to a pressured existence. We both travel frequently and need to be out in the evenings for business and social occasions. Fortunately, we almost never need to travel at the same time, so one of us has usually been home with our daughter.

"My husband has never been threatened by my career. He has been proud of my success and is willing to make the adjustments necessary to ensure a life-style with which we are both comfortable. He has always earned a larger paycheck than I; if this situation were to change, it would not represent a problem for either of us.

Equal partners share major decisions, especially financial, as well as the more mundane ones. These include such issues as running the house or deciding what's for dinner and who buys it. It also includes who cooks it!

Collins writes, "In my second marriage, we are indeed partners in many ways. While my husband has strengths in some areas as I have in others, we share our marriage responsibilities. We fortunately are able to delegate the duties that we do not enjoy. Because of our weekend home, it would be especially difficult to be responsible for the maintenance of two dwellings."

Said a psychiatrist in our study, "There is a growing evidence that marriages actually benefit from more equitable distribution of labor. Working wives who really believe in male/female equality seem to have *happier* marriages than those who try single-handedly to carry both the career and the homemaking duties."

Still, equal partners are quite unusual in many marriages. We have even met the wives of some of our business associates and have had them tell us in all seriousness that their husbands would not "let" them work. Our temptation at moments like that is to ask the woman if it is her husband or her father of whom she is speaking, and why she so readily accepts this decision, especially if it is not what she wants to do.

Another study participant told us, "My husband and I are more or less equal. I don't believe if either of us were too dominant, our marriage would have worked. Our marriage is also a business partnership. When we made a commitment to form our own company, which was some years after we were married, we both made an equal agreement of time and energy. It was clear from the beginning that we were peers."

When people marry as equals, the feeling of sacrificing or giving up something for the marriage tends to disappear. Instead, the marriage *enhances* the life of each partner, as Collins recounts from her experience: "Before I married several years ago, I had not expected to remarry. But I found the stage had changed for marriage. Now women *were* successfully combining many facets of their lives, the way men had done for generations. I didn't feel I 'gave up' anything to marry, or that I would become a lesser person, but rather that I gained a wonderful new dimension and freedom to my life."

One woman, in an equal relationship, told us, "As I was the only working wife in my suburb of nonworking spouses, I understood why my husband worked such long hours. I also knew why he often had to work on weekends. Thus, I was the only wife on the block who did not complain, which my husband seemed to appreciate." She believed her working was a commonality that made her marriage closer than the other couples' marriages.

The genuine understanding of an equal has its benefits. For Nycum, some sharing of work-related problems with her husband, George, helps her to keep her perspective: "Most of the work-related issues I discuss at home are management questions to which George brings thirty years of intensive experience. Since law firms are just learning to manage themselves as businesses, my access to a personal coach is quite an advantage.

"Sometimes I just cry on George's shoulder. When he feels the matter is just not as serious as I think it, he pats me and smiles, 'la pauvre'—French for 'poor you.' This signal isn't always well received, but it does tend to separate the serious problems from the garden variety, in my mind as well as his.

"I do not do the same for George. As an orphaned only child who never previously married, George is self-contained, and as a result, he does not seek that kind of support except in rare circumstances. Part of our success in living together is knowing when to give and when not to give advice and active support."

Dominant Women

Whether or not they themselves are successful, some husbands support their spouses' success while others do not. In an April 1983 article in *Working Woman*, Clifford J. Sager, M.D., a New York psychiatrist and marital therapist, stated, "Many kinds of men marry successful corporate women, and what may be ideal for one woman may be completely wrong for another."

It is very interesting to look at the partners that successful women select. Do dominant women select dominant men? Or do their personality and needs blend better with men who are less aggressive?

Some women are dominant by nature and always feel a desire to be in charge. They run their house and their relationships just as they run their office. It is difficult for them to let *anyone* make a decision that is going to affect them in any way. Dominant women can often be in conflict in marital relationships. On one hand, they have little respect for the spouse who is a pushover; on the other hand, they experience conflict if their spouse does not allow them to get their own way.

The skills required to climb upward, coupled with her forceful attitude, will not allow a professional female to be dominated for long. A relationship of dominance will not work, and most women soon sense this and seldom have a lengthy relationship with men in this category. Women who lead have a certain amount of forcefulness, and over a period of time, relationships with males who are too dominant and inflexible cause too much conflict and stress.

We know of several relationships where the woman is more dominant in the relationship than the man. In one case in our study, the respondent wrote, "My job came first, even before my children, and my husband slowly did less and less well to the point of changing jobs several times (necessary as my rising career called for moves), with each job having less responsibility. His ego was visibly shaken. Over time, I lost my respect for him, and we recently decided to divorce."

In another case where the woman is dominant, it didn't seem to affect their relationship adversely. She wrote, "More and more, I called upon my husband to do many tasks in the home that have been traditionally those of the woman, but he seemed to do them willingly. He seemed proud of my success and secure in our relationship." This is an example of a good blend of two different personalities representing a growth of one acceptable to the other.

Yet men who are married to ambitious and overly dominant women can often get the "short end of the stick." They do not get wives, at least not in the traditional sense. Working men need wives, just as do working women. They do not have a homemaker who provides them with hot meals when they get home, takes care of all their needs, does the laundry, and handles the dry cleaning. Nor are these men able to entertain the way they might otherwise have done. For some men, this is difficult to accept.

As a final word on the kinds of spouses high-achieving women marry, Collins talked in a May 11, 1987, interview, with Maryanne Vandervelde, Ph.D., president of Pioneer Management, Inc., in New York. They discussed her studies, which were published in the *Wall Street Journal* on September 29, 1980. Vandervelde dispelled the myth that dominant women are looking for "wimps." She said, "The husband who is both a non-achiever and an obstructionist is only about 5 percent of all successful women's husbands. What successful woman executive needs a man who not only makes less money and has less status, but is also critical of her efforts, disparaging of her associates, and unwilling to take household responsibility?"

Dominant Men

Because there is more of a historical precedent in our society, marriages where the husband is more dominant may chafe, but they don't seem to break up with the same frequency as those marriages where the woman tries to dominate. Since one measure of a professional woman's success is her ability to compromise and negotiate effectively, we found our respondents able to transfer this skill to their home relationships.

Understanding power is useful in understanding how a couple view their relationship. Neither wants to be powerless. However, the abuse of power, which occurs when power holders exploit those they control, signals problems for the relationship. The one who is seen as powerless can be less and less valued by the other.

Men who use strong tactics to control the relationship have a less satisfactory relationship with their spouses than those who share power. According to David Kipnis in *The Powerholders* (Chicago: University of Chicago Press,

1984), dominant partners also express less love and affection for their partners and are generally unhappier with the relationship.

However, there are always exceptions to every rule. One very senior level woman in our study attributed much of her success to her dominant husband—she wrote, "I was a public figure, and he was constantly in the background planning and plotting my every move as I climbed upward. Yet while his personality was more forceful, I felt our relationship worked because he seemed to have my best interests at heart." In contrast, another woman, married to a very dominant man, felt almost stifled in her domestic life. She told us, "He made all the key decisions without consulting me; although my career was a big success, our marriage was not."

The topic of dominant men caused mixed reactions among our respondents. One woman shared with us what her husband told her on her tenth anniversary. "He said that he hated to be so controlling, but he wanted me to be home. He told me he didn't want me out in the rat race all day. What this really translated into was that *he* needed the security and comfort of our relationship when *he* got home."

Several women in our study commented that their husbands dominated much of the conversation at home with their office politics and problems. One said, "Because I understand his problems, he always brings them home with him, and in this sense, he never leaves the office. I don't like it, but I seem unable to change the pattern."

Another wrote, "Earlier in the relationship with my dominant husband, I didn't dare make a salary. He kept reminding me I would only push us up into the next tax bracket, which he certainly did not want. He figured out what this would cost us, plus the high cost of day-care for our two children, extra help around the house, and a whole new wardrobe for a working woman. There was no way we could have afforded this! Then one day, I woke up and realized there was no way I could mentally afford *not* to go to work. So I started immediately. Sure, it was rough the first several years. Now sixteen years later, I make almost as much money as my husband and, because I am a woman, have much greater visibility!"

IMPACT OF WIFE'S CAREER

Although most men talk about their wife's successful career with a great deal of pride, they may nevertheless associate her after-work hours with their care and comfort. Men still want to be nurtured. And many men still resent being asked to participate in cooking and cleaning, or what they consider "women's work." But we are discovering that as women are adjusting to their new roles in the workplace, men are adjusting to the impact of their wives' careers and to their new role in the home.

The authors know from experience the effect a career can have on a marriage. States Nycum, "George and I enjoy my career. It introduces us to state-of-the-art ideas and fascinating people. It allows us to travel to interesting places under fortunate circumstances. For example, we were given a private tour of the old city of Jerusalem by the assistant attorney general of Israel, who had been city attorney and knew every stone and inhabitant. He was expressing his gratitude for my consulting with him and his staff on proposed high-technology legislation."

The authors' experiences are validated in the survey responses. Here are some of the mixed responses from our participants as to how women saw their careers impacting their marriage:

- *Positively.*
- *We are partners; makes our bond stronger.*
- *Makes me more vibrant, alive, equal.*
- *I have become the major breadwinner.*
- *I am less available to help with his career.*
- *No financial problems.*
- *He craves an ordinary wife to be home and wait on him!*
- *We are both in same field, have no lack of things to discuss.*
- *Since we travel extensively, we still greet each other as lovers.*
- *Limits his opportunities.*

One woman wrote, "As I achieved success, my marriage had several rocky periods. One one occasion, I actually filed for divorce. Then my husband adjusted his thinking and became more understanding of my career, and I changed my mind about leaving him. Finally we both accepted the relationship as it was, realizing we would continue to give a great deal of ourselves to our careers."

Another told us that she worked eighty-hour weeks and made all the money her husband had always wanted to make but never did. Now they have filed for divorce, and with a sense of humor, she said, "I am now wondering how much alimony I will have to pay *him!*"

Do our respondents' husbands view their careers the same way as the wives do? Not necessarily. Our survey reveals that the answers are mixed. After discussing this question with their husbands, our respondents wrote that their spouses feel:

- *Great.*
- *Wholeheartedly support.*
- *Very proud and admiring.*
- *My best critic, confidant, strategist.*
- *Would prefer normal family life.*
- *OK if meals are served on time.*
- *Was responsible for my becoming a professional person.*
- *Boasts in conversations to others; puts me down when alone.*
- *Deep envy because his success is not as public.*
- *Resentful and harbors these feelings.*

An engineer wrote, "My husband knew I would have a career before he married me. Otherwise, I would not have married him. My mother warned me not to 'put him off' with my career expectations, but I told her if he didn't want my career, then he didn't want me. My mother was horrified, but my father understood!"

Another woman told us, "My husband's mother was also a career woman. I would not have married him if he did not understand this kind of a mutual arrangement. It is important to know how your future husband treats his mother. He also encourages our two daughters as much as he does our two sons. Guilt and stress are inappropriate in a third-generation liberated home."

Along with many women in the study, Collins believes her second husband contributes significantly to her success. She jokingly says, "One way is that he 'gets out of my way' and lets me do it. This is no small thing. It is important to have an understanding that work has a high priority, and one does not need extra stress from a spouse who feels 'hurt' that his wife enjoys and needs to work additional time.

"My husband also contributes to my career by listening. Sometimes I bring home a problem that I am still wrestling with, and by just repeating it to someone who is interested, a solution can begin to evolve and sometimes I see the problem with a new perspective."

Gilbert notes her husband contributes to her career by totally supporting her efforts. "We solve together any problems that come up because of our life-style—from our child's illness to the lack of clean socks. Neither of us has *sole* responsibility for any area of our lives together. Without this support, I couldn't work at the level I do."

And Nycum adds of her husband, "Nothing is too difficult or too minimal for George. He solves sophisticated technical problems in my practice, and he picks up groceries. I know what it is like to succeed *in spite of others*. It is now a pleasure to know daily what it is like to succeed *because of another.*"

When we asked our respondents what they felt their husbands' major contributions to their careers were, they listed that he does the following:

- *Gives personal support in tough times.*
- *Has tolerance of my preoccupation.*
- *Cooks and shops.*
- *Stays home with kids while I travel.*
- *Supported me financially while I was in school.*
- *Urges me to move ahead.*
- *Lacks resentment over my earning double his salary.*
- *Gives intellectual colleagueship.*
- *Shares his professional projects with me.*
- *Sacrificed his career by not taking out-of-state job offer.*

One woman wrote at length that her husband had been especially supportive during the beginning of her career. He did this by contributing his time with the children when they were entering their teen years and were especially demanding. He supervised their schedule, kept the house running, and took the children to their various activities. And all the time he gave her the encouragement and emotional confidence that enabled her to begin at a low salary and work her way up to one of the top positions in a large organization.

Another told of a similar experience, "My husband supported me at critical times. His perception of the potential in me made me grow. Along with this was lots of TLC and understanding. While I always felt he encouraged me, this special support through difficult situations and belief in me made all the difference."

And still another shared, "The higher I climbed, the more difficult were my problems at work. I was in a field where few women had been. My husband understood the pressures I faced, and he was able to reassure me each morning. As I was leaving, he would yell, 'Don't let the bastards get you down!' I can honestly say I would not have persevered without him."

PROBLEMS IN DUAL-CAREER MARRIAGES

How *are* women handling the equality so recently won? Betty Friedan, in *The Second Stage* (Summit Books, New York: 1981), wrote that she senses something is going wrong. According to her, the women's movement uncover-ed possibilities, but it was also seen by both men and women as a root cause of the exploding divorce rate and soaring number of single-parent families. Friedan concluded that the women's movement was necessary to bring the freedom, but she thinks it is now time to restructure and move on.

In order for dual-career marriages to reshape and change, adaptations have to be made by both partners.

Adaptations of Women

Most of us would agree that it is the female who usually adapts the most, if problems are to be minimized and the marriage is to be successful. Issues such as relocation, relationship stresses, who pays for what (especially if her paycheck is larger), the nontraditional sharing of duties, and others must be resolved.

Struggles over power, along with questions of dependency and self-esteem, may also emerge as critical issues. Partners may even judge themselves and each other by the values of the workplace. And since men are still the princi-pal wage earners in most families, the women may take second billing.

The women in our study adapted in many different ways, and the out-comes did not always have a happy ending. One woman had a husband who received a teaching job in a college in the Midwest. She wrote, "Since my career in sales was just starting to take off, I stayed behind in the West, and we tried to continue our marriage by long distance. My job entailed a great deal of travel, and there were not sufficient financial resources for us to get together on a frequent basis. We were both fairly young at this time—under thirty—and we separated and divorced a year later.

"I had to choose between my career and my marriage. My husband want-ed me to come with him, but I believed that I would never again have an opportunity equal to the one that was being presented to me, and the possibili-ties for advancement were unlimited."

Another woman wrote, "My husband was semi-retired and decided to move to Florida to enjoy some of his hobbies. I remained behind in another state since I had begun a consulting business, and it was just getting off the ground. Our interests started to diverge on different paths, and it became impossible for us to maintain our relationship."

Gilbert has adapted to balancing a career and a marriage by understand-ing and communicating her priorities. "I know that my family is without question my first priority. No matter how compulsive an achiever I may be, my happiness is dependent on a stable home relationship. My husband and child make it possible for me to satisfy my need to work, but if my work environment made it impossible to give to my family, I would leave and find another job. However, I have not always felt this way."

And Nycum adds, "I know how devastating living apart can be to a relationship and am pleased that George and I have no business pressures to do so. I have known many couples whose careers have forced them to live apart, and I have rarely known a marriage to succeed in this circumstance. When it does, it requires great maturity of both partners."

Some people do manage to maintain a marriage or significant relationship over distance, and many of our national legislators live this way. However, to us, it certainly appears difficult and a marriage of this type needs a great deal of commitment on the part of both persons.

Jane Pauley discussed the adaptations of career women on March 16, 1985, in a TV special entitled "Women, Work and Babies: Can America Cope?" In quoting from the NBC White Paper that was written and produced by Bob Rogers, Pauley says, "There are no 'role models' for dual-career couples. The multiple role for the woman—worker, wife, and mother—is exhausting. Husbands often do not help around the house, of if so, it is usually minimum, and thus, the woman must put in long hours at home in addition to those at the office.

"It is very hard for women to do it all. Men, having no role models of men helping with the housework, feel 'put upon' if they are asked to help. Men can also feel deserted, as women share their emotions with those at work, and they feel left out. Men want more focus on themselves, the family, and the house.

"Other workers often don't see motherhood and a fast-track career as mixing. Pregnant women are not viewed as serious about their career, nor as committed to their career. When they become pregnant, promotions and advancement often stop. Some even are treated as disabled."

Pauley noted that working mothers say that finding good day-care is their biggest problem. "Experts agree that day-care needs improvement, but no one seems to have the solution. Some feel the government should take more responsibility; others feel that this would be too expensive, and the government should *not* spend that kind of money nor take this kind of responsibility."

Pauley summed up her TV special by saying, "It is a 'tough world' for the working mother. There is little recognition from society; hardly anyone is responding to this problem. The day-care issues are even more urgent for the poor, as they have fewer choices. It is a problem that all of us need to decide what to do about."

After Collins was interviewed by Pauley on "The Today Show" regarding mentors (October 25, 1985), they discussed women's problems in finding good day-care. Pauley, the mother of twins born in 1983 and another child born in 1986, said "This is a concern for many mothers. Parents are not trained to select good day-care. There is also a high turnover with household help, and psychologists say this is harmful to the well-being of the child."

Another area in which adaptations are necessary is the area of relationships with one's spouse. Stress in relationships that mean the most to us can occur as a side effect of the stress from our demanding occupational worlds.

Professional women often feel a need to have some measure of control not only over their job environment, but over their home life as well. Since tension results from constantly putting forth our best effort at work as well as at home, we need to pay close attention to the indicators that tell us how we are coping, and stress is one such indicator.

Gilbert talks about the stress she encounters. "Of course there are inevitable stresses. There are times when I feel as though I am coming unglued because of disruptions in schedules at work or home. Planning generally works for us, but every now and then the housekeeper is ill or the car breaks down, and I'm not sure how I'll get through the day. Luckily, my husband is relatively unflappable and doesn't react badly to disruptions. Since he works two miles from home while I currently commute eighty-five miles each day, he usually takes care of domestic crises.

"When my daughter was young, we purchased a home that was within two miles of our jobs. During this time, there were days when our daughter was home sick, and no care was available. Then we had to spend the day shuttling from home to work and take two-hour shifts to care for her. I have also conducted staff and other business meetings at home with my bedridden child in the next room."

One of the biggest problems that a career woman has is handling the stress of her husband's job in addition to her own. If her husband is also under a lot of tension, it will undoubtedly rub off. When a couple have similar jobs and feel a lot of pressure, they especially tend to share their concerns. This can lead to their never getting away from the office, since they bring their problems home to discuss with each other. Gilbert says, "I have asked my husband, who has his own successful career, if he resents not having a wife who is available to listen to him when he arrives home, or one who can go to the dry cleaners or get his shoes repaired rather than having to do these things himself. Luckily, at a stage where his peers receive just such service, his answer is still no."

Nycum finds that her husband, when under stress, simply likes to be alone. "The best I can do for him is to stay quiet and make no demands of my own. From years of living alone before his marriage, he learned to handle stress that way. Since it works for him, I'm all for it."

Collins comments, "My husband normally cuts off his workday when he walks in the house. And being a psychiatrist, much of what he experiences during his day is confidential. But when he is feeling stressed, I do for him what he does for me. I *listen*. I can ask questions or explore with him the outcome of the options he has available. We both feel close after these talks, and in a small way, I can reinforce how capable I believe he is of handling his situation. I also believe in 'hug therapy.' Hugs are a great way to relieve stress!

"But relationship stresses in general take their toll on me. I tend to carry an unpleasant family situation to the office and vice versa. I do not like conflicts and will go to almost any length to work things out as quickly as possible. I have been known to break a deadlock by smiling and saying, 'You want an arm? A leg? Here, take them.'"

Problems in marriage are causing many married couples who work to crowd therapists' offices. Dual paychecks may provide a better standard of living, but for a large number of couples, they also contribute to twin headaches. Many family counselors say their practices are now largely devoted to couples who cannot reconcile three often conflicting demands—his job, her job, and their relationship.

In a May 13, 1985, article in *Time* magazine, Patricia Kennedy, a psychologist in New York, commented, "Marriage, or even living together, has become every bit as much a business merger as it is an emotional commitment."

In part, the difficulties stem from the complexity of working couples' lives. There is only so much energy, emotion, and especially time to go around. When the career-minded pair finally meet at home, they are usually exhausted. Often their conversation is confined to work. Intimacy erodes; boredom sets in. Said one of our sample, "It's funny, but even sex can become another task that I feel I need to do; it satisfies physically but not emotionally."

Many couples in our study have found that a change of scene does a lot to relieve the stress between them. Stress is almost inevitable and should be planned for. Many schedule vacations as well as frequent weekends. Wrote one respondent, "Just the *thought* of such a break can act as a relaxant."

In November 1985, Sue Gilbert interviewed California State Senator Rebecca (Becky) Q. Morgan, who agreed with this approach. "My husband, Jim, and I review our calendars weekly to build in time together, trips away at the same time, and obligatory dinners. Since both of us often work sixty or more hours each week, our goal is one three-day weekend each month without job-related responsibilities. I am also learning to 'let go' of standards of excellence at home. The yard and garden are receiving minimal care, and a housekeeper-shopper for ten hours a week performs 'wifelike' services. And once a month I hire a window washer and a floor scrubber."

The wisdom of "letting go" of routine tasks should be obvious. And women should allow themselves to let go without guilt and without buying into the "superwoman image" of feeling like a failure because they cannot do it all.

Adaptations of Men

A husband can feel very much threatened by the success of his wife and can experience problems of self-esteem that make him and his career seem vulnerable. Thus his adaptations are very real. There are not many male role models for the men of our generation to follow in their marriage, nor are there many studies on husbands to see how they adapted to having a successful wife.

We discovered that the husbands who feel a part of the women's lives in our sample, and who play a supportive role, feel somewhat responsible for contributing to their success—and this seems to make a difference in how they cope.

We found that husbands adapt in different ways. As women work harder than ever to achieve professional success, some husbands complain of neglect. Many men feel their wives' successes somehow diminish their own. It's clear that the emergence of sizable numbers of career-minded wives has unsettled the balance of family power. What shocks some younger women is the discovery that the "liberated" men they married—the men who once agreed to share household chores, to delay having children, to support their wives' ambitions, and to strive for an egalitarian marriage—harbor many of the same "traditional" resentments.

Nycum's husband had to adapt to the tremendous number of social commitments that are a part of her normal working life. She comments, "George had been used to living alone, enjoying the performing arts, and reading for pleasure. Suddenly he was expected to host or attend receptions, meetings, and dinners for people he had never met before and whose careers were vastly different. Fortunately, he is a naturally congenial person and is easily very successful in this new role."

An example of a couple's not adapting is made clear by the following incident involving a female physician and a middle-manager in a corporation. Her income is more than twice his. They have recently had their first child (at the urging of the husband), and it is very clear that she expects the child to be more his responsibility.

She said, "I do not want to be involved in any of the middle-of-the-night feedings, evening or weekend babysitting, and I cite my longer-than-his hours at the office as well as being 'on call' many evenings for emergencies. This is a surprise to him and is an example of not working out in advance a most significant event in our relationship."

Many husbands said they support the notion of equality for women, but at the same time, some voiced a common complaint: "I didn't sign on to cheerlead a workaholic phantom who won't take my name, won't cook my meals, doesn't need my money, won't have my baby, and would rather make love to the job than to me."

Clearly a big area in which many husbands must adapt is in the issue of the paycheck, especially if hers is larger. Most husband's salaries have always been larger, but today, in some instances, the woman's is larger. It takes a very secure husband to feel proud and not intimidated or jealous when his wife's income outstrips his.

In our survey, we discovered that a significant number of our sample are the main breadwinners. We found of those answering, 47 percent earn more money than their husbands, 4 percent earned the same, and 49 percent earned less. If asked if this were a problem, only 20 percent stated yes, while 80 percent answered no.

We received many comments and interesting responses such as this one, "Money is not only an ego problem, but a life-style one. My salary encourages him to live beyond his means and tends to be a bad influence by his choices to do things I do—things he wants to do but cannot afford himself."

We also discovered 33 percent of the women in our study had higher titles and status than their husbands, 6 percent were the same, and 61 percent were lower. However, almost no one mentioned this as a conflict area.

If there are huge disparities in salary, it can mean there are huge disparities in job prestige and responsibilities. This can lead to dominance issues. On the other hand, we found some women with greater responsibilities than their husbands had lower salaries due to their field. Thus, the "power" each of the two individuals holds can be equal, even though her income is lower than his.

According to the U.S. Census Bureau, in the millions of American households where both spouses work, a significant number of women do earn more than their husbands. This figure will continue to rise. In a study conducted by *Goodhousekeeping* (October 1986), the wife earning more than her husband is, on average, over fifty-five years old and accounts for some 13 percent of the women in marriages where both spouses work.

Another area of adaptation for husbands is that of sharing the traditional domestic duties, previously the responsibility of the woman. As women accept a professional life outside the home, the demands on our time are such that keeping up the home by ourselves is impossible. Historically, men who held such positions have had the luxury of a wife, which we do not.

Husbands have begun to share women's traditional duties, and one way they are doing this is to help with child raising. Of those women in our study who had children, some 58 percent stated their husbands shared the responsibility. Thirty-one percent said they did not, and 11 percent responded that they helped sometimes.

Gilbert gives an example of how her husband shares the house duties. "Keith cooks breakfast and I cook dinner. In some ways this is unfair since we often go out for dinner, but rarely for breakfast."

And Nycum says, "Early in our marriage, I cooked while George sat patiently in the living room. He did this to support my need to be domestic. Finally we realized this would *not* work, and now George cooks and I clean up. Recently I have seldom cooked more than fudge!"

Collins comments, "My husband lived alone many years before we were married. This self-reliance around the house was one of the early attractions for me. He can do anything I can do, and do it well. And he is secure enough so that his masculinity is not threatened. While we eat at home only a few nights a week, we usually go into the kitchen, cook together, and stay until the cleanup is finished."

A clever article in the *San Francisco Chronicle* on June 7, 1985, with the headline of "So Who Has Time to Keep House?" reported that as more women choose paying careers, heavy housework is going the way of whalebone corsets and beehive hairdos. According to Claudia Bushman, executive director of the Delaware Heritage Commission, "People are quite proud of not having time to clean their houses. Women used to compete to have the cleanest floors. Now they compete to be too busy to do such things."

One of our sample humorously wrote, "The biggest problem with house-work is that men and children make 90 percent of the mess, and 90 percent of it is supposed to be cleaned up by women."

Many couples in our study reported having an agreement where the man does at least part of the cooking or other inside duties or they set aside a day over the weekend when both work on the chores. The latter arrangement was the most common, with each contributing to the domestic duties. Most of our respondents reported hiring help with the house and the yard and, in addition, used a cleaning service a few times a year for special cleaning.

In conclusion of the survey on the adaptations of dual-career marriages, we asked the question, "Who's the boss?" The most successful marriages were from those couples who answered, "We both are." Two-career couples represent a generation in transition. Whether these emerging professionals can succeed in their careers while keeping their marriage intact is one of the crucial socio-logical questions of the decade.

DIVORCE—WHAT NEXT?

In 1982, divorces in the United States hit an all-time high of 1.2 million cases, and more than half of the couples who divorced had children. Accord-ing to Linda Bird Francke's *Growing Up Divorced* (New York: Simon & Schus-ter, 1983), "Divorce is not a single event, but a series of events. Yet few people are really aware of what lies ahead."

According to the courts, the largest cause of divorce in the United States is stated as "incompatibility." What a large range of problems this covers! If men are left too far behind, they may satisfy their needs for gratification and being appreciated elsewhere. Many women in our study confided in us that if their husbands had only been more sympathetic partners most of their career difficulties would have diminished, and as a result, they could have made better wives.

Many problems lead to divorce—the timing of marriage, each partner's success and when it is achieved, the kind of marriage relationship, the domi-nance issue, salaries, stresses, home versus work priorities, and the division of domestic duties. These problems serve to cause pressures for the couple, which if not handled correctly can lead to the end of the marriage.

One woman wrote, "I preferred not to be married. It is extremely dif-ficult for someone like me, who is so career-oriented. I give most of my energy to my job; I did not know my husband would need so much sup-port. It would have been better for me to have stayed alone in the first place."

Extramarital affairs need to be examined when looking at causes of di-vorce, since this can be a major cause of break-up. One woman shared her view, "Although standards are changing, I do not personally think that many marriages can stand up to the threat of an affair. The perceived loss of intimacy with a partner makes the relationship undependable and a reevaluation of each other occurs. I think that faithfulness is the most important ingredient for a good marriage."

Some interesting comments were given by our survey participants regard-ing extramarital affairs, and a wide range of views were expressed. We found that many women increasingly view this activity much as does their male counterpart. Said one, "It is OK and an accepted part of the traveling execu-tive's life; however, affairs should never be confessed."

A corporate executive with worldwide responsibilities said, "It is not for me personally, but I would never judge what is right for another." And another opinion was, "As strange as it may sound, my affair has strengthened my marriage. It has added a 'zip and a zing' and has made my working life more enjoyable. I would not have worked as hard nor enjoyed my career as much if I had not had a very special relationship with my boss for almost five years. The extra travel and the long hours seemed tolerable, and even fun. And because I was happy in my work, my home life was more relaxed. It was always clear that I did not want a divorce, but I needed the extra support and comfort from my lover."

The answers to our survey question on extramarital affairs show a range of opinion:

- *If approve, no point in being married.*
- *I'd be foolish to jeopardize my good marriage.*
- *Totally emotionally draining.*
- *I couldn't handle.*
- *Intolerant of deceit.*
- *Have had several.*
- *Sometimes understandable.*
- *Fun and the spice of life.*
- *OK as long as partner is not knowledgeable about it.*
- *If it doesn't affect your marriage, do it!*

One woman stated, "Married men continue to want affairs with me; I'm burned out and shut off by their advances." Still another woman wrote, "If I could find someone who appealed to me sexually, I might be interested. Strangely enough, I have looked, but never found anyone worth the trauma or glory."

Another commented that she had been unable to change her husband's attitude about her career, which led to their divorce. She said, "When I got married in the mid-seventies, my husband and I shared a perception of the life we wanted. It included a station wagon, a house in the suburbs, two well-scrubbed children with perfect teeth, and a large white female dog.

"But when my children were old enough to go to school, I accepted a temporary job which was supposed to be for the summer only. I was surprised to find that my work became a great source of inner satisfaction, and as my responsibilities increased, so did my self-confidence. Finally, my job began to undermine my marriage. My husband couldn't imagine being married to a career woman, and as my power grew and my hours lengthened, his personality changed around me.

"One night, eight years after I began working, I proudly announced that I had received a promotion as head of a department in which fifty-five people would report to me. My husband's reaction is etched on my mind forever—he participated in my success by asking for a divorce."

Whatever the cause of divorce, what follows for the successful, high level woman? We found that a period of reassessment normally occurs. If she feels the break-up of the marriage was her fault and if the marriage mattered to her, then she may feel she failed in an important area. Failure can be hard to take for the upwardly mobile woman. As a result, her confidence level can be shaken. This can then undermine her in other areas where she had previously been successful.

However, if the divorced woman sees herself as successful at work, admired, appreciated, and compatible with others around her, she may be relieved that her bad marriage has come to an end. One woman in our study, who was recently divorced and was head of a division of a food company, wrote, "I felt I deserved a better male relationship and believed my divorce was in no way a threat to my ability to continue my career success."

After the end of a marriage or the end of any important relationship, we believe a woman should pamper herself. She should do whatever it takes to boost her ego, if she needs it, and to keep her self-image intact. She should draw heavily on support systems available—women or men friends, parents, or children. The importance in life of a network of loyal and loving friends cannot be overemphasized in a time of crisis.

Collins says, "When I first began living alone after being married, I counted heavily on my women friends for support and understanding. And as I began dating, I learned that because the man often does the inviting, the social friends were his friends. And when I dated someone else, I had to accept a whole new group of friends. But my women friends were constant and the glue that often held me together, and I just can't emphasize enough the importance of a loving and congenial group of female peers."

One woman in our study shared, "The end of a relationship always makes me take a good look at myself—both inward and outward. I normally bound into a self-improvement program by going on a diet, getting a new hair style, and delving into an evening course at my local university."

Nycum cautions, "The recently separated or divorced woman may not realize the extent of the emotional upheaval that she is experiencing and its effect on her judgment and behavior. This is a time to minimize other unnecessary changes and to keep a low profile in business."

Senior level women, recently divorced, are said to be too powerful and frightening for the new man. Sometimes we have noticed this to be true. The professional woman can often be so totally in control of every situation that she can be very intimidating to a would-be suitor, regardless of his position. At this point, her reactions to men may depend upon how she is feeling about herself as an individual. And if a man perceives that she has just chewed up and spat out another man, or used the relationship solely for her needs, he may feel it could also happen to him. Thus, he may not opt to enter a relationship with such a demanding woman.

Gilbert shares her experience in dating after her divorce: "I tended to meet men at the usual singles-scene places—parties and bars. Most assumed I was a teacher, stewardess, or secretary. When they learned after a few dates I earned more money than they did, they were usually threatened. Some did not call again."

Nycum looked for men who were comfortable with themselves and, therefore, who would not feel threatened by her career.

Collins's experience humorously points out how career and status can affect would-be suitors. "Before I remarried, I dated a variety of eligible men. Due to my job visibility and the people with whom I came in contact, I often felt I was quite intimidating to would-be suitors. I once had a blind date with a Merrill Lynch executive, and he seemed dumbfounded when I told him that two weeks before, I had sat next to Donald Regan, then chairman of Merrill Lynch, and several other key executives. He had never met Regan and couldn't adjust to the fact he was dating someone who had met the whole top team."

If a woman is competent only in her work, but not socially or physically, then she may be too powerful in one direction and not balanced. However, it has been our experience that a woman who is truly competent in her career is also competent in other areas.

One woman in our study commented that one successful man she was dating told her, "I kind of like going places with you. It's fun to have a girlfriend who intimidates my male friends!"

Another told us, "At the end of my first date, my new escort brought me home and said admiringly, 'You know, you are a real ball-buster!' "

In summary, we find that in love relationships, the successful woman usually chooses a successful man, although the man's success may be in fields unre-

lated to hers. Her new man is usually as self-assured as she is. When she
selects the right man, she will not appear overly frightening, and indeed,
he will see her as competent, interesting, and a real challenge. Certainly she
will never be dull!

4 Husbands of Superachievers

"Life?
Butterfly
On a swaying grass
That's all . . .
But exquisite!"
—SUIN (CHINESE PHILOSOPHER)—

Why does the marriage relationship work for some high achievers and not for others? We know that many men our age grew up expecting to be waited on by their wives and to be exempt from any housework. Not all men welcome the changing role of women, and we found there are few role models for men in dual-career marriages. Thus, we were interested in the impact of the female's recent success on her husband. Does it make him more proud and loving or threatened, jealous, and resentful?

To explore what it is like for men to be married to senior level women, the authors interviewed each other's husbands in December 1985. These in-depth interviews are included to give a firsthand illustration of the qualities and attitudes of a spouse that enable a senior level woman to realize her professional goals. The three interviews are followed by a survey of 100 spouses of senior level women, with questions covering four major areas: background compatibility; career attitudes; children and family; and future expectations.

THREE IN-DEPTH INTERVIEWS

The following accounts from the authors' spouses are drawn from those December 1985 interviews. These accounts may or may not be representational in all areas of inquiry. They are not meant to be. What is intended is that they give insight into marriages in which both partners are committed to their careers as well as to each other. In this section, the authors' first names are used, as that is the way they are naturally referred to by their husbands.

Richard F. Chapman, M.D.—husband of Nancy Collins (interviewed by Susan Nycum)

Dick is a fifty-two-year-old psychoanalyst, with a B.A. from Yale, a medical degree from Northwestern, psychiatric training at the Menninger Foundation, and psychoanalytic training from the San Francisco Psychoanalytic Institute. He is in private practice in Palo Alto, serves as a clinical professor of psychiatry and behavioral sciences at Stanford University Medical School, and is dean of faculty at the Pacific Graduate School of Psychology. He has been married to Nancy for four years.

When asked about the difficulties in being married to a high level career person, his response is immediate: "The difficulties? I don't think of the difficulties first. I think of the stimulation and advantages. I guess the difficulties are time and our schedules in terms of coordinating our activities together. There is some learning to do about each other's work, which is pretty far along at this point because we've known each other quite a while.

"Nancy's current work is in the medical field, which is my own field, so I know much of what she's coping with. The Palo Alto Medical Foundation deals with research and education, which are part of my interests also. So there is quite a bit of parallel and overlap."

It is this parallel and overlap that give Dick some of his greatest satisfactions, foremost being the companionate nature of his relationship with Nancy. They have common interests even to the point of coauthoring a book on the mentoring process. In addition to enjoying this shared research and writing project, Dick appreciates their similar life-styles and expectations. He finds that they have much to share by having lived in Menlo Park and being involved with Stanford for almost twenty years.

Successful joint careers are important to both, and the future holds a long-awaited freedom: "We have done the parenting of our children, and the next twenty years or so are ours to define as we wish."

Dick finds their shared interests so important that he cites it as one of the reasons the relationship works. Also factoring in their successful marriage are their similar ages—being in the same generation—and their dedication to professional excellence, each in their own field. He adds, "The relationship also works because I respect Nancy and actively encourage her to pursue her emerging interests."

Dick is clearly proud of Nancy's professional excellence and career success. He comments, "I define success as using your abilities and talents for the good of others, and I think that that fits her. She really uses her abilities and talents in a way that fits her and that others respond to. It's a pleasure to see how highly she's regarded by the people with whom she works."

In considering the implications of Nancy's success for him, Dick responds, "I'm mostly proud and happy. Her own enthusiasm about her work and her eager energy and the continued learning is just a pleasure to be around.

"There are times when she gets a little frantic or 'revved up,' and then I like to sit her down and tell her to slow down. But on the other hand, it's hard to be jealous of her when she's in a creative mood. Sometimes I think I'm envious of her skills. I think of jealousy as related to people, and I don't think people should be jealous."

What Dick values most about Nancy is "her loving enthusiasm, especially as it is shared with me." And he has never had the feeling that she values her career over their marriage: "When she gets an invitation to go somewhere to give an address, I do not feel like that is detracting from our relationship. It feels like a natural. I do get a little concerned when she gets preoccupied with her performance issues. Getting all 'revved up' makes her a good performer, but it is strenuous to be around her at this time! I especially feel her stress immediately before she appears on television or makes a presentation at a major meeting or conference."

Dick does, however, think that Nancy handles stress well. "She copes with problems by using problem-solving techniques. For instance, the choices for me are cognitive, affective, and behavioral. I think Nancy gets all three of them going. She is very good with actions and also about questioning her feelings and thinking."

Like most people, Dick admits to finding a difference in their relationship when Nancy is stressed and tired. He deals with that by first understanding the difference and then by using the weekend for quality, nurturing time together.

"Of course, there is a difference [when she is tired or stressed], and then I respect where she is. I get that way myself, and then she takes especially good care of me.

"I don't have the sense that I'm wearing her down, or that she is wearing me down. We get naturally tired from using our energies so much during our working day. We both keep long hours at our work. Apart from our full daytime schedule, we each spend several weekday evenings at writing, class preparation, committee meetings, or on other individual projects.

"Having a weekend home in Carmel Valley recharges our batteries, because here we have quality time by ourselves, and that can be an improvement over the weekdays. We especially enjoy our hot tub — sitting in it, we have a wonderful view of the valley, and our favorite time is getting up early and watching the sun rise.

"Sharing our quality time on weekends is important to us both. This is by design and also is a function of having a second home. For years, my Carmel home has been a place where I go to unwind on the weekends. And when I married Nancy, I set up an office there where she can work or do what she wants to do in her own space. And I have lots of room where I can putter around. It's a congenial setting, and Nancy works so hard during the work week that she needs a special place to go to and relax on the weekends."

In Dick's opinion, the largest problem in having a dual-career marriage "is that there are too many things to do and not enough time in which to do them; for instance, there are always several piles of professional journals and books awaiting attention and review, as well as correspondence to be answered."

However, "the greatest satisfaction is making enough time to do all the quality things together." Dick emphatically states that he did not pay a higher price because of his wife's career than he thought he would: "I knew what I was getting into! It has definitely been worth it, and I would certainly do it again."

Because Dick and Nancy both have children by previous marriages, they have become adept at raising two sets of children. Dick summarizes their approach. "We respect each other's primary relationship with our own children. Nancy has three sons, ages twenty-one, twenty-three, and twenty-five. I have a son, twenty-two, and a daughter, age twenty-four. Basically, we support each other's decisions.

"The youngest four are in college full-time, with Nancy's oldest living in New York and taking part-time courses, so they are visitors on holidays and during the summer vacations. The current focus is on the youngest who lives nearby. All seven of us get along fine. We came upon each other's children as they were entering young adulthood, so we do not have the background of their earlier years.

"I admit there is currently a financial drain due to having four kids in college (with the fifth taking classes) at the same time. This will change once the children are more independent, but handling their financial needs takes a lot of attention at this point. But this is age appropriate. We wish we had married earlier and had shared having the children together."

The similarity of Dick and Nancy's backgrounds made it easier to bring together their two sets of children. Many couples in a second marriage, of course, do not have two sets of children to blend into a family. Sometimes one person has raised a family, and the other has not but would like to. Dick comments on this situation: "I think that the biological drive is there, and if one has not had children, it is a key motivator. Especially in a loving relationship, it is basic to want to have a child with your partner. The realities around age, where you are, and the rest of the things you are doing are important.

"One of the basic decisions for people getting remarried past the age of thirty-five is a question of whether or not to start another generation. That is an individual matter, but it is harder to have the energy to make a twenty-year commitment to raising a child. But, professionally, I see a lot of people doing it. I am just kind of amazed when this happens!"

As well as understanding the challenges that couples face in regard to children, Dick understands what serious career women face. "The issues discussed in your book about the evolution of women's roles and careers are very timely. Being a member of the silent generation in the fifties lets me know how stereotypical women's roles were, and how far both men and women have come since then. For my daughter, this evolution makes perfect sense. Nancy's a pioneer in some of these ways. Her experience in having a talent and an ability to work in an organization is a major contribution. It's a pleasure to see it going on."

Dick is currently working with Nancy on their forthcoming book *Mentoring: Its Role in Career Development*. He comments, "My observation is that there are some major aspects of adult development around the mentor relationship. Mentoring is a very important part of career development, not just for women, but for men too. It will be interesting to research the man/woman issue in the professions. I have my own observations about women and men dominating different professions, and Nancy's observations may be different. What interests me is that there is a lot of overlapping between the settings in which we work and the people that we see."

Despite the overlapping of career areas, Dick finds that in midlife, he and Nancy have experienced a shift in their focus as individuals. "I believe that certain earlier conditioning exists. Nancy and I each had a number of years on our own before our marriage, and during this time, she relied on her sons to do certain things around the house, so that she really concentrated on her work.

"On the other hand, I had my career in place, so that when I got divorced, my career stayed constant. What I learned was to be by myself and take care of myself. I think this self-reliance was and is more expected of a man. I carry this out today by volunteering to do most of the menu planning, grocery shopping, and helping with the meal preparation. I learned to do all this while living alone.

"As one approaches midlife, the main issue for a man is how to make a relationship work. It is the reverse for a woman, who has been socialized to focus on relationships and much less on being independent and doing her own thing. Thus, the midlife transition for women has in part to do with bringing out the other side of herself.

"Nancy, having spent a lot of time and energy in being a parent and raising her children, can now focus on herself and her career, so this is a natural reversal for her. For me, having been so career-focused the first half of my adult life, I'm now more focused on the other side of myself, particularly in terms of teaching and mentoring graduate students. Thus, this is a reverse transition from Nancy's."

In conclusion, Dick offers his advice for a professional man who is thinking of entering into a relationship with a highly motivated professional woman. "There are two issues to consider—the personal side and the work side. It is important to be secure and pleased with what you're doing professionally and to have your own self-esteem in a good place.

"Then you have more of yourself to share in a relationship. I like the word 'companionate.' If you are companions, you look forward to sharing the years ahead. But it is key for each to have work that you are pleased with—this facilitates a constructive, interactional personal relationship, which is love and understanding."

Keith D. Gilbert—husband of Sue Gilbert
(interviewed by Nancy Collins)

For Keith Gilbert, the greatest satisfaction in his marriage to Sue is in sharing each other's successes. Says Keith, "There is a certain richness to the marriage that comes with both of us being involved in things that are exciting. And it is exciting to share satisfactions—this puts a certain 'spice' in the marriage!"

Keith, forty-four, has been married to Sue for fifteen years and is raising a daughter with her. An MIT graduate with both a B.S. and M.S. in Engineering, he is currently the group vice-president of the Devices Group for Watkins Johnson, a company in Palo Alto that is in the military microwave electronics business.

He finds that his relationship with Sue is enhanced because they are both involved in the business world and can understand and help each other. "I think it is very helpful for both of us to have been there in a business situation. If we need to bounce an idea or a problem off the other, we both know the kind of atmosphere we are dealing in, as we have had the experience ourselves. This helps in building the relationship between the two of us."

What Keith struggles with, as do most men who are teamed with high level career women, is the element of time. "By far, the greatest difficulty is the demand on time. Both of us have a lot of obligations at work, and we have to juggle those along with our relations with each other, our relationship with our child, keeping up with our home, and some degree of social life. This is difficult! For instance, travel has to be planned well in advance, as we both have many obligations at work. Without question, time is the greatest problem for us.

"Although not a frequent problem, conflicting after-hours business obligations are difficult with the responsibility of a young child. Because we were both busy one evening shortly before Christmas, our daughter helped me serve food at an employee Christmas dinner. She liked the experience, and the employees thought it was great!"

Despite the time pressure, Keith and Sue's relationship is a successful one. In citing why it has been so successful, Keith believes, "We are pretty well 'in sync' with each other. Certainly, the first starting point is caring about each other and having the same values, particularly in a pressure environment, where you have a dual-career marriage. It is also very important that your goals be similar. As I mentioned, time puts a lot of demands on us, and with that being the case, I think it would be very difficult for us both to be going in opposite directions with some of our desires. For instance, if my desire were to go skiing every weekend or participate heavily in other sports, then that would be difficult to match with Sue's desires, which are not in that direction. So we have similar values and goals, and that helps quite a bit."

As well as having insight into their relationship, Keith has insight into what makes Sue a successful business woman. "Sue is a very smart person—she has a very good intuitive feeling for making correct business decisions. I have certainly observed that in some of the decisions we have made as a couple, and I know that it carries over into her business career. When she gets a grip on a project, she just won't let go of it. She is like a tiger! Her concentration is tremendous, and she goes ninety miles an hour until she has the whole thing figured out with a nice, neat ribbon tied around it. She is very, very persistent.

"Sue recently spent a Sunday afternoon revising a client's business plan. Every time I looked in the room, she was concentrating, focusing on the task. She didn't stop until it was complete."

Keith seems to revel in his wife's success: "I don't think I have ever felt threatened and jealous over Sue's success. However, I do get this question from a number of people! I am very proud of her and her accomplishments.

I suffer occasionally with her when she has problems at work, but I certainly identify with her success, and I am very proud of it.

"One of the most interesting experiences I had was about six months ago, when my company had its quarterly management meeting. Our group executive decided he wanted someone to talk on strategic planning. He thought of Sue, whom he had met a few times, so she was invited to address our management group at Watkins Johnson on the subject of strategic planning. I found it quite interesting to watch the reactions of my coworkers! Some knew Sue fairly well, and others couldn't imagine the wife of one of their colleagues knowing so much more than we knew about strategic planning! It was a very interesting experience. And Sue seemed very pleased to make this presentation."

As Sue's career has evolved, Keith finds that she has become more serious about it: "I can sense that it means more to her. She has become more businesslike as she has become more senior. She is probably more impatient with trivialities—she does not 'suffer fools easily,' as the expression goes. Also, she does not like to waste time. She values her time more and probably has a little more difficulty relaxing than when we were first married."

Keith sees Sue's career as having the potential to rise still higher. "I believe she is capable of being the chief executive of a small-size company. It is hard to say how much her desires will be to move up the next step and become a CEO. I think a lot will depend on how she feels about the job she has now. But I certainly think she has the capability to do so if she wants."

Two high-powered careers seem to include some inevitable stresses. Keith comments, "Both of us operate in a fairly high-pressure environment, and this can be difficult. When we get home, we are still fairly wrapped up in that environment. Sometimes I can sense that Sue has a story to tell about her day, I have a story to tell about mine, and it can take a while to connect because we are each so wrapped up in our own day. One of the differences in how we approach this is Sue has a need to talk about what happened in her day, and I am more likely to 'veg' out with a newspaper. I tend to turn it off more easily and go away from the problem. She is more likely to mull it over and want to talk about it. I am more likely to intellectualize it."

In handling stress, Sue, according to Keith, "is more prone than I am to allow herself to react in an open and emotional way, which I think is probably good. She is able to vocally express her displeasure with whatever is causing the stress. She is much more prone than I am at showing anger at the situation. Usually she will go through an emotional and vocal phase, then settle down and deal with the problem.

"I was impressed when I followed her successful strategy in turning around the resignation of a key subordinate. She combined emotion and logic to convince him to stay in the job. The panic I know she felt didn't show in her discussions with him."

Keith explains how Sue solves problems: "Most of the time she copes with a problem by examining it, planning a solution, and attacking it. There are times when I sense that she gets overloaded, overstressed by problem situations as mundane as the housekeeper not keeping the house very clean, to solving the problem of getting Amanda to the dentist. I think there are times she gets overwhelmed by the magnitude of career, family and home life, social obligations—all building up together. But what she does is to attack the problem in a very logical manner.

"We depend on a reliable housekeeper for child care and cleaning, and the turnover of that type of employee is frequent. When that happens, Sue always pursues a number of approaches to finding a replacement—ads in the papers; calling employment offices at local junior colleges; checking with friends. So far it's worked every time."

For all the energy that Sue puts into her career, she puts equal commitment and caring into her family. That effort is certainly not lost upon Keith. "What I value most of all is her love and caring for me. I also value the determination she has put into making our family life a good one. She has made a lot of personal sacrifices in building our life-style and in making sure we are a good family with close relationships. She has certainly gone a long way toward helping me to see the value of communication between all of us, and the value of openness. She has pushed me to be a better person as well. So she has committed herself not only to her career, but also to us as a family."

And Keith has never felt that Sue valued her career over her marriage: "No, no, I have no question about that! We are both very careful to make sure that travel or business obligations do not overly interfere. And I think Sue would answer any question about me the same way."

Sue and Keith's commitment to their marriage is reflected in their commitment to their daughter, Amanda. "In terms of *time*, it is simply a high priority with us. Maybe when you have only one child, it becomes a higher priority because you know the events of their growing up are not going to be repeated. But since Amanda was born, we made a conscious decision that she would be a high priority in our lives, and we would not allow career decisions to overshadow that. I am sure there are times when Amanda feels one or another of us is gone for a long time period, especially when we are out for several nights in a row on business or social events. She may express some dissatisfaction, but never in a very serious way. We both have a very close relationship with her.

"As far as *discipline*, I would say that Sue is more the disciplinarian than I am, probably due to her nature, as she is quicker to react. Sue will get upset faster than I, for instance, if Amanda is not keeping her room clean. I am probably slower more by nature, and Sue is faster to react. Also, there are probably some areas in which it is easier for a mother to discipline a daughter, just by the nature of the sexes. We never have used harsh discipline on Amanda; it has always been more of a reasonable type. And this has worked for us. In some ways, it has been more like a business relationship, our discipline has been more like trying to reason with her. We try not to overwhelm her so that she withdraws from a situation.

"We have never criticized a test score our daughter has received; we believe she always does her best. We do emphasize meeting deadlines and obligations, always trying to use logic.

"Large *decisions* regarding Amanda are generally made by the three of us at this point. We do have a major decision coming up at the end of the school year, as Amanda finishes the sixth grade. We are trying to decide whether or not she should attend public school. Amanda wants to go, and Sue and I fluctuate, although we lean toward private school. We will probably be processing information for the next several months.

"The other large factor in handling children is the absolute necessity in getting good child care. In our case, since the time Amanda started school, we had someone pick her up at school, do light housework, and stay until we arrived home. We have always had good success in terms of the dependability of the housekeepers, but varying success in their ability to keep up the house! Certainly reliable care is essential if both parents are going to have a career.

"Our daughter has usually enjoyed our housekeepers, especially the younger ones. And she's learned to share responsibility with them, as during the serious house and brush fire in our neighborhood during July of 1985. Amanda and the housekeeper were away from the house when the fire started, but figured out exactly the most likely place to meet us. They were among the more calm people during the event. She handled a dangerous and frightening situation so well, it increased our trust in her competence to handle crises. Her home and possessions were definitely threatened, but she was able to let go of them and proceed to think about where we might live temporarily.

"The other thing that is interesting is how Amanda will react when she looks at our careers, having been raised in a very intense business environment. Our business often comes into the dinner conversation, and she will sometimes say, 'Why are you talking about business? Can't we talk about something else?' She is sort of half joking and half not. I have not seen any evidence that she is turned off by business, but it will be interesting to see where she heads when she is older."

When asked if he personally paid a higher price due to Sue's career than he thought he would, Keith responded, "No. When we were first married, I didn't think much about it. It seemed to be totally natural that both of us were working. At that point, both of us were at the start of successful careers. I did not think much about a family in terms of children—it seemed natural that we would keep on working.

"I would certainly marry Sue again, knowing how her career would turn out. There is, however, a price to pay—there is no doubt about that! There is that old expression, 'You get what you pay for!' I think the two of us have gotten benefits and personal satisfaction from a dual-career marriage. The price I pay involves opportunities missed to do things that we would otherwise have been able to do—mostly because of additional time or trying to mix two careers. For instance, vacations could be more easily planned; right now we have a tough mix of setting them up between the two jobs. Part of the problem is that there is not the 'traditional homemaker' handling house problems, and therefore, they are all shared.

"I could point to another benefit, and that is a certain amount of security in a dual-career family. If I were to hit bad times in my career or take a risk that did not pay off, then Sue's successful career would carry us. We have not taken advantage of this, but it is a factor that could be a real benefit.

"In summary, yes, there is a price in a number of ways, but I certainly consider the trade-offs worth it."

George H. Bosworth III—husband of Susan Nycum (interviewed by Sue Gilbert)

George Bosworth is married to a woman who, by standard definitions, is more successful than 90 percent of the working population. George says, "Susan is a senior partner in a large and prestigious law firm and is the recognized leader on high-technology law worldwide.

"I'm a very inner-directed person, so I believe that each person has to define success in his own right. But, when looking at other people, I would certainly see position, respect within the profession, earning capability, and opportunity to grow in ways that are both interesting and profitable in the future as measures of success."

George, fifty-two, has a B.A. from Cornell University and an M.A. from Harvard University in English Literature. He manages a large data communications network for Control Data Corporation and is also a consultant in this area. He lectures frequently on computer technology to lay groups and serves as an expert witness in complex computer litigations. He and Susan have been married for seven years and have one child who is Susan's by a prior marriage.

"A lifelong bachelor, I had considered marriage several times before I met Susan but never found just the right person. I am very particular, and Susan was worth waiting for." He values "her intelligence, her good taste, and her easy way with people."

Rather than feel threatened by his wife's very visible success, George is delighted by it: "It makes me feel happy that she's successful and she enjoys it, so that in turn is something pleasant for me to see. I think that the greatest impact is in the realization that she's *able* to be successful, rather than any specific things that come because of her success. Susan's success is not to be feared, but to be pleased about. And I believe she has still further opportunities for achievement, influence, and earnings.

"If I had to choose one tangible benefit from Susan's career, it is that we have good opportunities for interesting foreign travel. Susan often represents U.S. business abroad, is invited to advise foreign governments, and chairs international symposia. It's very pleasant to be able to travel a lot and be entertained—sometimes literally royally.

"Another benefit of Susan's career as a high-technology lawyer is the number of interesting technical people we meet. It is helpful to Susan and more fun for me that her clients and I speak the same language. When they realize the technical backgrounds and accomplishments they and I have in common, they know that Susan appreciates fully who they are, what they've done, and what their current challenges are."

George naturally enjoys the financial gain from having two successful people in one family. "That is certainly a plus, and we both enjoy what the other brings and the combined purchasing power that results from it." However, George is accustomed to living well and easily within his means. The dual-career household hasn't changed his life financially.

More important than material gain is George's satisfaction in loving Susan. For him, "the greatest satisfaction is when either on a business trip or otherwise, we find a time when we are both interested in being with the other and have the time to do it. We both think about it for weeks afterwards and keep referring to it.

"For example, Susan's birthday several years ago coincided with her return from consulting with the government of Singapore. I flew out and met her for a long weekend at one of our favorite places in Hawaii."

In considering the difficulties in being married to a high level and ambitious career woman, George comments, "I don't think there are very many difficulties, perhaps because I *wanted* to be married to a career person. The biggest difficulty is just the management of time, when either one of us is out of town or on an activity that can't be stopped. Sometimes the arrangements we've made have to be changed, and sometimes abruptly and suddenly. The management of joint time is the hardest to do."

When asked if it is lonely sometimes, George responded, "I suppose it is, but I'm sure that Susan feels the same way, too. For instance, when either one of us is traveling, it's presumably lonely for both of us in the sense that we're not together. But I think we're both mature enough that we can find ways of using our time."

Despite the demands of a dual-career marriage, George finds that his and Susan's relationship works because "we both work consciously to make it work. If we have problems or difficulties, we're fairly prompt to bring it up to the other and have an early-on discussion of it. One thing that makes our marriage work is that we have a large set of shared interests, and we share some attitudes as well. I think that these are by themselves pleasant things to have in a spouse. Those are the things that I measured when I met women, and they have been a factor in falling in love and deciding to be married."

In his opinion, the stability of their marriage has given Susan some freedom to realize how effective and resourceful she is in her career. "I believe she thinks of our life together as a base from which she can operate."

When asked if he thought that Susan ever values her career over their marriage, George commented, "There are times, and they probably occur several times a day, when all she's thinking about is her career. But, at other times, she's thinking about her marriage, and we've had relatively few times where there's been an explicit choice that she's had to confront. I talked about the management of time before as a problem, and that's one of the most frequent kinds of choices.

"It's often Susan who is forced to change the plan because her business is one in which she deals with many different companies' demands, and mine is one in which I basically deal inside one company. So she's more often the person who has to change, but I understand that, and it doesn't bother me."

George sees Susan as handling stress and coping with problems well. "Many people, women especially, have not been put into business stress when younger. This is an area that I've been able to help in occasionally, because I've earlier experienced patterns that Susan later experienced, and I can point out what might happen.

"It is an ongoing matter for Susan to continue to deal with stress, because the more she succeeds, the more situations occur with deeper and more frequent stress. But she's doing well in coping with this increased amount of stress."

When tiredness and stress are factors, George finds, "We're more likely to get into an argument or a misunderstanding as is anyone. But we are both people who remember what our activity has been, and in a more calm moment, we look back and laugh at it, or joke with each other because we were acting in stressful ways."

Furthermore, because they both experience stressful situations, they both understand those situations. "We can often anticipate what the other is going to face, and we are tolerant. We sometimes warn or at least tell the other when this may happen. This is one of the important support functions that comes from being married to a peer-group person. We both value the appreciation the other has of the demands we each face in our outside lives.

"One of the pleasures we find in our relationship is the different ways we approach a task or a problem. In our work, we each have to solve problems that have never had solutions before and a great deal of our business success depends on our ability to deal with state-of-the-art issues. We are both analytic and big-picture oriented, but I work best with a structure and Susan reasons often by analogy—comparing and contrasting the present matters to previous experience.

"It is fun to observe firsthand in domestic situations how the other person's mind works. Mostly our styles are compatible in a domestic situation, but sometimes we must choose. For example, in doing the income tax or trimming the Christmas tree, our styles work well together, but in cooking and serving a dinner party, only one style can be used or we bump into each other."

One important aspect of George and Susan's marriage is their relationship with Susan's daughter, Sue, whom each regards as a true joy, a mentally gifted, lovely looking woman with her feet firmly planted on the ground. "She even had the good sense to marry a man we would have chosen ourselves and whose family has become our friends.

"We compare notes a great deal. If we see Sue and her husband together we're almost sure to talk it over afterwards and see whether we can discern any new patterns that are present. And sometimes we compare them to us, back and forth. Susan's daughter is an executive at Esprit, and her husband is at Bechtel. Susan and I are both capable of giving some advice that isn't really parental advice, but business advice, and they appreciate that a great deal."

In return, "the children" are comfortable discussing everything range career choices to day-to-day technical or personnel quest George. His many years of managing professional people provide a of experience to help.

In summary, George exclaims that he did *not* pay a higher price due to his wife's career than he thought he would: "No. I knew it was coming!

"Oh, I'd do it again, I think it's extremely worth it. I'm very glad that I found Susan, and I enjoy with her the career that she has. If I were in a situation of marrying again, I would marry another career woman." And adds Susan, "Believe me, they would line up to marry him!"

SURVEY OF 100 HUSBANDS

To complement our spouses' interviews, Collins conducted a pioneer study of 100 male spouses of senior level women. We sought to discover why their marriages were (or were not) successful, how the wife's success and visibility affected the relationship, and if they resented the domestic pressures placed on them. Based on their replies, this revealing survey is one of the largest samples of its kind.

Our sample was asked questions covering four major areas: background compatibility (such as, age, education, salary, job title); career attitudes (such as, expectations of your spouse and her career, things gained and given up, pride or resentment of her career); children and family life (including, has her work impaired her role as mother? does her career make you spend more time in child care or household-related activities?); and last, future expectations (such as, will her career rise higher than yours? what will be her largest problems and biggest satisfactions?).

Above all, we wanted our respondents to answer the question: did you pay a higher price than you thought you would, and most important, was it worth it for you?

One man's response characterizes the general results: "I couldn't tolerate a passive, nonachieving wife; with all her ego and vanity, she is challenging, stimulating, activating, and the most exciting woman in the world."

The first part of our study explored background compatibility. We learned that the men in this survey come from many different early backgrounds, as do their wives. The following is a general profile that best describes our survey participants today: he is age forty-five, has a master's or other advanced degree, makes a salary of $75,000, is a professional person, is Protestant, is in his first marriage, and has been married an average of seventeen years.

Career Attitudes

Part two of our study centered around career attitudes and the early expectations that the men had about their wives' careers, what they had gained or given up as a result, whether they resented this, and the overall effect of their wives' careers on their sexual lives.

When the husbands were asked, "Did your wife's career turn out differently than you thought it would when you married?" the responses were almost equally divided between yes and no. One respondent shared, "My expectation from the beginning was that our life would be in 'high gear.' When I married my wife, I knew she thrived on stress and fast-paced schedules. She gets frustrated only when she is bored!"

Said another, "My expectations of my wife and her career have turned out as I thought they would. When I met her in college, she was intensely driven, and still is today. She can work anytime and anywhere, thinks vacations for the most part are a drag, and is happiest when working. Because I also work hard and enjoy my work, it has been a good match. But heaven help the poor guy who marries a woman like this and thinks he is going to change her."

And one respondent wrote, "I knew my wife was going to aim for the top in her career when I married her. So I knew this was a 'given.' But I had to learn that when things were slow and she could rest that this was the time she would create another challenge for herself!"

Many of the responses to the question "Did your wife's career turn out differently?" centered on the level of their spouse's success. Many of the men made such statements as "I did not know exactly how successful she would be (nor did she), but I knew she was the kind of person who was dedicated to climbing as far as she could, and I was also smart enough to know she would allow very little to get in her way, including our relationship."

Another wrote, "What made it [the relationship] work was our expectation that we would *both* change; as she grew, I grew, and while we did not always grow the same way, we were both experiencing new and exciting ideas, and we could relate to each other and understand what each was going through."

When respondents were asked to define what they meant by their wife's "success," they said that she has achieved the following: high salary, prestige in the community, higher status than most of their peers, influence on various committees and boards, and full individuality, with a solid identity not dependent upon him or his status.

Another wrote of his friend's reaction to his wife's position by saying, "I try not to brag around my colleagues who have wives with more routine jobs, but it is hard!"

They also pointed out that their spouses, as might be expected, were grappling with problems formerly unique to high level men and had solved the problems that used to trouble them at the beginning of their careers, such as equal opportunity, equal pay, and security in old age. A large majority commented that they felt their wives' success was based on overcoming many difficult situations and problems, handling more than their share of anxiety and stress, and putting forth a lot of hard work and effort all along the way.

When asked what they were forced to *give up* because of their wives' dedication to their careers, the respondents' most often mentioned answers (in order of frequency) were: leisure, friendships, entertainment, cultural activities, hobbies, and travel. Very few mentioned giving up sports in which they personally participated or living in an area not of their choice. One respondent seemed to sum up many feelings by writing, "I feel we have less time to enjoy life together than almost any other couple I know, but I don't feel her success has actually caused *me* to give up anything."

Elaborated another, "What did I give up? I gave up the 'normal relationship' one expects to have with the woman you marry. There's never a moment when she is not thinking about her work. It took a while before I learned not to take her long hours at work personally." And he ended somewhat humorously, "Because I love her, I feel the situation is hopeless, but not serious!"

One respondent shared, "I learned to give up routine socializing on weekends with my wife and our friends. She would promise not to bring work home for Saturday and Sunday, and every now and then she would actually keep her promise. But it never lasted as long as a month. Then she would say, 'Just this *one* weekend I need to work on a new project.' But of course as soon as she finished, another one would emerge—which would always turn out to be even more important to her than the one she just finished. Finally I had to come to grips with the fact that she didn't *want* to cut down her hours. Once I accepted this, the situation became tolerable."

The men in our study were as clear about their gains as they were on what they gave up. The key was which was greater. Commenting on what they had *gained* from their dual-career marriages, the men gave a variety of answers. The six most frequently mentioned replies, in order of ranking, were financial security made possible by two high incomes; a wide variety of investments; self-esteem due to their positions of authority; luxury auto; art and/or other collections; and the enjoyment of eating in expensive restaurants without considering the price. Aside from the obvious financial satisfactions experienced, many wrote that they were well aware of the respect they received from their male peers due to the status of their wives.

One man wrote, "When I first met my spouse, she was the first woman I ever knew whose career goals and aspirations were similar to mine. We felt the 'sky was the limit.' Now, years later, it is worth it all to have such an intelligent, understanding partner who understands my career demands and rewards almost as much as I do."

Another respondent praised his spouse, "My wife, a systems architect, is very competitive in all that she does. I have learned to turn this into an advantage which works directly for me. For instance, when she remodels our beach house, concentrates on her downhill skiing, or tackles our investments, I know she will master is until no one can do better!"

Many commented on their indirect gains. Said one, "I gained in subtle ways. I ran for public office and was elected. While my wife did not campaign for me directly, many people knew we were married, and I could not help but feel this was an enormous benefit."

Commented another, "I gained from my wife's business insights. We are both engineers, and she constantly talks shop, even when we are socializing. While I sometimes think she overdoes it, still I would rather talk about our work than about what many of our friends' spouses discuss—what the children ate for lunch and how the appliances are functioning. She is very bright and continues to give me suggestions and insights into problems I face at work. We have also coauthored joint publications."

Replied one, "My wife gets lots of strokes from her clients, which makes her feel positive and appreciated. She carries this feeling of self-worth over into our marriage, and she is a joy to be around."

The respondents were also asked what new personality traits emerged as their wives climbed higher. They listed an interesting combination (with no apparent pattern): assertiveness, self-reliance, resourcefulness, satisfaction with life, frustration, ambition, resentment, never satisfied with ordinary things, and emotional stability. Several added "anger" with the system that did not let them advance higher. Thus, while they did not agree on how she changed, most agreed that as she succeeded, she indeed *had* changed.

Yet one took exception and wrote, "My wife's personality did not seem to change as she advanced. She did not noticeably become more aggressive or develop a 'killer instinct.' In fact, her career did not go straight upward; she did not climb like the organized MBA with a road map that you read about. She would not admit to having a plan at all—she more or less drifted, sometimes upstream and sometimes down. However, with each drift, she managed to get a larger salary, but her personality seemed to stay more or less the same."

The men also pointed out that when given a choice their wives consistently seemed (at least to them) to select situations that were stressful. And this choice sometimes affected the respondent more than his spouse.

About two-thirds of the respondents did not think their wife's successful career, or any new personality traits, made her less supportive of him and his career. This is an important statement for professional women everywhere. And, overwhelmingly, the respondents did *not* resent their wives' independence.

The respondents were also asked when their wife felt the most stress in her job. In general, they felt that their wife's job was more stressful at the beginning of her career than after she had climbed to more senior positions. As a seasoned professional, she could concentrate on areas that matched her talents, delegate to others, and have more control over her work.

And when asked how their wives value their careers, one in six frankly responded, "She values her career more than her marriage." And the respondents seem to accept this.

We also wanted to know if the dual-career couple faced any special problems in their sexual life. As one would guess, the answers were mixed. Some men admitted to feeling a negative effect on their wives' sexual desires when they are under stress at the office. As one man wrote, "Is the Pope Catholic?" One illustrated the opposite and said, "My wife is head of marketing, and when she has just completed a large sale, she becomes a real tiger in bed!"

Another wrote, "My wife has become more manipulating of both sex and her work as she achieves more success. While I never knew a woman who enjoyed sex, simply and straightforward as men do, she has learned to use sex to manipulate me into getting her way."

Said another, "My wife is president of a fashion design company. During the day, she always looks so immaculate and acts so formidable. However, at night when we are close, our sex makes me feel she is human after all. It brings a tenderness which is very consoling—during this time I am not afraid to bare my soul."

The majority of our survey did not choose to write lengthy comments in this area, but one did share a humorous comment, "Sex after a hard day, nine or ten hours on the job? I sometimes think my wife would rather get paid than laid!"

While the questionnaire did not ask about extramarital sex, several of the respondents made comments in this area. Said one, "My wife seems so preoccupied with her job that when she has a deadline to meet (which is frequent), she comes to bed after I do, gets up before I do, and if I try to arouse her during the night, she angrily says she needs her sleep. This leaves me little choice, and I sometimes wonder if she cares."

Contrasted another, "I suppose I feel somewhat jealous when I see my wife pack and head out for another conference, which she frequently does, as my position affords little travel. But we have a very mature relationship, and I trust her completely."

Children and Family Life

Part three of our study concentrated on our sample's children and family life. About three-fourths of the respondents were parents, with an average of two children each. Although they stated that they did not think their wives' careers impaired their roles as mothers, they did state that as a result they spent much more time with their offspring. And while their wives' careers did interfere with their family life, only a handful claimed to resent this.

As would be imagined, several opinions were expressed, ranging from "My wife is an excellent role model for our three young daughters" to "There are times when she is greatly resented by each of our children, who know her career comes first unless there is a real crisis."

One husband wrote, "A main benefit of our two careers is that we are more sensitive to our children's needs on weekends. We put value on family outings on Sundays and seem to plan and do more as a family than most couples we know where the wife *doesn't* work."

Another responded, "My wife is a very controlling person. The more responsibility and control she has with anything, even the children, the happier she is. She wants to make a contribution to their lives and works hard at it. She is serious about their education and sets high standards. However, I accept and appreciate this."

Another respondent stated, "My wife exposes our children to her wide range of interests. As an example, once we were recently strolling in a garden, and she began to quiz them on the names of all the flowers. She made learning the new names a game."

Said another, "My wife's talents are in demand internationally. Not only am I proud of her, but the children and I accompany her on several exciting trips abroad each year. It is a source of deep satisfaction for us to see how respected she is in other countries as well as our own."

As a result of their wives' careers, there was great variation in the number of hours the men spent in household duties, but about ten hours per week seemed to be occupied with child-related activities. This included events with or without their spouses. One male spouse wrote, "I have become a fabulous cook, but then someone in our house had to learn, and after a few years, I realized it wouldn't be my wife."

Shared one, "My wife has great intentions, especially for celebrating holidays and special occasions, and she is very creative in planning these events. However, if she gets a business idea (as she often does), she is apt to get up in the middle of the party to sit in the car and dictate into the portable machine she takes everywhere.

"Sometimes she will even leave an important family celebration in order to make a long distance telephone call of thirty minutes or so. Once she was gone during the entire birthday cake festivities—this included the singing, the candle blowing, the speeches, cutting of the cake, and the presents which followed. Clearly she does her own thing, and it pays for me to understand what is planned so I can carry on, as I have to do this often."

Future Expectations

Part four, the final section of our study, covered our sample's future expectations of the next phase of their wives' careers and whether they would continue upward. We also asked for their insights and comments on what new problems and satisfactions this could bring.

When asked, "Do you think your wife's career will someday rise higher than yours?" over half stated, "It already has." However, over two-thirds said they were not paying a higher price than they originally thought because they were married to a successful career woman. And some 90 percent, when asked, "Is it worth it?" wrote yes.

When asked if they would be happier if their wives had *no* career, the vast majority (94 percent) stated that they would not. And all but three respondents said overwhelmingly that, if given a choice, they would again marry a high-achieving career woman.

Said one respondent, "My first wife was a typical 'hausfrau'—and it was so boring. All she could talk about was new recipes and what the children had done that day. Sure, I was interested, but there has to be more excitement and mental communication than this to hold a marriage together."

Another stated, "This is the first relationship I've had with someone whose career goals and ambitions are similar to mine. It's very stimulating and invigorating."

And added a third, "When good things happen to her at the office, she gets a real 'high' and that carries over into our marriage."

Summed up one, "My wife occasionally thinks more of her personal success than improved family relationships, but we know she is solidly there to count on in a crisis."

Dual-career marriages between two ambitious people face problems unique to this kind of relationship. When asked to comment on the largest problems the husband expects to face in the future, he lists: time for each other; cultivating friends; no energy left for me; the children; day-to-day housework; and issues centering on power and control. He anticipates his wife's attitude of supremacy on the job will continue to be hard for her to give up at home.

One man said, "Future problems? Of course. I remember one night going into a bar with a friend from work who had just filed for divorce. He was 'crying on my shoulder' about his problems and the end of his dreams and hopes. He began to tell me about how terrible it was when he found out his wife was having an affair. He described all the nights she came home late, and all the weekends she was away. It suddenly hit *me* that my wife was having an affair also—only it was with her work. I realized I could have coped better or at least had an equal chance with another man. But her work is a seducer with which I didn't stand a chance."

Another said, "My wife feels uncomfortable or anxious when she is doing nothing. It's almost as if she can't relax for worrying about her work! When we go on a vacation, which is rare, it's almost like she feels guilty for not working. Frankly, this is a problem for me, and I expect it will continue to be."

Wrote another, "My spouse has been promoted to the point where she is the only woman on her level. She seems to spend a lot of energy worrying about potential failures and making mistakes. She also spends a lot of time being concerned over her fear that others are saying negative things about her. She tries so hard to do a good job and please everyone that I think these concerns are unhealthy. In the future, she should stop trying to represent 'womankind' and just be herself."

Said one respondent, "My wife pushes herself much harder and works longer hours than I do myself. Also, when she is on a rush project at the office, she is apt to skip a meal or have her secretary bring her unhealthy foods like candy bars, potato chips, and Cokes from the office machines. So I worry about the problem of her health, but I do not believe she will change."

And said another, "I wish my wife had a more balanced life. She is president of a large professional real estate organization. She is committed emotionally to being tied to the 'fast track.' I believe she could survive a mastectomy, but I wonder if she could survive the recuperation period which would follow."

In contrast to the problems facing *him*, the husbands were asked to describe their *spouses'* major problems. They responded (in order): time for each other and the children; balancing a career and home; stress; lack of emotional support; and too much work. Thus, time was at the top of the list for both.

The men were also asked to list (in order) the greatest current *satisfaction* and rewards for them in their relationship. They said: security, personal freedom, a high standard of living, mental stimulation, peer relationship with wife, and community influence.

Said one respondent, "Our largest gain is the financial freedom my wife's salary (in addition to mine) gives us. Our hobby is investing—we have the ability to buy almost any stock or consider any investment that we want, and on short notice."

Another commented on the flexibility their two incomes gives them. He said, "We both work sixty-hour weeks for eleven months to be able to afford to play for one month. My wife totally throws herself into whatever she is doing at the office, and she likewise flings herself into doing nothing—which is our object—on our vacations. So, we do, for thirty days each year, what the Romans call *dolce far niente*—not merely 'doing nothing' but 'sweet doing nothing.'

"We select a different hideaway for each vacation. With a clear conscience, we indulge ourselves with finding the sun and the water, with sitting, gazing, smelling, and walking miles along the beach. We collect shells, watch our tan deepen, and achieve what we consider perfect peace.

"In short, we restore our souls. We replenish ourselves from our inner well. We don't think about our work, and we don't think about the people with whom we work. We tranquilize our senses, which are overabused by the bustle of both our corporate worlds. And for one month a year, we succeed."

Another wrote, "My satisfaction? With all her smart executive ways, she is still my little girl. She gets stressed from overwork and cross-country travel, and when she comes home all tired, I take over and give her back rubs. This makes me feel needed and like a real man, even though my salary and benefits are not what hers are. She leans on me when she is exhausted, and I love it."

And the husbands were asked to judge, in contrast to *their* satisfaction, their wives' greatest satisfaction. They replied (in order): self-esteem, independence, reaching her goals, influencing others, recognition, and financial success. It seemed clear that money was not their wives' prime motivator. In fact, one wrote, "She values her work for the satisfaction it gives her rather than for the paycheck it brings."

Conclusions

Many of our 100 male respondents stated they have never received a questionnaire of this type about their wife, and they were surprised and glad to have a chance to vent their feelings. Several told us they had never sat down before to actually write out a list of gains and problems from their dual-career marriage, and that they found this helped. One man stated that he planned to sit down with his wife and evaluate these questions every several years.

Final comments on "What's it really like to be married to a high level professional woman?" included such remarks as "We support each other," "Interesting," "I feel insecure and unneeded sometimes," "I cook more than I had imagined!" "Her job stress and tension causes conflict in our personal relationship," "Challenging," "We understand the other's similar goals," "We share professional growth," and "She's never boring." One man seemed to sum it up in his own way, and echoed many other replies, by writing in the margin, "With all our problems, it is still a lot better than being married to a low achiever!"

Elaborated one, "What's it like? Dazzling! She is always on-the-go, a study in 'rapidity,' even when not necessary; she frequently does two or more things at once; her mind is always one step ahead or shifting to the next task before she completes what she is doing; she's like a ballet dancer in constant motion!"

Wrote another, "I need high self-esteem so as not to be threatened by both her success and that of her company. Fortunately, I am a secure person, so I can enjoy her gains and achievements with her."

Summed up one respondent at the end of his questionnaire (and he echoed the thoughts of many), "With all my wife's crazy habits, all her lists, her late meetings and tight schedules, all her nervous energy, and all the long hours she puts into her job, she is the happiest person I know."

Another respondent told us he especially enjoyed replying to our survey. Attached to his questionnaire was the following:

WHAT'S IT LIKE FOR US? LIKE BEING ON A ROLLER COASTER!

Me: B.S. and M.S., age 44, Silicon Valley engineer, $75K/yr. (take home)

Her: Ph.D., age 42, pres. of her own company, $73K/yr. (take home)

Our situation: No kids, neat house, lots of toys, lots of ambition, lots of $$$, lots of technology and more than average marital problems, which I think we have worked through together and successfully.

Most couples are a major/minor pair. We are a major/major pairing. We set high standards for ourself and our spouse. Compromising is not easy for either of us—it is very hard for both of us not to tell the other what to do.

Characteristics:

- *We give each other lots of space.*
- *We are pretty independent.*
- *We trust each other absolutely, i.e., no infidelity doubts.*
- *Money control is an issue. We used to throw 100% each into a common pool. Now we each keep back a personal one-fourth. Makes us feel better about the control.*
- *The control issue is a big one. Who's got it? We try to work it out.*
- *My desire to 'drop out' is an issue. She's afraid I will be a dull fellow if I just goof around (i.e., manage our investments and do what I want technically or artistically on a 'don't have to make it happen' basis). I feel a little burned out after 20 years in the fast lane. Complex issue.*

Bottom line:

I am tremendously proud of my wife's achievements. It is a far better thing to be around someone who is intelligent, articulate, good looking, well paid, interesting, and competent than not to be. In fact, I wouldn't be, and neither would she.

We both place a high value on competency.

The value of this survey, the first of its type, is that it shows that the husbands of senior level professional women see their wives successfully combining their career and marriage and feel that the rewards that follow are well worth the sacrifices and personal life-styles required to attain these goals. Marriage can be a loving alliance of two economically equal people. Women's upward mobility with growing power, status, and clout in all professions is here to stay. And the good news is—their husbands are all for it.

5 Managing Children

*"The childhood shows the man,
As morning shows the day."*
—JOHN MILTON (PARADISE REGAINED)—

How do career women feel about motherhood? What is involved in terms of commitment, time, and work for those who choose to have children? These issues, as well as which child-rearing responsibilities can be delegated, day-care, and how children view their working mothers, are examined in this chapter.

There is no doubt that a dual-career marriage has an effect on the children involved. "Children in a marriage dominated by commitment to work usually turn out one of two ways: Either they are carbon copies, intense and hard-driving, or else they are exact opposites, beach bums or the equivalent," maintains Dr. Maurice Prout, assistant professor of mental-health sciences and director of behavior therapies at Hahnemann Medical College in Philadelphia (from Marilyn Machlowitz, *Workaholics*; Cranbury, N.Y.: New American Library, 1980).

Women with children are the fastest-growing commodity in the job market. A U.S. Department of Labor study in 1986 shows us that over half the American mothers with children younger than one year old work outside their homes. The study reported "profound" changes in the overall number of employed women, saying that the number of working mothers has more than doubled in the last fifteen years. This has caused a strain on both marriage and child rearing that traditional couples would never have faced a generation ago.

According to Linda Bird Francke in *Growing Up Divorced* (New York: Simon & Schuster, 1983), in 1982 divorces hit an all-time high of 1.2 million. This was double the number ten years earlier. While the percentage of divorces dropped in both 1984 and 1985, approximately 1 million children a year continue to be added to the ranks of those from broken homes; 12 million American children are now members of single-parent families. Sixty percent of children now being born may expect at one time or another to live in a single-parent family; nine in ten of such families are headed by females. And raising children alone requires an even more intense dedication than sharing the responsibility with another.

One of our respondents said, "As I became a parent, I tended to repeat with my children the patterns which I had experienced, and thus became aware of how they are transmitted from one generation to the next. The messages that parents give their children are enormous and form the groundwork for their roles as adults."

TO HAVE OR HAVE NOT

Whether or not to have children is one of the most important decisions ever made by either parent. At the time the decision is made, usually neither realizes the almost overwhelming commitment of some twenty-plus years that parenting requires. This commitment is in terms of personal time, finances, life-style, living arrangements, and in the overall serenity and direction of one's life. *The decision to have children is one of a small handful of decisions that forever changes our lives.*

As Nycum notes, "A lot of folks seem to have babies the same way others would acquire a puppy or a kitten. Their friends are doing it, it sounds like fun, and there is a great biological push to become a parent."

One woman in our study frankly wrote, "I was driven to have a child because I felt it was my link with immortality." Responded another, "At age thirty-six, I realized the time had really come for me to make a choice on whether or not to have a baby. I realized my childbearing years would soon end. I know my work was rewarding and fulfilling and had made me happy for the past ten years, but frankly, I wasn't sure what a baby would do for me."

Some women have grown up knowing that they wanted children. Such was Collins's experience. "I personally wanted children from as far back as I can remember; however, had I known I was going to be a single parent throughout most of my three sons' childhood, I probably would *not* have had so many children. But once having done so, there is no way I could ever part with any of them or choose among the three! Raising my boys and watching their various stages of growth and the development of their minds and personalities is one of the most rewarding experiences I have. It ties with the joy of seeing my children succeed on their own."

Like Collins, Gilbert had always wanted children: "I have always wanted a child, or children. I think this comes from the desire to experience *all* that life has to offer. I never knew how much I wanted to have a child until I had difficulty becoming pregnant. I realized then I would have sacrificed career success for a child. If I had felt it were possible, I would have liked more than one child. However, for me, the two-career life-style with one child seemed all I could manage."

Nycum states, "I never questioned that I would have children. My parents frequently told me and my sister as we were growing up how much we enriched their lives and often spoke in our presence of their pity for those who never had children. My mother stressed to us how much a part of life childbearing is and how much having a family means in one's later years, to both the parent and the child and to the sense of continuity with one's own ancestors and the whole human race."

Said one respondent, "The woman who strives for excellence in the workplace usually strives for excellence in the home, too. The supermother complex is common among my friends who combine marriage, children, and careers. We make the same demands on ourselves as mothers that we do as professionals."

A banker openly shared her experience, "I loved my husband, and there was no doubt that I wanted to marry and spend the rest of my life with him. . . . I was clear about this. But the most confusing question I had to later face was whether or not to have a child. Then we invited our best man in our wedding to visit for a weekend and he solved it for us (without knowing it). He brought his wife and their two young children. When we saw how whining and demanding his young family was, plus hearing how his wife quit her job because she felt so torn between the child-care issue and feeling overloaded at work all the time, I just *knew* it wasn't for me."

Another shared, "We didn't even discuss having our first child, as we just assumed parenthood came with marriage. But a few years after our baby was born, we spent a lot of time talking about whether or not to have a second one. Finally we decided that what made our careers and the close relation we shared with each other was sharing the responsibilities for just *one* child. This was manageable. Also, we both were concerned with what we would do if it wasn't born normal. Once we went through all our discussion and made the decision not to have another child, we never resented it. For us, having one child has allowed us to feel 'we have it all.' "

Most of our respondents felt that parenting should be entered into with equal commitment on the part of the husband and the wife, with both parents willing to spend whatever time was required. Gilbert says, "My choice to have a child was made easier by the knowledge that the responsibilities truly would be shared between Keith and me. In twelve years as parents, he has never wavered from this commitment. I see many other working mothers brought close to the breaking point by husbands who won't share the duties. It's hard enough to combine parenthood with two careers; if only one person bears all the child-rearing burdens, something has to give—the marriage, the care of the child, the career, or the health of the burdened parent."

One engineer in our study wrote, "I had my children before it was fashionable for men to share in the daily duties of child raising. Thus, the thought never occurred to me to negotiate a 'parent contract' as I would have today."

Still another woman in our study, an entrepreneur, jokingly told us she never felt much of a maternal instinct. "Frankly, I was not fond of children, and as I was growing up, I never babysat or took care of the neighbor's children," she said. She also made the comment that her husband would have liked instant teenage sons to go with him to football games, but it was not worth his effort either to get them to this point. For the first couple of years in their marriage, they put off making the decision. But then they said, "Let's not. For us, it is not going to work." She was recently asked if she ever regretted their decision. Her reply, "I may some day, but I can say that I have not as yet." And she joked, "I put all the money I would have spent on child raising into my wardrobe, and I can honestly say I am the best-dressed woman I know!"

Our survey revealed that 65 percent of our participants have children and 35 percent do not. The following shows how many children these women have:

NUMBER OF CHILDREN	PERCENTAGE OF WOMEN WITH CHILDREN
1	26
2	34
3	18
4	14
5	5
over 6	3

A small percentage of the women—13 percent—indicated that they had stepchildren, but none had more than four, and two was the number most frequently given. When asked if they would have children again, 90 percent in our study replied yes, only 6 percent responded no, and 4 percent stated that they don't know. One commented, "Children take too much time now that I am focusing on my career." Another wrote, "I don't know if I would have children again, but I would definitely get another dog. Dogs are the best help in rough times!"

We then wanted to know, if our respondents had no children of their own, did they plan to? Of the 46 percent who had no children, 24 percent of these said yes, 58 percent said no, and another 18 percent were not sure.

Some commented that they were beyond childbearing age. Several unmarried women said they would like to find a man with children from a previous marriage so they could share the children but not actually take the time to give birth to them.

We followed this question by asking those who had no children (the same 46 percent) if they wished they had. Of these, some 28 percent answered yes, 50 percent replied no, and 22 percent said sometimes.

Our last question along these lines was, would those who had children have preferred a different number? Thirty-three percent said yes, and 67 percent said no. One seemed to sum it up for many by writing, "One child lets me enjoy the joys of motherhood while leaving me free to enter the mainstream earlier, although at times I feel guilty that she has no siblings, which she often says she would like to have. Two would be too complicated for me to handle, and I'm not sure I could cope with any more. Being a mother and having so much responsibility is damn hard work!"

PERSONAL COMMITMENT TO MOTHERHOOD

There is very little evidence that male workers expect to make the same personal commitment to parenthood that female workers do. A study of family/work conflict reported in the *Stanford Law Review* (Vol. 34, No. 6, 1982) points out that most males do not expect to be equal parents, nor are their firms willing to give them the work flexibility needed for equal parenting. Thus, for many the family/work conflict remains primarily a woman's problem.

For women who do not want to take on the problems and responsibilities of parenting, alternatives are available. Foster parenting or supporting the many needy children in various parts of the world are two such alternatives. Another possibility is to assist in the care of children of family or friends. Several women in our study do this and find the contact to be a source of important relationships and pleasure. One woman wrote, "I care for my sister's two young children every other weekend. It is just right for me and I am relieved when Sunday night comes and I can give the children and all the responsibilities they entailed back to their own parents. Yet I eagerly wait for my turn to have them again two weekends later. As well as the children giving me pleasure, my baby-sitting is a welcome gift for my sister, who also works and appreciates time for herself and her husband."

For women who do choose to have children, the playing out of that commitment takes many forms and requires creative handling. In discussing her commitment, one woman wrote: "I traveled a lot and when I was in town, I frequently had to work at home in the evenings. When my daughter was in the fourth grade, she made it very hard for me to work at night due to her demands. So I set up side-by-side card tables in our family room. Then while one of us worked on a research paper on 'linear programming as the tool for cash flow prediction,' the other wrote on 'wild cats and bears in California.' "

Summed up one respondent who is president and CEO of a well-established company, "Motherhood is harder and takes more of a commitment than any job I ever tackled!"

While most women approach motherhood as a joint venture and responsibility between both parents, one factor that ought to be taken into consideration before having a child is the possibility that either parent could become a single parent. As Nycum notes, "Single parenting, like loneliness and poverty, *is* all that it is cracked up to be." She comments on her own experience as a single parent: "There were logistics problems, of course—such as studying for law school finals with a teething child screaming on my shoulder. But I believed that came with the territory. I was not prepared for the negative reactions of outsiders to my child simply because her parents were no longer married. No amount of time or energy I could spend with Sue could compensate. Thank God society's view of the single-parent family has changed!"

As to the single-parent home today, Nycum adds, "The difference in raising a child alone now and when my child, Sue, was growing up is like night and day. Today, single parenting is an accepted part of society. The child and parent each are regarded as normal people who, if anything, are respected for bearing a greater load than the two-parent family. It was not so in the sixties and early seventies when Sue was small, at least not in the professional, upper middle-class neighborhood we lived in. It was tough on Sue, and it was tough on me. We were each outside the norm in the judgment of our peers, and they often treated us as outsiders. Since our situation was my doing, not Sue's, I felt grief that she should suffer from it.

"The experience had two positive effects from my perspective. The first was we spent time together as *people*, not just parent and child. The second was that Sue became a responsible, thoughtful, and contributing member of the family unit. Compared with other children who were 'waited on' by their mothers, Sue is sensitive to others' needs rather than self-centered as many younger people from professional families seem to be. Finally, unlike a number of my nonworking friends, I do not look back in frustration at what might have been had I worked rather than stayed home and been just Mommy all day."

As Collins's experience also verifies, if this unfortunate event should occur and we become single parents, the responsibility for child raising almost doubles when it becomes ours alone. "Being a successful single parent was perhaps the largest commitment of all. I wish I could indicate something more positive about this experience, but the negative aspects seem to outweigh any positive ones. I suppose we were better off than those families with two adults who fought all the time or had other problems, but I certainly regarded with envy the model of a loving two-adult family.

"During my earlier career years, I never met another professional single woman who worked full-time and had the major financial responsibilities for child support. It was rough—there was no doubt about it. I often felt as if I were pioneering many of the rules. And some days, it seemed impossible!

"It was especially hard to be a single mother when the boys were ill. It was gut-wrenching for me to leave them at home, and it seemed that their degree of illness corresponded with my level of job responsibility for that day. And as a mother of three active boys, no one had told me just how much time I would be required to spend sitting in the doctor's reception room, waiting for our name to be called."

A management consultant in our survey wrote, "I married the ideal partner for me as well as the ideal father of my children. Unfortunately, he died, and I was left with four small children. What had all been manageable and carefree before, soon became a nightmare. I would never have had children if I knew I would have to raise them alone. But, alas, we have no control over death."

Time Required

By its very nature, motherhood demands an incredible personal commitment of time. The time involved can be as great as you are willing to allot—there is never enough! Parenting takes a great deal more patience, faith, and hard work than most of us originally expected. Even when children reach the magic age of twenty-one, the job is seldom finished.

What became clear to us as we studied the results of our survey was the extraordinary juggling act that having children creates. Wrote one, "It's a good thing children grow up—by giving up all free time for myself, I was able to successfully combine marriage, the children, and my career. But I don't think I could have done this forever!" Another shared, "All my time was spent on the baby, the job, and keeping my marriage together. Two was OK and manageable, but three pushed me to the edge."

The time involved in raising children is always greater than many women expect. Collins's experience agrees with this assumption: "I was ignorant of how much time it took to raise children. I somehow thought that if I could just get my sons old enough to tie their shoes and begin school that a lot of free time would open up for me. Then I discovered that the older they became, the more time they wanted me to be with them. My personal attendance at their activities—from horse shows to soccer games—became primary in their eyes. Even though I sat in the stands, they *especially* wanted me there when they performed. What worked best was separate time that each could count on."

Gilbert reflects on her time commitment to her daughter: "In the early years of my child's life, almost all of my nonworking time was spent with her. I returned to work within two weeks of my daughter's birth—pure insanity—but I wanted to prove the point that I was committed to my job. Now that she's a teenager, I don't need to spend as much caretaking time. I truly like and admire her and enjoy spending time with her as a friend. I'm somewhat indulgent and want her to be happy."

As all mothers come to realize, there is a distinction between simply "putting in time" with a child and giving quality time. Nycum illustrates this distinction with an unforgettable anecdote: "The time involved is either quantity time or quality time. When my daughter was small, one of our neighbors (in a very close neighborhood) threw herself under a train. She had spent day in and day out with her children and ultimately resented it to the point that there seemed no way out for her except to kill herself.

"Those of us who went to work believed that quality time with children is much more important than elapsed or quantity time, particularly when they were younger and, to some, were less interesting as human beings. Also, quality time was more important later, as they had a need to become people themselves and as we mothers had a need to let go."

Many women with whom we spoke seem to think a lot of time and attention is needed only when the baby is small and cannot care for itself. They fail to take into consideration the time needed years later when the child becomes a teenager and much counsel and guidance is required to see him or her successfully through these critical and formative years. Nor do they realize the extraordinary financial resources needed for a quality college education.

Said one respondent, "There is no doubt it takes a lot of time to take care of children and a home while juggling a job. But my tip is this—I don't think it is cheating to make things easier! It is OK to have help with the housework, help with the yard, and to use the microwave frequently. My advice has always been, 'whatever makes it easier, *do it*.' "

One woman in our survey, a vice-president for a consulting firm in Chicago, wrote, "I hope to sidestep some of the time requirement by searching for a husband with a ready-made family! I don't want to take time from my career to have children myself but would consider it ideal to marry someone with children already, so I could have the pleasure of stepmothering."

Wrote a high-tech executive, "I coped with the time demands by scheduling time each night with my children just like I would schedule appointments at my office. And I learned *not* to let unscheduled people or neighbors who dropped in interfere with this time. I gave one child from 7:00 to 7:30 P.M., and the other from 7:30 to 8:00 P.M. I spent this time in the child's room and did whatever he wanted."

Another said, "My career looks like a broken line. I worked twelve years before my children arrived. The time required to raise my children led to the decision not to work for several years; then I finally started back part-time for several more years. While I have been full-time for the past six years, I have never been able to get back into the excellent career stream with the prospects I had before I left the work force to have my children."

Obviously, raising children has its inevitable demands, and those demands begin with the birth process and preparation for it. Commented an attorney, "Since I was the first female partner in my firm and also the first to have a child, I was very determined to get back to work so as to reinforce my boss's notion I would return. I also felt I needed to show he had made the right decision to promote a woman to partnership. Therefore, I was back at work within a few weeks, which was a very foolish thing to do. I was exhausted for many months and would have recovered much quicker had I stayed home an extra week or two."

An old cliché in business states that no matter how stridently women promise to come back to work after the baby is born, they frequently change their minds once they look at their child. Gilbert says, "I have been occasionally disappointed by young women who have left to have babies but resigned when their maternity leave was up."

Nycum adds, "On the other hand, there are instances where the organization welcomes the woman back but penalizes her for that time off when she is reviewed for her next promotion, even though company policy states she was entitled to that time off."

It will be interesting to see the effect of the 1987 landmark U.S. Supreme Court ruling (*Lilian Garland*) that a state can require an employer to provide job protection for workers temporarily disabled with pregnancy. As Garland said, "Women should not have to choose between being a mother and having a job" (*Time*, January 26, 1987).

However, some women who change their minds about returning to work after having a baby may do so because of their expectations of life with a baby rather than their lack of commitment to the job. Several employees we know have formed parent-support groups in order to help new parents with all of the issues of working and parenting. Also many communities have classes in first-time parenting, and supportive relationships can be forged that help new parents cope with the realities of child rearing.

Responsibilities—And Which to Delegate

The fact that some child-rearing responsibilities *can* be delegated to others helps both parents feel they can successfully combine their home and career. Understanding what can and cannot be delegated might seem obvious, but it has its nuances, as Nycum points out. "Caring cannot be delegated in my opinion. Physical acts can. And knowing the difference between the two and what the distinctions are is all-important. This should be handled on a case-by-case basis and a time-by-time basis. Sometimes when a child is sick, one simply should not get a baby-sitter and leave the child. There are other times when a baby-sitter is the right thing to do for both the mother and child."

Decisions made from a context of caring do much to ensure that children grow up healthy and happy. When parents do select others to meet some of their children's needs, they should closely monitor the area delegated. If this is done, the child will adapt to the authority and concern of several adults.

Gilbert says, "I delegated day-time child care when my child was an infant, and I found a wonderfully warm, loving person to care for her. I think it taught Amanda at a very early age that there are many people who will love and care for us in life, not just our parents."

Nycum also comments, "I never delegated rocking-chair time. Even today, I get teary-eyed recalling my own mother cradling me in her arms in a big rocker when things—physical pain, emotional hurts, or things just too much to cope with—got beyond my powers to handle. The last time she did it I was bigger than she and we nearly broke the rocker, but the TLC was just as strong medicine as ever. While Sue and I haven't 'rocked' for years, we do still hug. There are just some things only Mom can do and of these, TLC is one of the most important.

"What I cheerfully *did* delegate was the part of parenting that is passive—I used carefully chosen sitters for after-bedtime sitting and as qualified chauffeurs after school. As a single parent I 'stretched' for private schooling and ballet lessons as I knew Sue had a highly gifted mind and physical grace. Our intellectual times—not just teaching, but interacting, were mind stretchers for each of us and fun!"

Based on her experience, Collins elaborates on areas that she believes cannot be delegated: "One area is the responsibility for your child's education. I believe you should give your children the finest education you can possibly afford and encourage them to be interested in reading and learning from an early age. I also do not believe you can delegate setting the standards of your home, and you need to set them high.

"Nor do I think you should delegate major responsibility to those children who are older, even though they are the most capable (I sometimes made this mistake). You also cannot delegate the spiritual development of your child. I feel this is clearly the parent's responsibility, and I cannot overemphasize the positive impact of religion in my life.

"I also believe you cannot delegate such things as the teaching of drive and motivation. I tried to teach my boys to 'go for it.' Sometimes the harder part in life is to figure out what you want, and the easier part is to figure out how to get it. But along with a philosophy of 'go for it' needs to be a mechanism for coping with not always achieving the goal, and children need to be given the freedom to 'fall on their face' from time to time.

"Drive and motivation go hand in hand with responsibility, and I have always felt it was a good idea for my boys to work outside the home. I felt this not only promoted a feeling of being able to take care of themselves, but gave them an opportunity to experience the 'real world.' All three, in turn, worked at an ice cream store.

"And all three also had daily morning-paper routes for many years. Each Sunday morning when the papers were giant-size, I would get up and help fold and put on the rubber bands. This was the one morning the papers were too heavy for them to carry on their bikes. Then we would pile in the car—boys, hundreds of papers, the dog, and both cats, who always perched on top of the papers. It was tough on my Saturday night dates, as I always wanted to get in early so I could get out of bed at 5:30 A.M.! This visible act was one way of expressing my commitment to them."

Other women also voiced the importance of taking the responsibility yourself for shaping the attitudes of young people. For many women, the way that they live their lives teaches their children some invaluable lessons. A woman banker wrote, "My work has had a powerful impact on my children's attitudes. My girls feel very different about their futures than do many of their peers. For my daughters, taking care of themselves and being independent persons is a given. They also are very, very aware of the conflicts. My sons have had to share equally in all household work. This has set them apart from *all* of their peers. They are appreciative of what I have accomplished and respect me, but they consider me to be 'different,' and that is not essentially positive."

Another shared, "While I was writing my Ph.D. thesis I did no housework of any sort and very little parenting. All the children were very conscious of the commitment and discipline required on my part, and it was as if they needed to be my 'wives.'"

As a NASA administrator put it, "What is important is that you teach children to cooperate at an early age. And they should have their jobs done before their mother gets home. In other words, the home needs to be handled with the same good management techniques that are used on the job. Teach your children that they are not helping you with *your* job, but that you, on occasion, help them with *theirs*. They should begin by being taught to do those jobs they can perform well, such as picking up their toys, putting their clothes in the hamper, or setting the table."

Another shared, "I soon found what I could *not* delegate was certain times when I should be with my kids. These times included school plays, band concerts, and trips to the doctor. I soon learned to tell my boss that I would not be in during these important times. While the men in my firm didn't do this, I feel if we professional mothers play strictly by the men's rules, we will be the big losers. And these opportunities to share will seldom come again."

Wrote another, "As a mother, you cannot delegate safety. Be sure to go over the safety rules of your home—how to call the police and fire department and what to do in other emergencies."

Nycum says, "I believe there are two things that are most important to being a successful parent, neither of which can be delegated. The first is to keep one's own emotional and physical health strong. As they say on the airplanes, 'put on your own oxygen mask first and then assist your child.' Money and time spent on health and emotional stability are an investment, not an expense. A healthy parent can provide the stability children must have, but an unhealthy parent creates instability and a downward cycle of problems.

"Secondly, I feel one should always be open with the children and share. Overprotection is a drain on the parent and really doesn't fool the children or truly insulate them from the fears and uncertainties that are part of growing up for anyone. Children should be treated as participants, or they can feel like victims."

Nycum recalls a proud moment of delegation. "When Sue was in junior high school, she eschewed a sitter and became a 'latch key kid.' She greeted me one day with the news that she had arrived at the door to find it ajar with marks of forced entry. Sue said she threw her books through the door into the hall and ran to the neighbors' house. The neighbors called the police and together they all entered the house and searched all the possible areas for hidden intruders. She had kept her head and was totally in charge of the event. She refused to call me at work because she was in control. Talk about delegating!"

Gilbert comments, "I delegate very little to my child since I believe school can be as demanding as a career. Amanda likes to cook and does make parts of meals on occasion, but this is not a routine chore. Her sole real responsibility is the care and feeding of her pets: two cats and a hamster.

"Many of my friends feel that children should have more household responsibilities than I give my child. My response is that my sisters and I were raised with few household duties (except the dishes) yet we're all competent homemakers as well as hard-working career women today. Actually, I've never minded housework and I like to cook; I think this is because these duties were not imposed on me in childhood."

Day-Care

For those of us who have children, child care can be a continual thorn in our side, but we must always remember it *is* possible to get good child care. Many of us have been doing it for years.

According to an article in the September 2, 1985, issue of *Newsweek*, corporate child-care centers tripled in the previous three years. The article pointed out, "Gone are the mornings when bread-winning husbands dashed off to work leaving behind bleary-eyed wives, awash in coffee and kids."

From 1970 to 1984, the percentage of working women with children under the age of six rose from 32 to 52 percent. And statistics show that, all things being equal, women with children under six years old make less than other women. As the number of career women with children grows, so does awareness of some of the associated problems. Many child-care programs are on the way, including some by such corporate pacesetters as IBM and AT&T.

Findings from a 1985 survey by Child Care Systems, Inc., a corporate child-care consultant based in Lansdale, Pennsylvania, show that half the 1,243 respondents had to make new child-care arrangements one or more times in a twelve-month period; parents lost an average of eight days a year to child-care problems; and 39 percent actually considered leaving their jobs because of the difficulty in finding good care.

Some companies that offer day-care services have benefited as a result: key employees have opted to turn down a job offered by a competitor at a substantial increase in salary. Said one woman in our study, "I recently declined a new offer due to the fact that the other company did not provide a day-care center." Used to spending some time with her child during most lunch breaks, she commented, "I told the prospective company they couldn't put a price tag on having my child under the same roof with me."

According to an article in *U.S. News & World Report* (November 25, 1985), it is estimated that some 80 percent of women now in the work force are of childbearing age, and 93 percent of them are expected to become pregnant at some point during their careers. With those demographics at work, employers may find child-care benefits hard to resist.

Most people, however, do not have access to corporate child care and must look at other options. Nycum offers her thoughts on day-care: "This is extremely important as one is trusting a lot of one's child to the care of a day person, and this is not just the physical well-being, but general nurturing and how the 'twig is bent.' Sometimes we don't realize this until years later.

"I think the key is to consider the kind of person we select, carefully looking at the age, intellect, and education of that person. He or she has to fit what is best for the child at the time. A nice, dull, motherly soul may be the kind of person who drives a bright and inquisitive child right up the wall; on the other hand, this would be just what the doctor ordered if the child feels insecure for any reason."

Nycum handled her daughter's early day-care by the following manner: "I did not work outside the home until Sue was in first grade, and not until second grade did I work outside the home past her school hours of eight to four. When she was small, I had an after-school teenager for a sitter whenever possible, and during the summers a teenage sitter all day. These young women worked out marvelously because they usually had siblings who came along and provided Sue, an only child, with playmates and a chance to be part of a family group.

"Once we had an au pair from Germany named Gertie. She was a law student and quite intelligent. Sue enjoyed learning about Germans and Germany from Gertie. It wasn't until months after her departure that I found out Sue had also 'learned' from Gertie that the Germans had won the Second World War!

"I used high school sitters—except for out of town trips when mature women came in—I joined baby-sitting pools whenever possible, and I prayed for good health for all concerned. As a single parent, I bought a house in the best school district I could find and worked as hard as I could to afford it. I found that led not only to a good education for Sue but also to congenial playmates and thus less of a burden for me. By forcing myself to work harder to support our choice of neighborhood, I kept looking for better jobs rather than settling with something 'comfortable.' This was a real win, as it turned out, because both my salary and the value of my house escalated and Sue's schooling and friends continued to be interesting for her."

Gilbert believes that excellent day-care can be found if you put some energy into the problem. She says, "I solved it as follows:

Age 0–2, exclusive care of Amanda by a woman in her home who could not have her own child. This was a wonderful situation; she was a warm, loving person.

Age 2–5, full-time nursery school. My daughter still remembers her time there and the other children with pleasure.

Age 6–present, a succession of high school and college girls who pick up Amanda after school, take her home or to activities, and do light housework. This has worked out well. Amanda enjoys their company, and I choose girls who are good role models for her."

Collins found that single working parents have unique needs. She says, "I found it an absolute necessity to have a live-in housekeeper and did so until my youngest son turned sixteen. A large part of my income went to pay their salary, but I felt it was the only way I could manage. Someone needed to be home, as my sons' involvement in sports and other activities meant that each had his own schedule. I paid more than the going wage, but I felt we needed continuity by keeping the same person as long as possible."

The women in our study who have children handle day-care in a variety of ways. Some of the methods that have worked for them are the following: hired baby-sitters; had housekeeper (live-in); used own mother; employed teenagers; alternated with husband; rented room to foreign person in exchange for sitting; pooled resources with neighbors; scheduled work around children's hours.

The largest number had live-in housekeepers. This was followed by baby-sitters. Almost tied with "day-time housekeepers" was the answer "sent children outside the home."

Even with an ideal plan, it is important to make arrangements for handling the inevitable crises that will arise. Collins, who went back to school for her master's degree when her children were small, says, "I will never forget the day when I was scheduled to take my first exams. It was a nightmare. On that morning my oldest son's bus for kindergarten broke down and because of this his class was canceled, and the sitter for the other two boys called in ill. Unfortunately, I did not have a list of supportive neighbors for just such emergencies, but you'd better believe I did from then on!"

When emergencies arise, children, too, need to be prepared to cope. They need to be taught what to do in a real disaster, and police, fire, and other important phone numbers need to be posted in a prominent place. In this way, the working mother will worry less about what could happen while she is not there. It is critical to educate our children to handle accidents in our absence.

Nycum comments on her situation with sitters, "My overall comment is that Murphy's Law applies to child care. If you really need your sleep, the child cries all night. If you really must keep an appointment, the child gets sick and the sitter cancels. The advance planning and flexibility that this instills in one is great business training as well.

"My daughter was born while I was in law school. She seemed to know when an important exam was happening and cut a tooth the night before. The ability to keep alert and keenly focused while exhausted serves me well now in long, protracted negotiations following a 'red eye' flight."

Many women in our survey reported that feelings of guilt for leaving their children are still with them. Shared one mother, "While some of my guilt ended when I could drop my daughter off at her first-grade class instead of the day-care center, I soon realized still other demands were placed on me. Within a short time, she had volunteered me to be there with home-baked cupcakes (chocolate, please) for the Thanksgiving class party, she needed me to take her shopping for a Girl Scout Brownie uniform, and she needed an immediate sheep's costume with floppy ears for the class play."

However, a University of Chicago study by Dr. Lois Hoffman found that children in day-care centers may develop intellectual, verbal, and social skills earlier than those children who remain at home. Dr. Hoffman asserted, "Research done has thus far not demonstrated adverse effects of quality day-care for infants and young children" (The Working Woman Report, New York: Simon & Schuster, 1984).

We are not aware of any study that has shown that children of working mothers do less well in life or are less emotionally secure than children whose mothers do not work. Thus, today with so many mothers working, women should put some of these feelings of guilt over leaving their children to rest once and for all. As one mother ended her questionnaire on children and child care, "I don't 'do guilt' anymore." Amen!

In summary, most American mothers are not home with their children, and most of us worry a great deal about child-care arrangements. In the early years it is especially difficult because we are not able to communicate with the child about how he or she perceives the arrangement. Once a child is able to tell us how he or she feels, we parents relax more and feel more assured that we are not damaging our child.

How Motherhood Affects Your Career

Nycum probably speaks for many women as she considers the impact of children on career: "I have to be candid and say that anything that detracts from the career has to be a deterrent to it. Sometimes supporting a child is the only reason to have a career, so attitudes will vary. I think we have all thought, 'Oh dear, if I just didn't have to leave now and pick up the baby-sitter. If I could just spend another half an hour!' And then there are times when the child is away in school or visiting a friend, and you think, 'Good Lord, if all I had was my career, how empty life would be.' "

As expected, the women in our study indicated that being a mother had a serious effect on their careers. Here are some of the ways that they felt that impact:

- *Could not do all I wanted to.*
- *Not able to be a workaholic.*
- *Negatively — has taken away some of my drive.*
- *Hindered my professional advancement significantly.*
- *Enjoyed both; feel neither suffered.*
- *Would have taken job requiring greater travel.*
- *Having to support two motivated me to attain.*
- *Wonderful counterweight to job pressures.*
- *Put me on different time frame from my male peers.*
- *No free time to relax!*
- *Had to accept less exciting assignments.*
- *Required me to rethink career direction and goals.*
- *Limited dinner meetings and socializing with coworkers.*
- *Helped understand those younger whom I supervise.*

Recent studies have shown that children play a major role in the earning power of women, women's continuity of labor force participation, the kinds of jobs women take, and the amount of effort women are able to bring to their career. Studies also point out that each additional child lowers a women's earnings.

Victor Fuchs, Ph.D., professor of Economics at Stanford University and author of several books in health economics, conducted a study of working women who made over $25,000 in 1983. He found that half of these women had no children and concluded that women who are serious about their careers have hard choices and trade-offs to make. And as the decreasing percentage of families with children shows, not as many women are choosing parenthood as did in the past.

In thinking about how having a child has influenced her work life, Gilbert comments, "I don't have as much time to devote to my career because I take my parental responsibility seriously. However, because my husband truly shares all responsibilities equally, I'm able to travel, attend evening functions, and fulfill my job responsibilities. And I should add, raising a child has not had a negative impact on Keith's career. In general, I wouldn't want to spend any more of my time or life working. In the past I've been too wrapped up in work, but would now rather have a balanced life."

One respondent, a sales representative for a million-dollar company, stated, "Motherhood has impacted my career *very* negatively. It has taken away some of my drive. I cannot spend as much time as I want at the office. This has significantly hindered my professional advancement."

Another said, "It was emotionally tough at the beginning. I had to insist on professional choices which would accommodate the time my children required. These choices were seldom the ones I would have selected had I not had children."

Collins looks back on her role as a single parent and comments, "Due to my seniority at Stanford, I accrued six weeks' vacation each year, and was able to negotiate two additional ones with no pay. So for eight summers, we headed to a camp for boys in the Smokey Mountains where I was director of the Riding Program. And for once, *I* could feel superior to the nonworking mothers who merely drove their boys to camp and left them for the summer. I was *there* to see my children achieve and grow!

"However, taking eight weeks off every summer for eight years was very hard on my career. As contrasted with the males in my organization, I came off not looking as dedicated and serious about my career. I never knew a man who would request that kind of time off. Thus, being a committed single parent was an awesome responsibility."

Says Nycum, "I recall an important and unexpected evening drafting session in our Boston office. My partner, Donna Sherry, took along her nine-week-old daughter, Caitlin, because both daddy and the grandparents were out of town and no sitters were available.

"I participated by conference call and enjoyed the interaction. Since the other participants were fathers, the situation was comfortable. Caitlin behaved like a trooper, only drooling slightly on the shoulder of one of the male partners. Later Donna and I finished up the papers by telephone when the baby was, by then, sound asleep in her own bed.

"Apparently that early experience was a trendsetter. Recently at age three, Caitlin dragged out a suitcase and was busily packing when her mother asked what she was doing. 'Oh, I'm going on a business trip,' was the reply."

WOMEN WHO LEAVE THEIR CHILDREN

As the struggle to combine parenting with career touches an increasing number of women, a once unthinkable situation is beginning to surface: some women are opting not to live with their children on a daily basis. They either willingly give up their custody during a divorce or choose to leave their children with relatives while they pursue their career.

While this is still the exception, of course, it is occurring with greater frequency. Often mothers forfeit custody due to lack of money to support their offspring and keep up the home. This is not the case for senior level women with their high salaries, but several executive women in our study with busy travel schedules gave up custody to be free of home responsibilities and to concentrate on their jobs.

One study respondent who opted not to raise her daughter sent the following summary of a recent study: children of employed mothers do better socially and academically than those of women who stay home. But researchers also found that children of employed mothers *whose parents are still together* do the best of all (from *News-in-Brief*, November 1986).

The well-known child psychologist and educator, Dr. Bruno Bettelheim, spoke at a dinner in Palo Alto sponsored by the Pacific Graduate School of Psychology, in June 1985, regarding the problems of parenting and the modern family. He summed up what is wrong with the middle-class American family in two words: high expectations. Dr. Bettelheim stated, "Entirely unreasonable expectations of children, of marital partners, and of ourselves lead to disappointment. Disappointment is destructive to successful family living. The American middle-class parents expect their children to do better than they have done. When this doesn't appear possible, the child gives up." We have also seen some parents give up, feeling both they and the children would fare better living apart. Some become noncustodial parents with varying degrees of success, frustration, and acceptance.

In noting the anguish of some noncustodial mothers, Patricia Paskowicz, author of *Absentee Mothers* (Oreville, Calif.: Universe Books, 1984), wrote, "Not long ago I went with my husband to a cocktail party, one of many such events I have to attend in relation to his faculty position at a large university.

"It should have been just another innocuous gathering, and it would have been if not for one significant factor: I'm an 'absentee' mother, a woman who gave custody of her three children to their father when he and I divorced. And that fact, I have learned, is like having a stick of dynamite strapped to me in a world full of pyromaniacs, forever fearing that someone will choose to strike a match and light the fuse. Anyone at all can do it at will. This time the destruction came from the department chairman's wife, a person I had not met before."

In describing the reaction of telling the chairman's wife that her children lived with their father in another state, she wrote, "The look of horror which spread across her face seemed like an eclipse of the sun. She stood there for a few seconds, utterly speechless, although her mouth was open in astonishment. A familiar anticipation of approaching danger rushed through me. This woman was reaching for one of those matches, and I had to stand there and allow her to use it. Without another word or gesture, she turned her back on me and walked away. I retreated to the nearest bathroom and cried."

Paskowicz personally conducted research on more than 100 absentee mothers but estimates that more than a million similar mothers exist. She believes most of them face a similar rejection and ostracism, which is seldom experienced by absentee fathers. She found that over 60 percent of absentee mothers experience emotional problems serious enough to require psychiatric help, and that the situation persists after an average of seven years from the time custody is relinquished.

She concluded, "In our society, the absentee mother is seen as having refused to accept her life assignment . . . she is seen as unfeeling, irresponsible, narcissistic, and obscenely ambitious. These feelings are prevalent in spite of the fact that in certain instances not only is it in the mother's best interest, but also in the *children's*."

One accountant in our study said, "I had my child close to twelve years ago. I left my baby with my parents during the week (rural setting), while I worked in a nearby city. It was highly unusual for a woman to leave her baby, and I had to cope with this feeling of guilt; in fact, I worried for several years if I was doing the right thing. This was made even more difficult by the negative criticism which I received from my husband's mother. She constantly told me, 'If you wanted to work instead of stay home and care for Ben, you should not have had him in the first place.' This was especially hard because I did not need to work for financial reasons. While I finally came to grips with the fact that I could *not* convince her that it was OK for her first grandson to be with my parents during the week, it still took an emotional toll on me."

Another said, "I share custody of my children, and what this means is that they live with me six months and with my ex-husband the other six. This is mainly due to my job, which requires me to be in Europe six months each year. While I am a noncustodial mother I find it stressful as I want to give 100 percent to both motherhood and to my career. I miss my children when I travel, and they tell me they miss me also. Not being with them at night to hear about their day really hurts."

Wrote a telephone executive, "After my divorce, my children lived with me for a number of years. I was then offered a one-year fixed promotion to be the division manager in another state. I knew it would be the end of my fast-track career if I turned this down. So my two children moved in with their father and his new wife. After twelve months when we again became a family, they constantly reminded me they had received a great deal more attention from their father than from me."

One respondent wrote, "My children, ages eleven and thirteen, live with their father, and it seems to work best for all concerned. I am gone a lot, and while we had a cleaning woman when the children lived with me, it seems they were continually behind in their homework and into mischief. While I thought the children's father was a lousy husband for *me*, I must admit he is great for *them*."

A university professor in our study said, "The key thing is for a child to have continuing positive contact with the absent parent, whether it is the noncustodial mother or father. This means that fathers who want custody can have it, mothers who want help with parenting can get it, the children can be better off in some important ways, and human frustration can be reduced all around."

For example, we know of two very successful women who chose to let their children live with their husband after their divorce. One woman was head of a start-up company, and the other a successful psychiatrist. Each woman had one son, and both the husband and the child opted to live with each other.

This decision did not interfere with the women's career, nor with their status within the community. While both women lived far away from their children, they saw their children in the summer and during some holidays. As far as we could tell and according to what both women told us, they had a fine relationship with their offspring. But the two women confessed that when their young son came to visit, with all the assorted pets and bubble gum, it threw their work schedule as well as their house into chaos!

We know, too, of an absentee mother who is a successful lawyer. She and the children, all girls, seem to see nothing unusual in their situation.

They spend summers and some holidays together just as many divorced fathers and their children do. The key, then, is to look at each family member as an individual and to make a plan that is best for all.

THE CHILDREN'S VIEW

Only 7 percent of all American households are the "Ozzie and Harriet" type (according to the "Orange County Commission Study on Status of Women," *Liberty Street Chronicle*, July 1985), in which the father works and the mother stays home and takes care of the kids. As more and more women enter the work force, researchers are beginning to study the psychological and social effects this may have on their children. How do children feel about their mothers working and being left during the day? And if the children had their choice, would they elect to have their mother work or not?

One respondent told us, "During the early years of my son's childhood, he compared my going to work with his doing 'homework,' which he did *not* enjoy. He seemed truly amazed when I told him how much I loved my job!"

Since most high achievers in our study expressed high job satisfaction, we learned that it is important to teach our children that we *enjoy* our work.

Pride in Mother's Success

An opportunity to hear a child comment on her working mother was given at a seminar on March 8, 1986, at Stanford University, entitled "A Stanford Focus on Professional Women." Sarah L. Clever, age fifteen, appeared on a panel along with her mother, Linda Hawes Clever, M.D. (clinical professor at the University of California) and her father, James Clever, M.D. (chief of staff at the Pacific Presbyterian Medical Center in San Francisco). According to Sarah, "What makes our family work is that we put each other first. This means sharing household responsibilities; for instance, my father does dishes and the Sunday laundry. We try to eat dinner each night together. This often means waiting until 8:00 P.M. when my father gets home.

"My father drives me to school each day, as my mother leaves by 6:30 A.M. After school, I try to find a variety of things to do before I am driven home. This includes waiting several hours in my mother's office. But at least there I can do my homework. But it seems to me that I do spend a lot of time *waiting*! I wait a lot in order to fit into their schedule.

"My mother's job has been a real plus for me. I get to travel with her sometimes and meet interesting people whom she often brings home with her. I plan to have a career, too. When I was six I was sure I wanted to be a doctor, then I went through several changes, and now I may want to study law."

Nycum says of her daughter, "Now that Sue is grown up, we often discuss how she felt when I worked. When she was younger, every place I worked welcomed Sue as a frequent visitor. She is still remembered at Christmas by former colleagues of ten or more years ago. Sometimes when she was small, I'd get a call at odd hours during the day, 'I want Mommy,' and sometimes when I was at work, I'd call up just to hear her voice.

"Today we have a close relationship, albeit a loose one. Sue is an executive and happily married to a rising young engineer at Bechtel. She and her husband live in Tennessee, but we talk often. We are friends, but neither gives unasked advice unless the situation is critical—for instance, 'Mother, you really should update your after-work wardrobe' or 'Sue, those fingernails are a mile long.' Since we trust the other's judgment and goodwill, we take heed. Because the relationship is easy, formality is unnecessary. I recall a call from college, 'Mom, can we celebrate Mother's Day next week? I've got something else on this Sunday!' My reply was, 'Heavens, yes.' I knew I was loved—everyday."

Nycum says, "We visit weekly by phone and additional times when the spirit moves us. It's more personal than letters and not costly during low-rate hours. We also plan trips here for Sue and Bret so they can keep in close touch with us, Bret's folks, and their friends.

"We have a bedroom all set up with their things. It connects through a bath with another bedroom just right for future grandchildren. We do not expect to entice them into spending time with us but to provide them with a base of operation when they are in northern California."

When we asked our survey participants to give us their children's positive thoughts on how they view their working, one mother replied, "Because our time was scarce, my son voiced that my job seemed to make us closer knit to one another. We regarded each other as friends."

A physician wrote of her children's opinion, "They always felt my work had a very positive influence. I had a better relationship with my children than did their peers with mothers *not* employed. They told me they respected me more."

Commented another, "My children always told me I was a good role model for them. My eldest daughter is in third-year law school, and the others are achieving appropriately. However, I have always expected them not only to succeed, but to excel."

And another perspective from an executive in charge of a worldwide division of her organization: "My children told me that my job, which required constant travel to foreign countries, enriched their lives and broadened their perspective. I always brought home books and handicrafts from the countries

I traveled to and shared this with my children. While they did not enjoy having me gone for weeks at a time, my travel gave us a lot to discuss, and they looked forward to having an update with each of my trips."

In Collins's opinion, "It has been my experience that children seem to view their successful mothers with great pride, much as they do their fathers. This is a trend that will continue as women progress up the professional ladder. My three boys have always been very proud of my career, especially in the last several years when my book was published, I was on TV, and my picture was in newspapers nationwide.

"But because I worked during their early years, I was first viewed as different from the mothers of their friends. This had advantages and disadvantages. I always felt that our time together was real quality time, and after all, this is what all parents strive for. We tried to spend one weekend a month away from home—our favorite places were Asilomar at Pacific Grove or Pajaro Dunes, south of Santa Cruz, California. I was the only mother they knew who arranged monthly outings, probably brought on by the fact that I was gone all day during the week and I wanted to make our weekend time special for them."

One respondent who manages political campaigns wrote of her daughter, "My work and my outspoken stance at the office inspired her to be a leader in the women's movement, and it has caused my son to have great respect for women of achievement."

Said another respondent, "My twin sons express appreciation for the time I gave to them from my busy schedule. While I worked full-time, I encouraged them to develop their own interests and I tried to share these with them. For example, both boys swam competitively, and three days a week we left home at 6:00 A.M. to drive thirty minutes for their swimming lessons. From there, I dropped them at school and continued to my office. Nothing, but nothing, interfered with this schedule! Although I did not pressure them to swim, once committed, I did encourage them to 'stretch.' I expected them to practice outside their lessons, and I always felt because of the driving effort I made, that they tried extra hard."

Other women in our study gave a variety of answers to how their work favorably impacted on their children:

- *Gave incentive to continue their education.*
- *Expected all mothers to work.*
- *Made more self-reliant, independent, and assertive.*
- *Enriched their lives.*
- *Expected me first to be their mother.*

- *Gave us more to talk about.*
- *Taught them to juggle many responsibilities.*
- *Gave them pride in my accomplishments.*
- *Caused them to respect women's capabilities.*
- *Made them feel a part of my success.*
- *Impacted insignificantly, if at all.*

Elaborated one high-technology senior vice-president. "My daughter is very independent and often reminds me of the day she turned twenty-one. I had sent her an air ticket so she could fly home from college, and the two of us could celebrate with a festive birthday dinner. As the dinner hour approached, I was caught in a meeting. First my secretary called to tell her to open the champagne and have a toast to herself, then an hour later, she called back to ask my daughter if she could please begin cooking the surprise dinner herself!"

Gilbert comments on her daughter's perspective: "My daughter is old enough now to understand why I need to work. Whenever I make comments about the possibility of retiring or taking time off, she tells me that this would be a mistake. 'You'd go crazy,' she says. I'm afraid she doesn't have much respect for nonworking mothers, which is not my attitude at all. She surely intends to be a working mother herself. She seems to be proud of what I have achieved in my work. She is also proud of the fact that I'm a good cook and have nice friends. For me, the lesson is: we are not one-dimensional beings, and we have choices. I want to live my life according to what makes sense for me and my family at any point in time. I hope my daughter does the same."

Nycum comments, "I am thrilled that my daughter recommends me to her employers for legal services. That is the ultimate compliment. She is delighted when I receive honors and awards, and I'm told she 'brags like mad' about me to her friends who are law students or young lawyers. I have been interviewed by her friends for school newspapers and asked to speak to groups she belongs to. She also nominated me for Volunteer of the Year of the Palo Alto Junior League."

One legislator in our study told of her experience, "My son complained at an early age because, as a city official, my name was always in the newspaper. The other children at school constantly questioned him about it, and this embarrassed him because he couldn't answer their questions. As he got older and understood what I did and its importance, he took pride in explaining it."

Another respondent wrote, "I worked in industrial sales, and my children were always pleased that my name would be listed in the upper 10 percent of all salespeople. But I felt the key to what made my 'mother-child relationship work' was *love*. In my experience, I strongly believe you cannot over-love! I also feel you can not *over-encourage* a child. This makes the child feel self-confident, which will lead to his or her becoming a productive adult. Of course, a structure or framework is necessary, but within this, love is the key."

It has been our experience that children, for the most part, are not harmed by their mother's working. In fact, as they get older, they are usually impressed with the success and status of their mothers. And for them, her salary often means better clothes, homes, cars, and more exciting vacations. In general, their life-style, while different, can be superior to a family with only one income. And as children enter their teens, they often say they are glad their mothers do not stay home and live their lives through them as do many mothers of their friends.

The Negative Side

There are two sides to how working women's careers affect their children, as there are to every issue. The subject of childhood stability of the offspring of working mothers was studied by Amitai Etzioni in *An Immodest Agenda: Rebuilding America Before the Twenty-first Century* (New York: McGraw-Hill, 1984). Etzioni lamented the fact that droves of women have joined the labor force with little attention to the children left behind at home. He sees the "ego-centered mentality" as the chief villain in America and believes that many Americans are deeply committed to a philosophy of self-fulfillment — a feeling that ego needs, sensation, and excitement take priority over the needs of others, including spouse and children.

Etzioni feels that the first step to combat this is not to accept the idea that skimping on child care is acceptable if the reduced time spent is "quality time." He believes few children are so resilient. He said, "The fragmentary sociological studies on such children suggest that at least for significant numbers of the children considerable and lasting psychic damage is caused."

Etzioni is not the only person who believes that children are under a new threat. A growing level of stress may be attacking the physical and emotional health of children and young persons, according to pediatricians at the Palo Alto Medical Foundation in Palo Alto, who say they see many more stress-related conditions now than in the past.

Dr. Harry E. Hartzell, chairman of the Department of Pediatrics at the Palo Alto Medical Foundation said, "Girls are probably under more stress than they were in previous generations. They want to pursue careers and be competitive in the job market. They also want to be recognized for their intellectual capabilities. On the other hand, they have needs to be loved and to be loving. Sometimes it's very difficult to meet all these expectations."

He further commented, "Children today have expectations which are often difficult to meet. For the first time in this country, children will have to accept the possibility that they may not be able to live or travel as well as their parents did."

Stress levels that children and adolescents feel often are linked closely to how they feel about themselves, or their "self-esteem." A child with a poor self-image will feel higher levels of stress even when facing a modest challenge than someone who feels confident and good about himself.

Child psychiatrist Dr. Bruce Bienenstock, also at the Palo Alto Medical Clinic, voiced his view about how some of today's parents are communicating their expectations to their children. "We seem to be thrusting our children right into our own distress about the meritocracy (achievement-based society) in which we live. We often don't give them a chance just to experience being cared for by parents who can concentrate on what their needs are. Parents seem so terribly preoccupied with their own achievement—and just making it—that many, many of them, as much as they intend or want to be connected to their children, are overwhelmed with trying to survive themselves.

"So what I find," continued Bienenstock, "is that children really feel a sense of abandonment. The children then try to be more like their parents: do better in school; be more successful; be more attractive; be thinner. Children show that kind of distress by depression and a lack of positive self-esteem, because what they are trying to achieve is one of the aims of adulthood, not an aim of childhood."

Nycum knows there is another side with dark moments: "Sue learned early that as a single-parent, working-mother family we could not do or have everything that the two-parent traditional family did and had. That taught Sue the value of scarce resources, including time management. She also learned to be self-sufficient. Today, she is an excellent manager and leader of people. The self-confidence she has from knowing herself and her inner strength is a backbone of her present widely admired poise and presence."

Gilbert, too, comments on the negative: "I am noticing that more and more women feel trapped in the superwoman syndrome. Sometimes they achieve all their career goals, and yet the rewards and the applause don't make up for the sacrifices. My daughter has seen me cope with achieving more than I ever hoped I would and has also seen me go through the process of deciding that there is much more to life than career success and material gains. Having seen both sides of the coin, I believe she'll have the basis for making rational choices in her life."

Collins recalls with amusement asking her sons if they planned to marry a woman like herself. "Heavens, no," came an immediate reply from her middle son. "I want a wife who stays home and cooks brownies!" They joke about this remark even today, but at the time, Collins admits, she was hurt.

From our respondents, we received the following comments about the negative effects of their having careers: "My daughter, age twenty, says she will *not* be a working mother. She is having regular counseling and feels very resentful over my being away so much," and "My son told me the whole time he was growing up he felt I never really put him before my work. He says I seemed to be always thinking about my job and reminds me of the many times I brought my work to the dinner table."

Other women in our study gave the following replies from their children:

- *Sometimes felt took second place to my work.*
- *Missed many warm dinners!*
- *Resented my absence during school functions.*
- *Felt I was too tired to play games as other mothers did.*
- *Yearned for a mother who baked.*
- *Suffered because they did not have a mother who chauffeured!*
- *Was sometimes neglected.*
- *Occasionally felt overlooked and lonely.*
- *Were sent away to boarding school.*

The New York Times Magazine (September 9, 1984) published an article, "The Working Mother as Role Model," by Anita Shreve. In it she shares a humorous comment by a three-year-old girl, whose mother is a businesswoman described by colleagues and friends as so well-organized that she is called a "superwoman." The daughter announces that she wants to be a father when she grows up. "Why?" an adult friend asked. The little girl had no trouble answering, "Because mommies work too hard."

In sharing her insights, Nycum looks at both the positive and negative sides of combining children with careers: "I think it is some of each. I can think back on poignant vignettes where my daughter was growing up, and I know that pride in my success did not compensate for the loneliness or personal needs at times when Mom was just not there. On the other hand, I suppose the same thing might have happened if I had been playing bridge or doing a volunteer job.

"I think it is good for female children that their role model is a person who is her own person, and not a woman who lives entirely through her children. This enables the child to be more independent, more willing to take risks because only her own life is dependent on her, and not her mother, who is living vicariously through her.

"On the whole, I think my daughter is very happy now at what I have done. But I suspect that when she was very little, there might have been a time of fear and uncertainty and concern about where she fit in, and possibly what would happen to her since we were a single-parent/single-child household. But if the proof of the pudding is in the tasting thereof, we have done a very good job of our cooking!"

In summary, we believe that the impact that a mother's career can have on her children should be understood; we also strongly believe that the quality of motherhood need not be impaired when a woman chooses to have both a family and a high level career. Children are bound to say that they spent fewer hours with their mothers but probably will also admit that due to their mother's prestige, high salary, and interesting life-style, they had many advantages that their peers with nonworking mothers did not have. They also comment that even though they spent less time with their mothers it was quality time and they were satisfied.

While some view the change in women's roles as the end of a system that provided a warm and comfortable home life, most women and young girls are pleased that they can express their talents and no longer are dependent on a male head of household to have sole responsibility for earning the family income. And most men and young boys seem delighted with the new opportunities and freedoms that their daughters and sisters are experiencing.

We do not personally think that children of professional women are deprived of a stable, happy, or loving childhood. However, in making the decision to have children, parents need to understand that the commitment to a child *is* enormous, and the child's needs—emotional, physical, and financial—must be considered throughout his or her entire lifetime.

6 Ambitions for the Future

Most women in our study are in the upper echelon of our working society and have experienced a high sense of success in their endeavors. Rather than bask in past and current accomplishments, however, senior level women continue to look forward. "We are different women from the women we were ten years ago. No, not just older. Stronger. Bolder. Surer," said Dame Nita Barrow of Barbados in her opening-day address at the 1985 U.N. Conference on Women.

Not surprisingly, women's ambitions for the future focus on three areas: equal status and salary as men in comparable positions, elimination of prejudice and chauvinism, and more political clout.

EQUAL STATUS AND SALARIES

Many survey respondents commented that there had been times in their careers when they performed equal work as their male counterparts but were not given equal pay, equal status, or equal titles. As one respondent wrote, "We have successfully infiltrated the middle levels, and now the key issue is to have equal room at the top."

Before really appreciating the impact that senior status women as a group have made in the work force today, one must understand both where women have come from and how few have made it to senior status. In 1986 only 1 percent of working women earned over $50,000, compared with 9 percent of men. And not even one in ten women earns over $30,000, compared with one in three men (from *U.S. News & World Report*, December 29, 1986).

While employment has declined in most industrial countries around the world, the United States has created some 20 million jobs in the past ten years. Who is filling these new jobs? Women. They are flooding into the job arena, boosting both economic growth and stability. They are also pushing harder each year for equal pay, and they are making some impressive gains.

In reviewing her career, Collins finds certain periods of discrimination: "When I first graduated from college and worked for a Fortune 500 company in New York City, my salary was equal to the recently graduated men coming into the organization in similar positions. Several years later as a freelance journalist in Europe, I also made an equal salary. However, since then, the salaries of men in similar positions have been somewhat higher than mine, even though I have similar responsibilities. This view is expressed by many women in our study.

"The most flagrant salary violation of equal rights was with my first job after I moved to California. Although my responsibilities and title were exactly the same as those of the man I replaced (I even used the same office, desk, and chair), my salary was lower. However, in the late sixties and early seventies, this was common practice. Many women also echoed that in earlier jobs they were often given equal *work*, but not the equal pay that should have gone with it."

In contrast to most women, Gilbert has been fortunate in the area of compensation: "Because my responsibilities as a financial officer usually included knowledge of payroll, during my executive career I know that I have usually been paid the equivalent of men in my position and on a par with the men in the organizations for which I have worked. There were many times early in my career that the promotions seemed more difficult to obtain, and it took me a little longer to earn the title of vice-president than it did my male peers.

"I recently considered a 25 percent drop in salary in order to join a fledgling health-care company. The job carried with it substantial equity in the company. I looked around enough to feel with certainty that men who take a similar career step earn the same salary."

One respondent wrote of her nonequal status: "I was discriminated against in a most subtle manner. I progressed in an orderly fashion in my organization until I was the only female in a group of five vice-presidents, all reporting equally to the president. My salary was on a par, as were my benefits and responsibilities. What was interesting was my office. I was the only VP *not* to have a corner office (reason: 'there are only four corner offices and they are occupied').

"I was the only VP to have a small desk and a small couch and conference table (reason: 'your office is smaller and it looks better'). I thought if I waited until one of the four either left or retired, I would be the next in line for a corner office. No way did this work. Some junior (male), appointed to VP at the retirement of one of the four, was assigned to the vacant corner office (reason: 'if he doesn't get this office, we may lose him'). I tried all of my logic, and then all of my feminine wiles, but here I am, still in the smaller office."

Another woman in our study stated, "I put some of the blame of women's low salaries on other women. Often women are in a position to influence another woman's earnings. While they should not overly favor the female getting more money than the male for the same work, they should make a concerted effort to see that the earnings are more equal."

Nycum sums up how the future looks: "I certainly think that equal status in salaries for senior level women is a nonnegotiable event for the future. Something must happen—I think it will happen. I think it will for one reason: it is no longer necessary in the information age to have any physical strength in order to be a very successful person. In fact, one can be handicapped in many physical ways and excel in this new 'cerebral' dependent society, where the elite are the brightest and most assertive. Thus, the macho reasons for higher salaries in the 'man's world' will no longer exist."

There are only too many surveys that clearly point out that women in similar positions to men continue to earn significantly less money. One such was made by the Rand Corporation in 1984 and pointed out that, while women are closing the gender gap in the workplace and are expected to experience a dramatic surge in income over the next twenty years, they will still lag far behind their male colleagues. The southern California "think tank" pointed out that women's pay has climbed from 60 percent of men's in 1980 to 64 percent in 1983. And according to James Smith of the Rand Corporation (and author of the *Rand Report* article "Women's Wages and Work in the 20th Century" in October 1984) these figures are much the same today (telephone conversation with Collins on May 20, 1987). If the trend continues, women will earn about 74 percent of men's income by the year 2000.

Despite some hard-won progress toward equality of the sexes, data compiled by the U.S. Department of Labor's Bureau of Labor Statistics show in another study that women's earnings are generally much lower than men's—even in the same occupation. For example, women lawyers earned only 71 percent of the salaries of male lawyers, and women doctors' salaries totaled some 81 percent of the salaries earned by their male colleagues.

While the gap between male and female wages remained essentially unchanged between 1920 and 1980, it has begun to narrow rapidly. Since 1980 the real purchasing power of women workers has increased by 3.3 percent while that of male workers has dropped by almost as much. At the same time, the wages of women ages twenty to twenty-four have closed to within 14 percent of the wages of men in that group. Because of the closing experience gap, women's pay will increase an average of 15 percent faster than men's between now and the year 2000.

And in another survey, in 1983, by Korn/Ferry, 300 of the highest-level executive women were studied in posts ranging from vice-presidents to presidents of some of the nation's largest corporations. Richard Ferry, president, said the firm decided to conduct the study after it found clients increasingly seeking women for key executive positions. Two-thirds of the executives surveyed earned between $50,000 and $125,000, and 2.7 percent earned more than $200,000.

The study shattered the stereotype that women are unwilling to sacrifice for their careers. It shows women are willing to work long hours, accept risky assignments, and travel and relocate as necessary. Spokesperson Lucy Adams of Korn/Ferry confirmed these findings are the same in 1987 (telephone interview with Collins on May 20, 1987).

The average woman surveyed in the Korn/Ferry study was forty-six years old and earned $92,159 annually. By comparison, the firm found in a similar study several years earlier that the average pay for men in such jobs was $116,000, a "disparity" that becomes greater with inflation.

They also discovered that the typical female top executive had been with her current employer for thirteen years, after having worked for two other firms. Ferry reported that these women "paid a price" for their impressive titles. The typical respondent works an average of fifty-three hours a week, spends thirty-three days a year out of town on business, and believes her social life suffers as a result. A minority of women, 30 percent, said they worked more than fifty-five hours a week.

Almost 40 percent of these successful women said that the greatest obstacle they had faced at work was being a woman. And 70 percent believed men in comparable jobs receive higher pay.

OVERCOMING PREJUDICE AND CHAUVINISM

A second major goal for women is to eliminate prejudice and chauvinism in the workplace. While federal and state laws forbid discrimination, subtle forms of sexism often prevail. Although such prejudice is expressed in unequal salaries and status, that is only one manifestation of it. Other pervasive attitudes affect a woman's ability to function effectively.

Gilbert, who has fortunately not suffered salary discrimination, discusses those other, destructive attitudes: "In areas apart from compensation, the discrimination that I felt has been real, but subtle. Behavior on my part as well as that of other female executives with whom I have worked is frequently interpreted differently from that of our male colleagues. I have been described as manipulative by one superior while at the same time being told I had the highest integrity; when I asked him to explain examples of what he meant, he could not.

"A female executive in the same company was called 'bossy' by her superior. When was the last time any of us heard a man described as being 'bossy'? Assertive and forceful, yes, but bossy, no! I know I have been more controversial and more closely watched than my male colleagues—a price of being one of the only women at my level."

Simple awareness of this problem does not erase it, and Nycum still remembers an example she experienced early in her career. She says, "After graduating from Ohio Wesleyan University, I found that my B.A. Degree, Phi Beta key, and 10 cents could buy me a cup of coffee, and so I went to secretarial school in order to get any kind of a job. After a while I decided to enroll in law school, an idea planted by my former husband. Although my employer knew of it and applauded the activity, he continued to assign projects that interfered with my attending a particular class. Nevertheless, upon my graduation from law school (and while in the meantime retired temporarily to give birth to my daughter), he offered my old job back and stated that he had never had a secretary who was as good. He wanted me to know that having taken time out for law school and having a baby in no sense lowered my value to him."

In noting the problem still exists today, Nycum points out: "I wish I could think that it is just a matter of having all the fifty year olds who went to boys' schools and never learned how to treat women as *people* retire. I'm afraid that is not the case. My working daughter tells me that young men in their twenties are still being chauvinist. I certainly see it in men in their early forties. I don't know on whom to place the burden for this. I'm not sure that it was totally the responsibility of the fathers of these younger people. I have a suspicion that there are still some mothers who are training their little boys to think of women as other than equals.

"I would like to see a lot of energy spent in the classrooms of the early grades on wiping out the bad habits that are apparently still being fostered at home. We need textbooks that are nonsexist, work assignments and team play that are nonsexist, and all the rest that helps get rid of the notion that there's any reason under the sun why a person should be a male chauvinist—and worse yet, brag about it."

Collins reinforces how widespread chauvinistic attitudes are: "I still hear some men I work with continue to call women 'girls.' I find this undermines any power or feeling of equality for women. Unfortunately, this is a natural attitude for many men in their sixties, who are true gentlemen and who wouldn't purposely hurt women's feelings.

"It has also been my experience that many celebration lunches are held at private clubs that do not admit women. Granted, these places are prestigious as well as elegant. However, when such places are selected, the men shift the 'blame' to the *establishment* that makes the rules and not to their choice of selection. And, thus, many victories are celebrated only by men at these locations when, in fact, women had a significant role in making the success happen."

Collins adds further insight into the female struggle with prejudice: "I find there is an interesting phenomenon regarding prejudice—and that is *how* power is perceived. Some women tell me that as a woman, it is hard to *get* power from most men, especially those older."

Nycum perceives, "I can't imagine any woman over forty who hasn't seen prejudice in her working relationships. I recall Mary Templeton's comment about walking into a meeting where she was initially regarded as a 'piece of fluff.' Mary worked through that perception as quickly as possible, in her case, to take control of the meeting. I think everyone has faced that.

"One time I was in a group of managers, and the boss said, 'Why don't we take a break now, and let's all go to the john and talk this over.' I asked if everyone would be comfortable if I was there, or whether this was just his idea that we should all go to the bathroom together. They all laughed, and he blushed deeply. It was quite clear that he meant that 'all of us men' would go, he had not thought of me as a woman at all."

Commented a retail executive in our survey, "I recall a meeting several years ago in which I was told by a visiting executive who was not used to working with women, 'If you have other things to do, don't feel you need to attend.' I attended anyway (and was the only woman), and it was one of those meetings that couldn't have gone more perfectly from my point of view. It got bogged down several times, and I just happened to come up with acceptable solutions. I recommended a plan of action and helped decide how to implement it. When the meeting was over my boss came up and said, 'Had you not been there, we would not have gotten half as much done.' I knew the man who was unclear about my attendance was also impressed."

Nycum says, "I have found that when faced with prejudice, the best thing to do is not to acknowledge but to ignore it." And Collins adds, "I think many women have gone to a meeting when someone there senior to us has seemed a little surprised we were there. My advice is to get tough mentally and prove that we belong. So, sometimes prejudice, if we are prepared, can work in our favor and bring out the best in us."

But, notes Nycum, "On occasion, junior level people don't understand when it is really inappropriate for them to attend a meeting. As a boss, there are times when I have to indicate to a junior level person that he or she may be excused because he or she doesn't have the judgment to realize that sometimes the very senior level people want to discuss something that isn't appropriate, not because of gender but because of level. This isn't gender prejudice, but simply a situation that isn't appropriate for their level of participation."

One woman who has certainly earned the laurels and power within her field is Mary E. Lanigar, an expert in the tax field, who was the first woman to make partner at Arthur Young. In an interview on November 11, 1985, with Collins, she looked at her career and commented on overcoming chauvinism: "During the war, there were a lot of women entering all the public accounting firms. The majority of them were basically bookkeepers rather than people with professional training. Right after the war, everything changed. Many of these women got their husbands back who had been overseas, or they married someone who was returning. And as was typical of that generation, most of them immediately stopped working and started a family. So that by the fifties, there were almost no women left in public accounting. You could almost count them on your hand!"

When asked if she would have been made a partner earlier if she had been a man, Lanigar responded: "I think probably not, although there was considerable resentment among some of the men because I made partner. So I don't think there was any discrimination. I do think, however, that one of the reasons I probably made partner was that I had started to go to law school, and it was obvious that if I wasn't made a partner I might have other alternatives; so this had some effect."

In looking at accounting as an attractive field for younger women, Lanigar commented: "The number of women going into accounting today is absolutely amazing. Almost 50 percent of the new 'hires' are women. Although there are not that many women in partner positions, they are not that rare anymore. But in the grades below, which are management positions, they are making good strides.

"One thing to remember is that accounting firms do a lot of transferring of their personnel, and women frequently have restraints on their moving because of their husbands' positions. Frequently today you have to take into account the two-career situation. If the husband has a position he wants to hang on to, my guess is that 75 percent of the time it is the wife who must decline the transfer. It is more unusual for the husband to say, 'You take that wonderful opportunity, and I will find something else.' And this can't help but hurt the woman's career and chances for her promotion."

Discrimination is such a universal problem that the Ford Foundation authorized a major study in 1980 aimed at advancing women's roles and opportunities around the world. In a paper entitled "Women in the World," it states, "Sex discrimination is a universal problem. It exists in varying forms and degrees, but everywhere girls' and women's basic rights, opportunities, and development are circumscribed, and societies are deprived of their skills. Sex discrimination is a costly constraint on productivity. It pervades all institutions with strong reinforcement from culture and custom. Whenever and however it exists, it is unjust. Women's significance as workers and producers has been consistently denied and obscured."

Attempting to overcome prejudice and chauvinism is a problem that senior women often face. Even Jeane Kirkpatrick, the former U.S. ambassador to the United Nations, says that she has faced discrimination. In an interview published in Newsweek (January 14, 1985), she said, "Any time a woman is involved in nontraditional roles, she is likely to encounter certain kinds of discrimination. And one also develops an ability to bear it in certain perspective. I go and read a good book, listen to some Bach, absorb myself in music.

"Most of my outrageous experiences have come with the media," she commented. "One was the report that I left a National Security Council meeting and stalked across the Rose Garden. This was so funny because it happened to have been a glorious sunny day and I had 10 minutes free time. The roses were in bloom, and I was strolling in the Rose Garden smelling the roses, absolutely engaged in a real sensual delight. And it came out in the news media, 'enraged, she stalked out.' "

Gilbert notes, "During a job search a few years ago, I targeted the role of chief operating officer as one for which I believed I was ready. Many of my former male peers told me my references as a general manager are excellent. I was told very candidly and straight forwardly by several venture capitalists that 'women aren't COOs yet.' I did, however, achieve my goal despite the apparent discrimination."

Lawrence D. Schwimmer, head of the Chicago-based Schwimmer & Associates and author of How to Ask for a Raise Without Getting Fired (New

York: Harper & Row, 1980), discovered that prejudice and chauvinism still prevent many women from advancing faster up the corporate ladder, but females also can hurt their own chances for success. Schwimmer wrote, "The chauvinistic attitudes of traditional executives—90 percent of whom are men—are a major obstacle, although chauvinism has become more subtle. Sex bias shows up very clearly, though, in the double standard often applied to men versus women. Men are given opportunities not offered women, and women are hurt by stereotypes.

"There are a lot of old biases about what women can and can't do. A woman is going to be scrutinized far more closely than a male. And women are less skilled at playing the corporate game. The societal conditioning has not given them the same advantages that men have had. One of the classic examples, of course, is sports, where young boys begin to learn very early the importance of competing as a team.

"Women have been socialized to be very honest and forthright, and there-fore bring a certain naivete to the world of business. They tend to fall victim to certain myths, one of which is the idea that the business world will be fair."

In commenting about office politics, Schwimmer stated, "Women are less inclined to believe work is, in fact, a game with rules and customs that have been fashioned by men, who have controlled business for centuries. There are some classic ways that a woman's power is undermined, and one is by interruptions. Men seem to freely interrupt women and women seem to tolerate it."

Mary Cunningham, former vice-president for strategic planning of Joseph E. Seagram & Sons, Inc. but better known for her previous position as vice-president of Bendix, resigned her position several years ago. She blamed it on persistent sexual harassment, another classic way to undermine women.

The Cunningham saga is one of the better-known examples of how a perceived sexual relationship is harmful on the job. Whether or not she in fact had an affair with her boss, William Agee, then president of Bendix, became secondary; what was crucial was that the employees perceived their relationship that way to the point that she lost her effectiveness to operate.

Cunningham, giving her side in an interview with *U.S. News & World Report* (published on November 29, 1982), said, "Women who want to succeed in business still face far-reaching discrimination." When asked what her experi-ence at Bendix taught her, she replied, "It taught me there is a form of sexual harassment far more subtle than the kind people frequently talk about.

"The harassment most often cited is the passing comment in the hall, the physical attempt to abuse a woman in the workplace. Sexual harassment of the form I experienced is more far-reaching more frequent and much more powerful in its impact. . . . I'm talking about the attempts to undermine a woman's credibility—to take away from her accomplishments through rumor or innuendo by assuming that the only way a woman could accomplish something significant is to have a sexual affair with her boss. It's a gradual erosion of a woman's credibility and sense of self-respect, with the goal of destroying her effectiveness."

Many respondents in our survey had stories of personal harassment and blatant chauvinism. One respondent, an aerospace executive, dealt with this in a most unique way: "I was on the golf team at Florida State all through college. Then I went to work for a large company and was soon transferred to southern California. I found myself working with a group of executives (all men) who did not know my background. I also discovered they were big golfers and made a point of taking major clients to the club every Wednesday afternoon. I laid my strategy carefully and maneuvered to host a man who I knew was not only a hot prospect for a major contract, but was an excellent golfer.

"I subtly dropped my news in the staff meeting that I had made reservations at the club for the following week and needed two more for the foursome. Pandemonium reigned. They couldn't have been more shocked if I had told them our client had gotten me pregnant with sextuplets.

"The actual golf day was one of the more unforgettable in my life. Two of the most senior level men in our division (as well as two of the firm's best golfers) joined us. I played my usual brilliant game, clucked in sympathy when their balls went in sand traps or hit trees, and in my unobtrusive manner, *beat the hell out of them*."

In one of a series of articles on executive women published in the *Wall Street Journal* on October 29, 1984, author Helen Rogan wrote of what she considers the senior level woman's most serious obstacle—her sex. She wrote, "The 'pioneers'—the women who were the first to reach management level in their company—were asked what they considered the most serious obstacle in their business careers. Only 3 percent cite family responsibilities, and only 12 percent blame the lack of a formal education. But a good half of the women name reasons related to their sex—including male chauvinism, attitudes toward a female boss, slow advancement for women and the simple fact of being female."

Rogan's poll found, "Men are prejudiced." Others summed up their feelings by saying, "We are not considered seriously. We're a social issue, not a business issue. This is a subtle but far-reaching discrimination."

Equity in Board Positions

In comparison to men, few women sit on boards. Because many organizations are managed and run by boards, it is important for women to be a part of those groups that are wielding power and making decisions. Nycum cites the need for qualified women and the difficulty in finding them. "Unfortunately in so many, many cases, the problem is not do companies want to have women on boards, but can they find a competent, qualified one to serve?"

Even when offered a board position, women should not accept simply because of the status equated with such an appointment. Nycum states, "I have begun to be very selective in accepting board positions and I serve only when the board is active and not a rubber stamp for management. I also serve only when I can make a contribution to the organization and when I fully understand the operations of the company so I can make informed decisions."

Collins finds satisfaction in serving on boards and currently serves on several. She also works with boards and comments, "Getting excellent board members is darn hard work. And when you do, they need to be thanked and recognized in a way that is really satisfying for them. Few organizations could afford to pay a trustee what he or she is *really* worth."

Rita Ricardo-Campbell, Ph.D., senior fellow at the Hoover Institution at Stanford University, sits on several boards; she states, "There are three reasons that women are not currently serving as outside directors on more boards. First, not many women are CEOs—thus the female pool for directors is small. Second, the women who have made it do not have high visibility and are not well known. And the third is a lack of enlightened board chairmen and by this I mean those who are convinced that women are intellectually equal to men and who will push for women as board members."

Mary Lanigar, a retired partner at Arthur Young (and the first woman to make partner), has become somewhat of a professional board sitter and finds it a great second career. She is dedicated to the boards on which she serves and believes it to be a commendable way to contribute to the community. She encourages senior level women to accept board invitations.

Lanigar says, "I learn a lot from being on boards, and I hope that I also contribute something. There is a degree of prestige in being associated with well-known and well-managed companies, and it is interesting to get to meet other directors and to get to know and work with them."

At the same time, Lanigar cautions against blindly accepting any board invitation that comes along. "If the company has a doubtful reputation or has some obvious problems, then I think one takes a great risk by going on that board. Some advice I always give is to learn all you can about the CEO and his personal style of management. Make sure he is someone you want to work with."

Thus, while senior status women should certainly aspire to board positions, we need also to be aware of the hard work and commitment involved, as well as the possible pitfalls.

MORE POLITICAL CLOUT

Many women in our study stated that they believed only through entry into the political arena could women achieve true equality. Wrote one respondent, "Women's growing political power is slow to be felt. We have the first female astronaut and Supreme Court justice, but still male attitudes have not changed that greatly."

One woman who was recently elected to her state senate commented, "Politics is certainly a passage to power. Many women are not aware of their own personal stakes in the affairs of government. Few women seem willing to run for public office and to assume that responsibility. While the number of women elected to public office in the last decade has quadrupled, they still hold only about 12 percent of the key positions in the United States.

"I am not convinced that more women will run in the future; it seems that younger women today are looking for money, and they will not find it in politics. However, they will find power," she said.

Gilbert comments, "It seems to me that women are being elected with increasing frequency to local, state, and national office. As more women aim for these offices, I believe our numbers will increase. I am not sure that the average citizen perceives any office other than the presidency of the United States as truly powerful, so it does not surprise me that we can make inroads to lesser offices. I would personally be surprised to see a woman elected to the presidency in my lifetime."

Collins is strong in her support of women in politics: "When an exceptionally qualified woman runs for political office, I go out of my way to support her. I went door-to-door in our neighborhood for a woman running for the local school board, and I assisted Dianne Feinstein in her successful campaign for the mayor of San Francisco. I also supported Becky Morgan in her close race for the California State Senate. I help both with my time and my pocketbook.

"I believe women must work together if we wish to achieve more political recognition. So few significant positions in government are held by women, and more will not be achieved if we do not make a united effort to get more qualified women elected. So often women have a hard time winning their first campaign, yet many make very successful politicians, winning the confidence of men and women equally for their second race."

State Senator Morgan might well serve as a role model for other women entering politics. She got her start in politics in 1973 as a member of the Palo Alto School Board and went on to become a Santa Clara County supervisor in 1980.

Morgan's rapid climb up the political ladder continued in 1984 when she became the first woman senator from northern California. Her race for the Eleventh Senate District seat (San Mateo to San Jose) had been her toughest. Only two women ever had been elected to the state senate before her.

Morgan won her race by a 15,000-vote margin of victory over her opponent Arlen Gregorio. Their combined expenses, reported at $1.4 million, made it the most expensive state senate campaign ever waged.

In a November 1985 interview with Gilbert, Senator Morgan revealed her commitment to her work. "Being a senator has been a goal since I was a teenager. It provides the opportunity to serve the public, to pull together ideas and to provide the leadership to translate them into action, and to attain recognition. I do not have aspirations beyond being state senator at present. I've met my goal—anything else is frosting."

In choosing a career in public service, Senator Morgan has obviously made sacrifices. "I have sacrificed confidential friendships and relaxed socializing. Were it not for a successful and sharing husband, I would also be giving up material comforts and luxuries such as travel. Some $35,000 in salary and $15,000 in per diem must support a residence in my district and a Sacramento living space as well as all other expenses for a single-wage earner . . . not close to the six-digit figures being earned by my Stanford MBA classmates. The number of friendships outside the office are limited but are maintained through dinner out, tennis, and skiing."

In Morgan's estimation, however, the benefits far outweigh the sacrifices. "It is worth it. It's a chance to guide change, and to bring a businessperson's perspective to government tempered by concerns for our environments—personal, corporate, and global. It's worth it so far. It's exciting and fascinating."

Unfortunately, Senator Morgan is in the minority: the percentage of women at all levels of govenment is woefully small. In an age where equality between the sexes has received much national attention, the participation of women in politics is shockingly inadequate. Although women today are seeking elective office in record numbers, their climb is a slow struggle against society's deep biases and stereotypes. According to the National Women's

Political Caucus, in 1987 there were only 24 women out of 535 members of congress. In the state legislatures, although the number of women serving has tripled since 1969, they hold only 1,157 seats out of 7,461; only 92 women are mayors out of 832; and in the largest cities, only 3 women are governors out of 50.

As Nancy Hoch, unsuccessful Nebraska GOP candidate for the U.S. Senate said, "We are 52 percent of the voting-age population and ought to have women in top positions" (*U.S. News & World Report*, October 8, 1984).

Women still seem to attract unusual interest in nonrelevant issues when they run for office. This was illustrated when Geraldine Ferraro ran as the Democratic candidate for vice-president in 1984. Much of the news media on her campaign centered around not just her qualifications but also on her size-6 dresses, her relationship with her businessman husband, and whether a female vice-presidential candidate should be kissed in public.

As Maureen Dowd reported in the *New York Times Magazine* of December 30, 1984, "No one knew what Geraldine Ferraro was supposed to be. She did not remind you of anyone who had aspired to the inner sanctum. So every time she spoke, you had to make up your mind all over again whether she was good enough, tough enough, smart enough, honest enough to be the archetype. There was no navy blue suit so redolent of power it seemed invisible. There were instead, skirts flying in the wind, pocketbooks clutched at news conference. And you caught yourself thinking incongruously: A Vice President with a purse? A Vice President whose favorite expression is 'Gimme a break!'?"

And according to Dowd, "Many observers predict that the growth of female political power, combined with the pioneering candidacies of Ferraro and others, will crowd out the remaining biases that have kept elections a man's world. Women already are dreaming of their own presidential candidate in the near future."

At the 1987 Eleanor Roosevelt International Caucus of Women Political Leaders held in San Francisco, women gathered from around the world to discuss ways in which more women can gain office. Kathleen Staudt, a political science professor from the University of Texas, urged women to work with other women and form networks, emulating the ways men have traditionally organized political groups. "Women get political power by working with other women," she said. "Political parties are one way, too, but history has shown that women have been used by parties."

Barbara Mikulski, U.S. senator from Maryland, told the conference, "I got elected because I spent fifteen years pounding the streets. Don't hang out with the think-tank crowd to figure out what's bothering people. Focus on the grass roots, on the day-to-day local issues. That's the incubator for the women's movement."

WHERE DO WE GO FROM HERE?

In discussing where women go from here, our sample has diverse opinions, yet most agree they still have some unfulfilled ambitions. While many were at the place in their career where they could take it easy and rest on their accomplishments, still, they had ambitious plans for the future. Said one, "I certainly don't plan to slow down. I have always been the kind of person who is 'one step ahead' of the task I am finishing so that I can mentally shift in high gear to the next as soon as I complete the one I am on."

When asked about personal work-related ambitions for the future and where she would like to go from here, Nycum replies, "I hope to continue my active career forever. Retirement is not necessary in my field, and I eschew it. I wish to continue to help shape the course of high-technology law as it develops and to advise clients throughout the world doing business in the everchanging legal climate.

"I enjoy rendering project specific advice on particular transactions or resolution of particular disputes. I like to provide strategic advice for structuring new products and services, guiding entry into new markets and responses to new legal challenges. I have been performing these services for clients who range from the boards of multinational corporations to the officers of start-up companies, and I wish to continue such active 'lawyering' throughout my career."

She continues, "In the past several years I have also been counsel to national governments and supranational organizations such as the United Nations and OECD on technology law, and I hope to continue these activities. I have always been accessible to law schools and other university departments and plan to continue to be. I want to continue to practice, write, and lecture in my field and by so doing to keep learning and growing professionally. The most fun of all is that I plan to work with younger lawyers and business people coming along in their careers. In a professional sense, that is the best form of immortality."

Collins says of her goals, "I sometimes ask myself where I want to be in five and ten years. In the next five, I anticipate continuing my full-time-plus active career, and I plan to stay in the development area of promoting health care. I like to see dreams and plans that are good for mankind become a reality. It is very satisfying to see a concept evolve and unfold and then become operational.

"In ten to fifteen years, I will be close to retiring from a full-time job. But one never really 'retires' from the world. While trite but true, I embrace the cliché of wanting to leave the world a better place than I found it. And I believe I can do this by continuing to serve on my current boards and having an impact in the policy-making and guidance of these organizations.

"I also want to continue writing, as I am a journalist at heart. I am currently writing my third book, *Mentoring: Its Role in Career Development*, which I am coauthoring with my husband. Then I hope to write a romantic novel with historical importance tracing my own family back thirteen generations to the *Mayflower*.

"I am satisfied with where I am today and feel I have accomplished more than I imagined I would when I finished college. In the next decade, when my career ends, I hope to continue putting energy into my family and hopefully into my future grandchildren. I want to hand down to them the importance of good health: this includes the proper diet, exercise, and moderate living. Because, without this, it is hard to put the drive into and reap the enjoyment of a successful career. When it is all over, how would I like to be remembered? For my courage, expertise, loyalty, and generosity."

When asked about their ambitions for the future and where they wanted to go from here, most of our sample answered in terms of their career. One response reflected many: "Women should work together as a collective group. We should support each other in our campaign for women's rights. Only lately have we made extraordinary gains in the job market, and with such a vast store of work experience, we must continue our quest for the top jobs which still elude so many of us."

One corporate executive commented that she wanted to train talented younger women below her in obtaining the skills needed for the highest level jobs and to keep them from not "hitting the glass ceiling" as she had. She said, "I would like to make it easier for them to get through the system's invisible barriers. In comparison to my male peers, I had to accept several parallel positions before I was finally permitted into the inner sanctum."

However, a certain number of respondents had big noncareer plans in totally unrelated fields. Said one, "I hope to get my pilot's license"; said another, "I have signed up for a trek to Nepal." A third wrote of going on a safari, and a fourth mentioned enrolling for a Ph.D. in counseling. A fifth told us she wanted to head up a philanthropic board and *give* money away to those less fortunate.

An executive recruiter who owns her own company said humorously, "Where do I want to go? I want to go to *lunch*! I haven't taken a social lunch in probably five years—they are either business meals or I grab a sandwich and eat at my desk. I have just decided to 'give myself permission' to have at least one 'fun' lunch a week from now on. I have always set my personal standards higher than those of others around me, certainly higher than is demanded of me, but I have always been this way."

Gilbert comments on her work-related ambitions, "My future career desires are several. Having helped start a new company, I want to see it grow and flourish. Beyond the current challenge, I hope, will be many more—at least for the next twenty years.

"It would be fair to characterize me as 'driven' in the past. I followed the path on which I was put somewhat blindly but always with great energy and drive. I worked hard and was rewarded with promotions, greater responsibility, and financial security. I gave little thought to my values and whether or not I truly enjoyed what I was doing.

"Twice within the past year I have chosen to make a change. The first time I left a company where I had been employed for thirteen years and had been richly rewarded with position, status, and salary. However, after reaching the status of vice-president of corporate development, I felt I had few challenging options left to me, and I feared I was stagnating.

"I then chose a small start-up company, also in the field of health care, where I felt I could make major contributions. I very quickly realized that I had made a mistake: I was working well below my capabilities and for someone who did not delegate and was less experienced than I. The description of the job I thought I was taking bore little resemblance to reality.

"So, for the first time in my life, I took a breather. Having worked nonstop since age fourteen, I felt it was a good time to rest and get caught up with who I am and what I wanted. My sabbatical lasted less than three months, but it reaffirmed, for me, that I'm on the right path.

"I believe the best is yet to come. The challenge of building a business is one I welcomed since it will stretch me to learn new skills. I am fortunate to have a good team, and this reinforces my belief that we can continue to learn as we progress through our careers."

Women's recent gains have left their mark on all levels of social, economic, and political activity, thus reshaping society's attitudes about the worth of women in the labor force. Encouraging the next generation of women, stabilizing organizations, and maintaining a clear focus on women's advancement will be essential to women as they continue to make their vision of top positions a reality.

Where do we go from here? As a biologist summed up, "We [women] *will* get there, but we'll go a lot faster and further if we join and go *together*."

In conclusion, high-achieving women today have ambitions similar to their male peers, both short and long term. They have committed themselves to careers of hard work and long hours. Women's growth in top-level jobs will most likely expand until it equals men's. Their emergence has made a difference in the entire work force, and with so many choices, more options will open up for both sexes. This should result in a stronger economy, utilizing the expertise of both sexes, which will be essential to meet the business challenges in years to come. In proving themselves victors over their peers, women are demanding the spoils they deserve but have not always received—equal status and salaries and more political clout.

7 Is It Worth It?

Never measure the height of a mountain,
Until you have reached the top.
Then you will see how low it was.
    —DAG HAMMARSKJOLD (MARKINGS)—

Few women of senior status who have tasted freedom, known job satisfaction and recognition at the highest levels, and experienced the affluence that comes from a sizable paycheck would return to being content with less challenging career positions.

As discussed in earlier chapters, reaching senior status for some women has involved many sacrifices—marriage, good relationships, children, friendships, and leisure time. Although most women are able to identify a price for their success, others say, "*Nothing* is a price anymore."

In assessing where they are now and in looking at where they have been, we discovered that senior level women would, in general, follow the same upward career paths over again.

WHAT PRICE SUCCESS?

For Collins, "There is a huge price to pay for success. Any woman who tells you that she can hold down a high level professional position (not a job but a career), raise children, be a good wife with a home and social life, and not suffer for it is not telling the truth. It just isn't possible!"

In examining what she personally paid for success, Gilbert candidly looks at the failure of her first marriage. Her story is representative of several women in our study, who chose between a career and a failing marriage. "I married at twenty-one without thinking through the consequences of an early marriage or my choice of a husband. It is only now, many years after my divorce and subsequent successful remarriage, that I fully understand what caused the failure of my first marriage."

For Nycum, one price paid for success is use of energy. She adds, "But since I have an enormous amount of it, it hasn't been an unreasonable price to pay. Emotional relationships have also suffered when I have made inappropriate choices of mates and tried to make a silk purse out of a sow's ear. I have learned that it just can't be done. It's much better to find a mate who is a silk purse to start with, and once that happens, life can be absolutely marvelous."

In addition to the more obvious personal sacrifices, many women in our study stated that they paid a price in facing discrimination every day. The discrimination that many face is draining of time and energy and is sometimes so subtle they are not fully aware of its negative influence when it happens. They feel that the key issue now is whether women will ever be accepted in any large numbers in the top ranks.

We heard an often-recurring theme regarding the price of success for many of our respondents. Said a computer firm executive: "The cost was a large one. I was transferred six times in eight years. Each time brought greater marital and personal problems. And moving from one new city to another brought unbearable pressure to my two children. They had a harder and harder time fitting into new communities, and finally they stopped trying altogether."

Said a lawyer, "I know my experience is overstated, but it *is* true: so many successful male executives are taken care of by a wife—including entertaining, maintaining a clean house, and assuming the major responsibility for the children. A woman can't compete with constant sexism in a tough job market while devoting herself to her family as she did twenty years ago. The price for me is to be continually late, to feel like I have one more ball in the air than I can possibly juggle, and to feel I am not doing *anything* as well as I know I could."

A president of a psychological-testing company stated, "I still believe women have to work harder than men to succeed. For me, the big price to pay is the constant effort to be exceptional."

Observed a vice-president of an apparel manufacturing company, "Many of my female classmates who had visions of moving up in management in the seventies are beginning a mass exodus in the eighties. Some of my most intelligent friends in the corporate world feel they have 'hit a wall' and are resigning in favor of spending more time at home or in favor of self-employment. This has been their price."

A judge told of the price she paid with her parents. "I struggled for thirty years to gain their approval, as I was always reading and studying and was not social as were my two sisters." And she humorously added, "Now I have spent the past ten years trying to escape all the approval and attention they began lavishing on me as soon as I became successful!"

Below are some of the briefer responses to the question of the price our respondents pay:

- *Hard to have time for relationships — some men are not comfortable with my visibility or career interests.*
- *Necessity to substantially alter my life expectations; my work has consumed all my time and interests.*
- *Body stress — results in migraines, ulcer, tenseness, irritability.*
- *Jealousy from many other women, formerly my friends.*
- *Wrinkles, grey hair, bunions!*
- *Envious of my husband's lighter schedule and time for vacation travel.*
- *Not available when my family needs me.*
- *Divorce — one of the major issues was success (his and mine).*
- *I have lost my anonymity — I am a public figure now.*

Collins observes, "One price for me has been to eliminate many activities that I enjoy from my twenty-four-hour day. I have chosen to let go the ones that are non-work-related. In other words, I rarely attend social events. However, as I do often get bored with small talk and parties, this is not a great sacrifice. But I do like to get together with colleagues after the business day with a glass of wine to discuss our work and how our lives are going. These relaxed, yet structured times still achieve a goal.

"I also try to 'give myself' to my family. While this does not happen often enough, I believe the greatest gift a busy person can give is yourself. I try to save some time each month to fit into each family member's agenda. This can include going to my college son's soccer game or driving the hour up and back to San Francisco to have dinner with my stepdaughter. And within this setting, I try to have time (albeit limited) to discuss important issues and find out where each person is in his or her life. I firmly believe that it is the *quality* of the time that counts.

"I am sure my emotional health is better since I have achieved my current status. Now that I have more authority, I can set my own schedule, drive myself really hard, and psychologically, this works for me.

"I almost have no leisure time now, but again, I suppose this is by choice. I constantly keep a list of all that I need to accomplish each day and check it often. Probably the most relaxed I ever get is each Sunday morning when my husband makes the coffee and brings me breakfast in bed with the morning papers (we take three, including the *New York Times*). I also linger over the weekly magazines. This leisure reading probably lasts for several hours, and I love it!"

In expanding on the price she paid in her early work life, Gilbert says, "I was raised in a family whose values were attaining a good education, achieving success, and contributing to church and society. My parents were not from upper-class families, nor had they attained college degrees, but they had worked hard to provide a good life for themselves and their children and hoped their children would do the same. I assumed that my husband would share these values and that we would walk off into the sunset to the house on the hill, two cars in the garage, high-paying jobs, and 2.4 children.

"My husband's parents were from lower middle-class backgrounds and valued security above all else. Although his mother had a degree in education and taught school and his father had a management career, the family did not highly value success. Obviously, with these disparate backgrounds, our expectations were different.

"I wanted, more than anything, to complete my education. My husband did not much care about his. So, I cajoled, pleaded, and argued him through school, trying to fit him into my mold. He would finish college only on the condition that he did not need to work at the same time. Since we needed to eat, I worked full-time and went to school full-time. I worked at a management-level accounting job during the day and went to graduate school from 6:00 to 10:00 P.M. every night while he took ten undergraduate credits in college.

"When we finished our educations, the pattern continued. He got a management trainee job with an insurance company but took so much time off to fish, read, or rest that he lost his job six months later. Then followed a long period of unemployment, with no ambition on his part to find another job. He wanted to leave our urban home and head off to the wilderness, finding jobs wherever we could and maintaining a simple life. I wanted to continue my rapid career success.

"After five years, we split up. I am embarrassed to admit that it was he who first realized our marriage couldn't work, and he chose to run away—taking all our savings and our car. I was able to accept the inevitable and went on with my life.

"When I last heard of him, he was working in a civil service job and enjoying his life. I was not willing to forgo my ideas of success, career, or life-style in order to save my marriage. I have never regretted this decision."

Now forty-three, Gilbert finds that she is no longer willing to accept harmful situations in exchange for further success. "I want to spend time with my family, enjoy my friends, and have some leisure time. I feel I have earned the right to do so. Part of this desire stems from having worked nonstop all of my adult life. Although I certainly am willing to work hard, I would not accept a situation that did not allow me to be a whole person. For example, when I travel away from my family, I realize that I would not be willing to accept constant separations at this stage in my life. And, it is foolhardy not to have enough time to exercise, eat properly, and relax. I have gone through long periods of devaluating myself to the extent that there was no time for me. I will not do it again!

"In general, so far I do not feel I have paid too high a price for the success I have achieved. There have been times of enormous stress, too little time with my family, and minor physical illness including an incipient ulcer. Luckily, none of these periods had serious or lasting adverse consequences.

"As I have mentioned, I always have had the full support of my husband. Because he has a successful executive career, he understands what is required of me by my job, and he does more than his share so that I can do what I want to do."

Looking back on her career, Nycum expands, "Emotional and physical health are both a cause and effect of a successful career. Most of us, when we are ill, realize that the most precious commodity we have is our health. And I'm afraid I have taken good health for granted a great deal of the time.

"Leisure and personal time can be a sacrifice that we make, but the other side is what would we do with it if we had a lot of it? Look at all the retirees who drop dead because of boredom. The few moments that I steal away from an energy-packed day to do something just for me are very valuable. To have an opportunity to see a part of the world I probably would never get around to seeing unless I were there on business is also very, very valuable. Somehow these times are much more treasured than the endless summer months that I suffered through as a child waiting for school to start again in the fall."

We heard of one woman who paid a rather humorous ego price. Heidi Roizen, president of software company T-Maker, was having dinner with Steve Jobs (president of Apple Computer), Bill Gates (chairman of Microsoft), and another woman (who was a past president of a software company). The two men were mentioned by name in a social column, and she is later quoted as saying, "I didn't even mind that whoever saw us didn't even know we were in the industry too—but at least they could have said there were two attractive blondes at the table!"

Concluded a TV executive, "Success has left me little time to do things I used to enjoy: sewing my clothes, refinishing furniture, leisure reading, cooking (fortunately my husband cooks), and polishing silver (which I enjoy!)."

Despite sometimes substantial sacrifices, we discovered most of the women in our survey are satisfied with their personal lives and have no immediate plans to change them.

THE REWARDS

Almost all high-achieving women mention tangible rewards when they speak about the benefits they receive as a direct result of their work, and most cite financial rewards as a key benefit of their success. However, there are many important intangible rewards as well. These latter benefits include respect, recognition, independence, fulfillment, an increase in self-esteem, interaction with interesting people, greater equity in relationships, and a life of choices.

One woman, an entrepreneur living in California, has a life-style that is not atypical of a high-achieving woman. She worked hard to get where she is—sometimes eighty-hour weeks—and now she is enjoying it. She currently has two residences with her husband, a pool and hot tub, and two Mercedes-Benz 450 SLs. She travels extensively to such places as Europe and the Far East. She happens to be a very attractive woman and wears her designer clothing well. Fortunately for her, her income is such that she does not need to spend it all to maintain this life-style. She has extensive investments in real estate, the stock market, and precious metals, and her financial future appears secure.

Not all of us are as financially well off as this woman, but we did discover that many respondents have such a life-style and choose to work hard to continue it.

Nycum, too, is forthright about what success has brought her: "Oh, I love the goodies—I love the accoutrements of success. I was in New York recently and had a few moments to kill between appointments. I walked into a store and was looking at something, and the owner of the store said, 'How about buying this?' I answered that I didn't have the money to spend, and he said, 'Lady, you look like you could buy this whole place!'

"Then I started to take stock mentally of the toys that I had accumulated and was sporting on that occasion. It was true—there were a number of tangible, generally accepted signs of success in the form of jewelry, clothes, hairstyle, and the fact that I was in New York, shopping in a very fashionable part of town between two very interesting business meetings and on the way to have lunch with *Fortune* magazine. I like that!"

Collins, too, cites tangible and intangible rewards. "The biggest reward is simply feeling good about yourself—feeling you have done your best while maintaining your integrity. I am not sure there is a simple answer to why some people work so hard while others just seem to settle for getting by. The psychic rewards—recognition and status with your peers, the feeling of contribution to society, and the job title—all play a part."

Gilbert says, "The most important intangible reward for me is freedom—a sense that I can make it on my own with the hand I was dealt at birth. I also need a sense of accomplishment in my life."

One of our respondents said, "My reward is getting up each morning and having my work be where I would most like to go. I have 'taken time to smell the daisies,' and the daisies are my work."

Shared a public officer: "Winning my public election two years ago was my biggest accomplishment. This was all the reward I needed for all the many hours of getting my campaign in order. The feeling I experienced when it was announced was just indescribable. For me, the rewards are being able to concentrate on the really important issues in our national work world—ethics, leadership techniques, increased productivity, and a greater market share for U.S. goods."

Stated an executive in research and development: "What I really want is to totally escape from *any* responsibility at home. I hate and loathe housework—this includes making breakfast, cleaning, and the laundry. My job lets me afford help. *That* is my reward at home! I do as I want and pay someone to do what I dislike. And my reward at work has been my relationship with the many people and my two mentors who have gone out of their way to help and encourage me."

Below are some of our respondents' shorter answers on the key benefits and rewards that come from their success:

- *Independence, freedom, and ability to choose my own hours.*
- *Interesting life and the ability to make decisions that affect many people.*
- *Recognition, respect, and contribution to betterment of society.*
- *High self-esteem, participation in projects outside work, such as developing an art collection, building a library, or aiding with a symphony.*
- *Feeling of confidence from doing a highly demanding and technical job well, and one that few other people do.*
- *Election to trusteeship and directorships.*
- *Knowledge that I am among the brightest and best.*
- *Being a good example for my daughter.*
- *Opportunity to participate in public policy and exchange ideas with many of the intellectual giants of my generation.*

As delightful as the material benefits are, however, Nycum finds a deeper reward in the nonmaterial ones: "The intangible rewards—the feeling of contributing something—are much more important to me. The person who simply occupies space and time is the person I pity most in this world. He or she has the greatest gift—which is life—and isn't living it to the hilt. I am.

"I'm stretching, I'm thinking, I'm learning, I'm reading, I'm roaring with laughter, and I'm sobbing with sorrow, but every minute of the time, I'm *alive*, with the ability to enjoy the contribution, accomplishment, being with intelligent people, being respected, and being able to respect others. Most of all, I like having the feeling that, whether by freight train out of the blue or long-term illness, my demise will find the world a little farther along in some way—if just by some kindness or by some contribution in intellectual capability—than when I entered it."

To those who know Nycum, her contributions are noteworthy; her desire to contribute is not a hollow one. Many friends and acquaintances envy her job and her admirable success. Because of her expertise in high-technology law, she meets many national and international figures: legislators, parliamentarians, presidents, entertainment figures, and the heads of major corporations. Like other senior level women, she values her ability and opportunity to contribute as well as the rewards she gets from such a contribution.

Collins elaborates on the rewards. "After writing my book on mentors, I find I am often invited to speak at conferences. I enjoy the travel, first-class accommodations, and meeting so many interesting new people. I was recently in Dallas speaking to a national conference on 'Women in Natural Resources.' I remember the carefree, heady feeling when my speech was over, and I treated myself to a trip to the original Neiman-Marcus store. It seemed to be one of those rare times when I didn't have a problem in the world and had a whole afternoon just for *me*. And last year when I spoke to a Fortune 500 company in the Denver area, I received $3,000 for the day, which I immediately spent on special items for my family, including a treat for my middle son's entire fraternity. I felt good I could make so many people happy by doing what I like to do! We have all experienced times in our life that we would like to return to—this day is one of them."

Gilbert comments on an unusual reward she recently gave herself. "I decided to take a several-month sabbatical. I did this for several reasons: first, because I felt I deserved it after working nonstop for thirty years. I was also tired and run down; I had a winter filled with strep throat and several cases of the flu, a most unusual circumstance for me. Also, I needed to clear the cobwebs and think very hard about what I would do next, and I felt that this would take some time.

"I was amused to find that I began to operate at home the way I operated for years at work. I had two projects going at once, and long lists of things to do each day. I redecorated the kitchen, relandscaped the yard, scrubbed the shower (the first time I had done this since we moved into our house years ago), and reorganized every closet. This was in the first month! I also repaid every social obligation we had accrued over the years and caught up with my friends. Clearly, I need a strong sense of accomplishment in my life.

"As a person with a background in finance, I appreciate the security that the tangible rewards bring also. After a few months of my sabbatical I realized: 'Wait a minute—there's a terrific opportunity cost here.' If I can earn a large salary working, it's foolish for me to be doing these projects around the house for which I would pay a fraction of my salary.

"I do like the goodies—a nice house, clothes and vacations, and private school for our daughter. We are fortunate to be at a stage in life where my husband's salary alone can provide this life-style, but my salary can add to future security. And we recently bought a Mercedes, which I have always wanted but have denied myself due to my innate frugality.

"In summary, the two intangible rewards—freedom and a sense of accomplishment—are what I gain most from working. I believe I can continue experiencing these feelings and still maintain a reasonable level of financial security while building a new business. If not, it will have been a lot of fun."

Most women, we learned, enjoy the feeling of independence that their work brings. They have a sense of being in charge of their own lives. Their satisfaction comes from knowing that they need not rely on anyone else for their livelihood but can count on their own abilities. With this independence comes a sense of freedom—a woman's choices can be her own.

Several in our study listed the satisfaction of helping others as their greatest reward. A government employee said, "My salary lets me make a difference. Last summer I almost single-handedly saved the summer theater in our town."

Another added, "One of my relatives wanted to open a camp for underprivileged children in New Hampshire. I was able to become a major stockholder in the land costs, and I felt that I was making a significant contribution to humanity."

IS SUCCESS WORTH IT?

For every woman, the trade-offs and benefits must eventually be pitted against each other in one final question: is it worth it? For the most part, once the professional woman realized all the pitfalls, problems, and demands of a successful career, the conclusion was favorable. However, many are not willing to sacrifice so much to achieve earlier goals and expectations.

Gilbert expresses the sentiments of many with her response: "Most of the time it is worth it. What else is there? When I consider the alternatives—life as a homemaker, life in a dead-end job, life as a volunteer—then I know it's worth it. Sometimes it is hard (having a child, home, and executive career is no *picnic*), but whoever said life should be easy? Human growth can only occur by testing ourselves with such struggles. It's a juggling act, and the more experienced and mature we become, the easier it gets."

Collins gives a resounding yes: "For me, the price has been well worth it. A hundred times so! It is almost necessary for my makeup to feel I am making a contribution, and this carries over to my career, my family, and the various boards on which I serve. I believe I would be driven to have a career at any cost, but the understanding and support that I receive at home has been the frosting on the cake. It is what makes me smile as I work hard! I feel sorry for any woman who has not worked out her home situation and the compromise among all those involved (and it *is* a compromise), because her lot will certainly be a more difficult one.

"But my climb has not been an easy one. I often ask myself, is my track up as invigorating as I believe the top will be? I don't think life is to be lived with the object of getting to the peak. To me, the climb to the top should be fun and exciting, and life should be experienced each step along the way."

Nycum says in a word, "Yes. Having spent time in the last year with people who knew that their lives were ending forced some thinking—how would I change my own life? Although I would have done some things differently, perhaps made some changes earlier than I did, there aren't any regrets that I have spent the years or the energy the way I have. So in the final analysis, I have only joy at looking at the amount of time and energy expended, and I look forward to doing more of the same kind in the future.

"Sometimes I have moments when I have said to myself or to my family, 'Oh, gosh, why am I doing this' or 'I wish I could be like so-and-so who has a lovely tan and a good tennis stroke.' Then someone in the family who can say things directly to me says, 'You couldn't stand yourself, and we wouldn't like you if you were any different.'

"So it has been worth it. In fact, I'd have to look very hard for situations that would be to the contrary. Sometimes I think I'd give anything to go sit on a desert island or the equivalent for a week or so. But this thought doesn't last long enough to change my life-style."

Gilbert says, "If I won $20 million in the California state lottery, I know I would still want to work. In periods of low energy, or when I'm burned out or dissatisfied with my job, I've thought 'the grass is greener on the other side,' but when I had the opportunity to back away from my job with the chance not to work with no change in life-style, I've realized that I really *do* want to work!"

Nycum feels it's important to pace herself and warns against burnout. "People of both sexes get into syndromes, where they must keep on pushing when they really need to back off; perhaps experience would show if men are better at realizing that and then take time off—women just seem to keep going until they drop," she says.

We also wanted to know if money, power, recognition, and influence brought happiness to our respondents. When posed with the question, "All things considered, are the benefits of success worth the cost?" almost everyone in our survey responded yes. Only two indicated a no. And some women weren't quite sure: "I think so, but it's still a 51 percent/49 percent decision. My sixteen-year-old daughter recently said, 'I respect and admire what you have done, but I don't want to have to work as hard as you did.' She feels she missed having a family around her. But I don't think I would have been a good mother to a larger family."

Another woman rationalized: "I never took the time from my career to marry. I recognize the possibility that at age sixty or seventy I could wonder whether I should have married a rich man and had babies. But if I have such thoughts, I hope they occur to me on a lovely cruise ship somewhere in the South Pacific."

Commented an HMO executive, "I finally made it to the level in which I was included in the senior management meeting. I was very proud, but when I attended my first meeting, my boss, who introduced me, sounded like he was giving a five-minute apology for my being a woman. He mentioned, 'we will all have to clean up our jokes,' and ended by saying, 'as you can see from her appearance, she will add a lot to the looks of this board!' Never a word about my competence or my past achievements, which led to the promotion. I had to bite my tongue and swallow really hard and often. So sometimes I can't help but wonder if it was worth it."

Said an insurance company owner, "We are being swamped with claims relating to job stress—this includes burnout, anxiety, nervous breakdowns, manic depression to just plain mental fatigue. These claims have doubled in the past several years and are rising. However, only seven states recognize mental stress as grounds for benefits from workers' compensation; in California, one of the seven states, claims have risen by 40 percent in the past five years. If it is worth it, why are women, now in positions of increasing authority, filing so many claims?"

A college dean said, "I know that I would be completely frustrated staying home every day not using my mind. Perhaps if I were independently wealthy, it would be OK—then I would have funds to pursue any intellectual challenge I was interested in. There are days, however, when I'm frustrated, depressed, and exhausted, and I ask myself, is it worth it? Then I am not so sure."

An engineer added, "Absolutely. I am very lucky. I have a wonderful marriage and enough success to pay for all my hard work and long hours."

Commented a cardiologist, "Has my career been worth it? Sometimes I ask myself if *life* has been worth it. And, on occasion, I sometimes have doubts! Fortunately, it doesn't last long! Success is only worth it if you keep both your perspective and your sense of humor."

Stated an editor: "Of course it is worth it. I embrace the saying by Sir James M. Barrie, 'Nothing is really work unless you would rather be doing something else.' "

Below is a representative sample of the shorter, enthusiastic "yes, it's worth it!" responses that we received:

- *Success is liking what you do—of course it is worth the cost!*
- *Yes, as long as I keep perspective—when I begin equating money with success, then I distort the meaning of success as I choose to define it.*
- *Success is worth it, but one must hang on to basic human and family values along the way. Loyalty and generosity should not be given up.*
- *Yes, I worked very hard to get through medical school, working in the evenings. I now have a successful career, a good marriage, and three marvelous children.*
- *Yes, it is an exciting time for women; but they must work with man and not bruise his ego.*
- *With my upbringing, yes. But sometimes I wish I could settle for the typical "Dick and Jane" suburban middle-American life. But I know that is unreal, and I would go nuts from boredom. I seem to thrive on crisis and confusion, and I guess I will just keep on doing what I do.*

WHAT WOULD YOU DO DIFFERENTLY?

From their experience, senior level women have gleaned some insights into what choices make the career path a bit smoother. We asked ourselves as well as our respondents whether they would do anything differently if they knew at age twenty-five what they know today.

For Gilbert, "The changes I would make are minor. After all, it's the total of our experiences that make us who we are. I would have gotten help at home sooner; I would have gotten an MBA instead of entering what became a too-early and bad marriage; I would have moved on from a boring job earlier than I did. Changing either of the last two choices, however, may have had other, worse consequences. If I could only change one thing, it would be *attitude*—a stronger sense of my own worth and value."

Most senior level women would not argue with Gilbert's focus on attitude and how important it is to understand one's own value in the business community. With that strong sense of self-worth comes the confidence to move more quickly through career challenges, as Nycum points out: "I have thought about what I would do differently. It would be to recognize changes that I needed to make earlier. I always tended to take a long time reaching conclusions, and once I reached them, say, 'Why didn't I do that years ago, or weeks ago, or say it yesterday?' That's what I think I would have improved on.

"I am a risk-taker, but I'm a risk-taker who ponders the risk for quite a while before actually getting around to doing it. I think if I were to do it over again, I would take some of these risks earlier, and I wouldn't have so darn many data points accumulated before I decided it was the only thing to do. I would see the handwriting on the wall in bad situations, and I would get out of them faster. I'd see the opportunity in a good situation, and I'd run after it more quickly. I think I'd take advantage of my contacts instead of letting them take advantage of me, which, if anything, is a product of the culture in which I was raised."

Given the opportunity to alter her choices, Collins pinpoints two specific areas. "First, I would have learned to delegate more at an earlier age—both at the office and at home. I learned this the hard way and through necessity. I often stayed up late at night to organize a dinner party for the following night or remained behind at the office to complete a project. It may take some extra time to train your support group, but it is well worth it in the long run. I am such a perfectionist, but with training, there is no reason that you cannot achieve the same high standards through others.

"The second thing I would do differently would be to leave the one job where I did not get along with my boss sooner. I wish I had realized earlier it was not a matter of who was 'right' and who was 'wrong.' Nor was it a matter even of whose work was superior. It was simply a matter of realizing *he* was the boss and would be backed by the Old Boys' Network. I wish I could have understood earlier the male ego and how office politics *really* work! My mentor finally helped me get the situation in focus, and I was able to land an even higher job, but for a while, it was a time of great conflict."

Our respondents had a lot to say on what they would do differently. Responded a dentist: "I have ended up exactly where I wanted to be. Who can say if I had not done things as I did where I would end up? Life cannot be plotted. You cannot advise someone to take steps '2, 4, and 6' and tell her that she will end up on square '12.' The combination may be so that it puts her on '20,' or it may tell her 'return and start over.' Luck and timing are two essential ingredients that cannot be calculated and must be added to all formulas for success."

Stated a chemist for a Fortune 500 company: "About fourteen years ago, a younger, less-experienced male was promoted to a job which I actively sought. A year later, I resigned. What would I do differently? I would have resigned the day his appointment was announced. During the year I stayed, I was expected not only to *show* the new manager what to do to be profitable, *do* a good share of his work, but to *smile* while he received all the accolades for such good management!"

Added an urban planner: "I would have learned sooner all the long hours which I worked did not pay. Instead, I would have worked a normal eight- to nine-hour day and been much more political. It is who you know that makes a difference. I would also have made more effort to be a member of the 'in' team. I always preferred working alone so I could achieve greater results in a shorter time. But, as a consequence, I realize most promotions came slow for me and were harder to get than they were for the men on my level."

Stated a stock broker, "When I finished college, I was so happy to get a job with a prestigious company that I just settled into my position. During the first five years, it seemed appropriate for younger men to pass me by. One day I said, 'Whoa, I may be known for being an expert in my area, but I can also do more.' So I decided to concentrate on moving up. It worked fine, and I've been doing it ever since. So my advice would be—don't get too comfortable in that first job. Know that you need to grow; find a mentor who will teach and encourage you. Set goals and priorities and work 'smart' to get ahead."

Noted a graphic artist: "Be a more effective public speaker. I could always write what I wanted to communicate, but put me in a room with 100 people and my voice would crack and my heart would beat so fast I thought everyone could surely *see* my blouse heave! You cannot have power if you can't be heard! I finally hired a voice coach and spent endless hours in her office rehearsing the simplest speech. Although I'm not totally at ease now, I can do it and do it well. I wish I had done this many years earlier."

Stated a solar designer: "I wish I had learned earlier what it takes to be the best—motivation and the determination not to give up."

Said a government employee, "I would have federal corporate compliance order (Revised Order 4), issued December 1971 by the secretary of labor, passed sooner. This required prime government contractors and subcontractors with fifty or more employees and government contracts of $50,000 or more to set specific goals and timetables for moving qualified women into all levels of the work force. Although it took a lot of earlier tokenism, time and court cases, the early seventies marked the beginning of women on the way up. I graduated ten years prior, so what I would do differently would be to have enacted earlier legislation which would have given me a sooner thrust into management."

Below are shorter responses from our respondents on what they wished they had done differently:

- *Majored in a different field, chosen business courses instead of music.*
- *Been more of a specialist, not so much a generalist.*
- *Not have married and started my family when I was so young, and also I would have selected a more prestigious school for my education.*
- *Acted more self-assured earlier. I'm now aware of the importance of presenting a self-confident, assured facade, regardless of the situation.*
- *Fought back when treated badly instead of slinking away.*
- *Trusted my judgment more, been more aggressive and more daring. I would have been more attuned to the bottom-line results, making the company more profitable sooner.*
- *Not been so afraid of failure.*
- *Would have gone to a therapist years ago to learn more about myself and why I reacted to things the way I did. I would have shed "The Cinderella Complex" a lot sooner.*
- *Would have worked harder to become a very skilled "corporate player" instead of believing that position, compensation, and recognition would come from doing a good job.*
- *Find a mentor sooner and listen harder.*
- *Would have taken out a loan to have more child care instead of a new carpet and refrigerator.*
- *Paid more attention to life outside my work.*
- *Not allow fear of change to keep me from making career move.*
- *Picked a husband who would have been more supportive of my career.*

With a bit of humor, Nycum notes that marriage continues to be a means of advancement, both socially and financially, for women. "My grandmother and my mother—and I'm sure everyone else's—said that the single most important piece of advice they could give any lady was to marry a wealthy man. I've never done that, but I think it is true: it is possible to advance oneself faster in fifteen minutes at the altar with a good marital choice, than it is in thirty years in a career. I have a number of friends whose success has been in spite of poor marital choices and many whose success has been independent of any marital relation. But I've seen a lot of ladies with no more talent get a lot farther because they made the right choice of spouse. And that normally means a spouse with an earning capacity at least as good as and a circle of acquaintances at least as strong as the woman herself. So, if I had it to do over, what I would do differently, I believe, is to marry the Aga Khan!"

Thus, in summary, although a number of senior level women in the survey indicated that they would not change anything, the majority of the respondents would have made changes such as the following: taken more career-related courses in college; married later in life (or not at all) and to someone supportive of their career; received more help at home (especially for child care and housework); gotten more formal training earlier in their career; had more confidence to make a career change when appropriate; delegated more (both at home and at work); and worked "smarter" with mentors and been more political with those higher up.

Specifically, Rear Admiral Grace Hopper suggests, "Learn everything you can, get every book, read them all, take every opportunity to go to any public, free displays, meetings in whatever your field is. Listen, meet people, collect information, because the day you stop learning is the day you start to die. So, the answer is to keep on learning. I say keep on working, go ahead, and do things." She so aptly epitomizes the spirit and the secret of the successful woman.

Rear Admiral Hopper, now age eighty-one, ends with some spirited remarks for those aiming for meaningful careers. Her advice is "In the first place, if it's a good idea, go ahead and do it, because it's much easier to apologize than it is to get permission.

"And the criterion they gave me when I left midshipman school was that 'for the good of the ships at sea, do it!' I think this is a very important attitude. If you're a little scared about sticking your neck out, then I'll give you another motto to use: 'A ship in port is safe, but that's not what ships are built for.' Let's all be good ships and sail out."

Hindsight is valuable only when used as lessons either for ourselves or for others. The hindsight reflected here may be useful to other career women in that it defines areas of difficulty from the perspective of those who have been through it. Nycum warns, "If we say 'Had I done that or the other differently,' we may be altering the fabric of what we are and perhaps it wouldn't have worked. If I'd been more of a Doberman pinscher and less of a Saint Bernard, maybe the Saint Bernard lovers out there wouldn't have been helping me."

The selection of choices is always an individual act and plays an important part in the lives of successful women. For these high level women, their sense of freedom and independence is enhanced because they have had a hand in shaping their destiny. The role of choice constantly reinforces the importance of work in their lives. We discovered that our respondents' work itself is as important to them as the rewards that follow. We learned that senior level women would not give up their careers even if finances permitted them to maintain their current standard of living; indeed, they would choose to "keep on working."

We hope *Women Leading* has better armed and prepared aspiring career women to make *their* choices by giving them a glimpse of the achievements, failures, problems, and rewards of our own lives as well as those lives of the 160 women in our survey. Once we women understand the personal lifestyle and many sacrifices required to attain a senior level status in our career and are willing to commit so much of ourselves to achieve these goals, the rewards that follow are and will continue to be well worth the hard work, sacrifices, and commitment required to attain these goals.

Bibliography

Bergmann, Barbara R. *The Economic Emergence of Women*. New York: Basic Books, 1986.

Bird, Caroline. *Two Paycheck Marriages*. New York: Pocket Books, 1982.

Bryant, Gay, and the editors of *Working Woman*. *The Working Woman Report*. New York: Simon & Schuster, 1984.

Collins, Nancy W. *Professional Women and Their Mentors*. New York: Prentice-Hall, 1983.

Deal, Terrence E., and Allan A. Kennedy. *Corporate Cultures*. Reading, Mass.: Addison-Wesley, 1984.

Ferraro, Geraldine. *My Story*. Toronto: Bantam Books, 1985.

Gallese, Liz Roman. *Women Like Us*. New York: Morrow, 1985.

Gilligan, Carol. *In a Different Voice*. Cambridge, Mass.: Harvard University Press, 1982.

Halcomb, Ruth. *Women Making It*. New York: Ballantine Books, 1981.

Harragan, Betty Lehan. *Knowing the Score*. New York: St. Martin's Press, 1984.

Josefowitz, Natasha. *Paths to Power*. Reading, Mass.: Addison-Wesley, 1982.

Kanter, Rosabeth M. *The Change Masters*. Beaverton, Ore.: Touchstone Books, 1985.

Machlowitz, Marilyn. *Workaholics*. Cranbury, N.Y.: New American Library, 1980.

McCormack, Mark H. *What They Don't Teach You at the Harvard Business School*. Toronto: Bantam Books, 1984.

Schaevitz, Marjorie Hansen. *The Superwoman Syndrome*. New York: Warner Books, 1984.

Welch, Mary-Scott. *Networking*. New York: Harcourt Brace Jovanovich, 1980.